JENNA'S WAR

Undead America

Leah Rhyne

MuseItUp Publishing
Canada

MuseItUp Publishing
14878 James, Pierrefonds, Quebec, Canada, H9H 1P5

Edited by Lea Schizas
Layout and Book Production by Lea Schizas
Print ISBN: 978-1-77127-685-6
eBook ISBN: 978-1-77127-623-8

For Charles and Zoe,
because there's no one else
with whom I'd rather share the apocalypse

Acknowledgements

An Entire Series of Thanks

No book gets written without significant amounts of help from the author's friends and family, and this particular book is the culmination of a series. I began writing it in November of 2010; how fitting it will release the day before the first of November, 2014. Four years gone, but what a lot of work to show for it!

So much has changed in four years. I've gone from being a full-time software technician to a full-time writer and mom. My child's grown from age two to six. My husband and I have four more years of marriage under our belts. I'm a different girl than the one who wrote the opening lines of Zombie Days, Campfire Nights.

And I have so many people to thank. Here's a list of the ones I love. You should all know why you're here. Whether it's been a word of encouragement here, a cup of coffee there, I love you all and am better for having you in my life. So here goes. Let's hope I don't forget anyone.

Charles Zoe Andy Wendy Jonathan Daniel Colette Zeke Joshua Kira Jenna Morgan Kayla Mary Keith Harriet Louisa Barbara Iris Allison Jason Layne Andrea Marissa Jen Penelope Shauna Sandhya Lewis Pat Meredith Jessica Renee Dino Emma Lauren Rob Amy Tina Debra Kim

Whew

Whether or not you know it, you've all helped shape this book, and for that I thank you tremendously.

Undead America

Zombie Days, Campfire Nights
No Angels
Jenna's War

Lesson 1: Sometimes you have to trust people

In the Middle of the Night: Will

The barn was cold, so cold my toes swelled inside my sneakers as I sat, waiting in the dark. I blew on my hands, hoping to thaw them, hoping to get the blood molecules flowing through my veins again, but it was no use. Frozen they'd stay, at least for the time being.

The scrape of wood against floor, both swollen with age and rot, made me jump as the barn door pushed sideways into its nesting place. My heart flipped, just a little, as a body appeared, standing in the doorway and backlight by the moon's glittering reflections in the snow. The snow covered everything outside with a blanket so thick and so deep and so heavy that we were trapped, stranded in a falling-down farmhouse deep in Nebraskan farmland.

My stomach growled, a lone sound in the night, as the thick figure in the doorway moved forward. Now the sound of cloth scraping cloth filled the surrounding space, along with footsteps so heavy and loud they were offensive. I cringed, leaning back against the wall, away from the thud…thud…thud.

"Are you ready?"

Sam's voice, too, was foreign in the night. Something about the snow, the dark, warped everything, changed sound waves and pitches until they were hardly recognizable.

But maybe that was my brain, working itself into a swirl of thoughts and memories that it didn't want to face. Maybe I needed to stop thinking and focus.

"Yes."

"Good."

Sam paused and closed the door behind him. Immersed in darkness, I calmed until the small scratch and bright flare of a match broke up the night again. He lit the wick of a lantern and then turned it up, the flame burning low and warm. It reflected off the object beside me on the floor. I reached for it at the same time as Sam, and we almost bumped heads.

"Watch it," he said, setting the lantern down and picking up the hack saw. "I'll handle the cutting."

"You sure? I'm really…"

"Yes," he said, fixing a knowing glance toward me. "Let this one be on me. If it works, you can always do it next time."

I nodded and turned to the table. There it sat, the body of….no, I won't say his name. Names are for people; dead people don't need names. But he was one of the biggest people at the house, up until he died. The pneumonia took him fast, so fast his body didn't have time to shrivel on its path to death. I'd already peeled off the frozen remnants of his jeans, leaving his tattered boxers on as though keeping his private areas hidden would make it a little easier to…

"Hey, man, wake up. I'm about to start. Back away."

"Right."

Sam leaned over the exposed leg, his face in shadows. He set the knife down on the table, just for a second, as he scratched his head.

"Here?"

"No," I said, pointing upward, as near to the groin as I dared. "Start there. Cut down, not across. It'll make for longer…"

"Right."

He palmed the handle of the knife, which sparkled in the lantern light. It looked almost beautiful, poised over the white, fleshy, hairy leg.

"We'll have to burn the hair off," I said.

"No," said Sam. "We don't keep the skin."

He sucked in a breath and slowly, tentatively, slipped the knife down. The tip penetrated barely a millimeter before he stopped, his hand poised above as though he was a statue ready to sacrifice a virgin over a sacred altar.

"What's wrong?"

"It's stuck." He reached up with his free hand to tug on his beard. "It's frozen solid. I don't think a knife'll cut it."

I nodded. "Then we need to use the…"

"I know."

He walked to the corner of the barn, disappearing entirely after leaving the small circle of light cast by the lantern. In the darkness, he fumbled and stumbled. Finally, he returned. "Got it."

Standing over the body again, he raised the small axe over his head. He pulled on the safety glasses I'd brought for just such an occasion. "Ready?" he said again, though there was no need, as he didn't wait for an answer.

With a grunt he let the axe fall, using momentum and his own strength to plunge it deep into the fleshy thigh. The crack that followed was bone as Sam raised and slammed, raised and slammed, the axe repeatedly. Soon, the blood in the leg began to thaw, warmed by friction and the faint lantern beside it. I pressed a fist to my mouth, willing myself not to make a sound when the leg detached, and Sam raised his eyes, looking at me through glasses splattered with blood that burned black in the night.

It's just a body. It's just science. Muscle, bone, blood. Nothing more, nothing less. It's just a body. It's just science. Muscle, bone, blood. Nothing more, nothing less.

"Right," said Sam. "Now that's done, I think I can cut in here…" He demonstrated, sliding the knife beneath the skin, warming it with his hands as he cut and rolled and sliced.

And soon we worked together, carving the thick, sinewy flesh in strips from the bone.

Chapter 1: Jenna

"Meat's meat," said Sam, thumping the butt of his ancient shotgun against the dull hardwood floor. A sound like an actual gunshot rang through the room, and the gathered collection of ragtag survivors sat up a little straighter. "We need to survive, and to survive we need protein. I don't care where it comes from."

He paused, letting the words sink in, and I stared at the ground beneath my feet.

Winters in Nebraska—or at least that winter, since it was the only one I'd ever experienced—were hard. The chaotic thunderstorms of the fall gave way only when the furies of blizzards took over, with snow falling so thick and heavy and fast we found ourselves paralyzed, stuck in a farmhouse whose walls cried out in agony against the winds, and whose roof sank beneath the snow's wet, heavy weight.

The number of refugees in the house dwindled, slowly at first but then picking up speed as food stores disappeared and with them, the will to live. We did our best, languishing within the snowbound farmhouse, but suddenly our best wasn't good enough. Nothing could have prepared us for the dull, aching boredom and the vicious, vengeful starvation of a winter trapped inside the home we once considered paradise.

"Maybe we can try the snowshoes again," I said, not daring to look up. For the truth of the matter was, Sam had a point. We were starving

—not slowly anymore, but daily, with gusto. I rarely ate more than a few mouthfuls of rice a day, squirreling away my shares of food for Sadie or Rosie or Will, who were younger and needed the nutrition more than I did. Hunger was a monster worse than any zombie. It tore at you from the inside out. It made your stomach seize with cramps so painful you dropped to your knees in the middle of a crowded room. It made your head throb and your hands shake, forcing you to question any decision you'd ever made, because every decision you'd ever made somehow had landed you there, in the midst of the terribly long process of starving to death.

Even though it was barbaric, I couldn't help but sometimes think with longing of the piles of preserved meat—human meat, the meat of the refugees who'd already succumbed to death—stored in the unused barn less than a hundred yards from our house. I couldn't help but sometimes remember with a sudden, lurching, hopeful churn of my stomach, the scent of burning human flesh that filled the air as we once, a lifetime before, mounted our escape from the fire-eaten city of New Orleans. Even though I knew with every ounce of my being it was wrong, somewhere deep in my stomach, as I stared at the swirling pattern of battered wood beneath my feet, I couldn't help admitting: Sam definitely had a point.

As if reading my mind, Sam thumped the shotgun against the floor again. "You know that won't work. Our snowshoes are tennis rackets with straps. That's it. None of us knows the first thing about how to actually use them. And anyway, there's nowhere close that we haven't already swept clean of anything and everything useful."

His words were daggers, sharp and edgy. I forced myself to look up. From across the room, Sam glared at me. Closer than him, his brother Michael, once my husband but now a silent shadow hovering on the outskirts of my daily routine, glared at me too, but for so many different reasons. Beside him stood Simon, his face gaunt beneath a long, graying beard, leaning his near skeletal frame against the old chest of drawers that stood by the foot of his bed. His wife Allie sat beside me, her hand occasionally grasping mine, with fingers so bony and lean I could barely stand their touch.

Me. They all stared at me. As if I'd have all the answers.

"Well, then, what the hell else do you want me to say? Okay, fine. Bust out the meat. Skin the bodies, dry their flesh on some kind of metal out in the sun until we can't tell what it is anymore. Make it jerky. Isn't that what they did in that movie about the soccer team? Fine by me. People who want some protein can eat it. Go for it, Sam. I don't care anymore."

My head throbbed in time with my quickening heartbeat, and I cast my eyes back downward. "Next thing I know, you'll be wanting to eat Chicken."

As if on cue, my little black dog looked up and nuzzled my hand. I scratched his ears, refusing to look up.

"For God's sake, Jenna, what's wrong with you?"

Great, I thought. Now it's Michael's turn to tell me why I'm wrong. I pulled Chicken closer.

Michael's voice grew louder as he gained momentum. "I never knew you were such a monster. Sam, here? That doesn't surprise me. But you? You're nothing but a cold-blooded killer, aren't you?"

I raised my head, tears cold against my cheeks. I hated them. I hated him. I hated everything. "You'd like to believe that, wouldn't you? You'd like to believe that I'm a killer. But I'm the only one who makes any decisions around me, and let me tell you: they suck. *Suck.* So until you're ready to step up and stand in my shoes for a minute, Mr. Holier Than Thou, I'm done listening to you. And I'm done letting you pass judgment on me like you're a god or something. And I'm done with everything."

I hadn't realized I'd walked to the door during my speech, but suddenly, there was the doorknob in hand, and with no one trying to stop me I flung the door outward and stomped off down the stairs. The eyes of starving people found me as I walked, but with a hateful glare I backed them off as I continued my march to the basement.

* * * *

"Whoa, there. Down girl," said Will as he emerged, ashen and dusty, from behind the curtain partition he hung to separate his sleeping area from the rest of the dim, cavernous basement. "Ease up on that thing or you're going to break your hand."

I paused, arm drawn back for another punch, the heavy bag swinging sickly from its rusted chain, and turned to face Will.

"Whoa," he said again, his eyes widening. "What happened to you?"

"Nothing," I said, and I let the punch fly. My fist connected with the old, battered leather. A jarring rattle flew up my arm and into my shoulder, and my knuckles wept bloody tears. The pain was good though. The pain took my mind off what had happened upstairs.

"Yeah, right," he said. "You need to stop letting them get to you."

"Easy for you to say." I punched again. "You stay down here, day in and day out. You only have to deal with Rosie, Sadie, and me. You don't have to deal with *them*."

I punched again, a combo this time. Right-left-right-right. I'd be a killer in a boxing ring.

Will backed to a post and slid down to sit. He crossed his legs and rested his elbows on his knees. With his wild, brown hair and big eyes dominating his small, thin face, he looked much younger than fifteen. And then, as he sighed, he sounded much older. Ancient, even. The juxtaposition of the two made me pause.

"Sorry," I said. "Rough day."

"No need to apologize. Do you want to talk about it?"

"No. Not at all actually."

"Okay, that's fine. We can talk about movies instead. What was your favorite movie, you know, before?"

I made a face. "I don't know. Does it matter? It's just…well, Sam wants to start eating…well, he wants to start eating…God, when I try to say it, it just sounds that much worse, but he wants to start eating…"

"The people that died," Will finished for me.

"Yes! How'd you…oh, never mind, it doesn't matter. The point of the thing is that he actually *has* a point, but it's too disgusting and barbaric and I can't even think about it. But then Michael about bit my head off just for admitting he had a *point!*"

"He does have a point."

"What?"

Will laughed. "You just said so yourself. He has a point. We're starving. Dying. There's a decent source of protein readily available out in the barn. But the question is, are you ready to take that step? Because that's a pretty big step to take."

"I don't know if I am. Sam sure seems to be."

"Okay, so what are your other options?"

I stared at him. Will with his baby face and genius IQ. Will who was biding his time until spring, he said, until he could set off in search of someone with the facilities to test out his crazy plans for curing or at least immunizing the world against the zombie plague that had brought us all to our knees. Will who sometimes seemed like the only person I could talk to in the entire farmhouse full of people. "Are you sure you're just fifteen?"

"As sure as I was the last time you asked me. When was that? Yesterday?"

I laughed, and sniffed, and wiped at my nose with my sleeve. "I hate that I'm such an ugly crier," I said. "But no, I don't think we've exhausted all our options. We've still got some food left, some rice and some beans and stuff. We've searched a lot of houses, but not all of them. One of them might still have a snow mobile or something. That would help us broaden our searches again."

"Running on what gasoline?"

"So we'll find gasoline, too. Make something happen. Save the world or something. Who the hell knows. But there's gotta be another way. A *better* way. To *live,* not just to survive."

Will stared at me. Those eyes—they killed me. "There *is* another way. Sam's way. It's still on the table."

Suddenly, it was all clear. "No," I said. "We're not there yet. Like you said. Or at least *I'm* not there yet."

"Well then, now you have your answer, don't you?"

"I can't stand you sometimes. You know that, right?"

Will's face broke into a grin, and it was like the sun coming out after a storm. "I know," he said. "That's why you'll miss me when I'm gone."

"Shut up about that. I'm definitely not ready to talk about that."

"Spring's coming soon."

Upstairs, the whine of rusty hinges and the clatter of Chicken's toenails against the rough wooden steps told me someone was coming. It was time to go tell everyone my decision, and I was ready to deal with the repercussions again. I smiled back at Will. "Later," I said. "Not right now. Right now I have to go. But thanks for the chat!"

He leaned his head back against the post, and suddenly he looked tired and unwell again. I blinked and turned away, pretending not to see how much starvation affected him, too.

"I'm coming," I called up the stairs, and I turned the light off as I reached the top. Will preferred being in the dark.

* * * *

Somehow we managed, though more bodies were added to the piles of the dead out in the barn, and though the snow piled up beyond the windows of the house, and though no amount of shoveling could manage to get us more than a few feet beyond the barn. Some of us stayed alive, even on the longest nights winter threw at us, and somehow we managed not to kill each other. Though, from the way Michael looked at me, no matter what I said or did, I sometimes wondered if it wouldn't have been better for him if I was dead.

But I couldn't afford to think thoughts like that. Thoughts like that were poison, and they'd kill me faster than any bullet…or any zombie.

I went about the business of taking care of my dwindling group of refugees, taking heart in romp-sessions with Sadie and Chicken, in the warmth of their small bodies pressed against mine in the night. I learned to avoid Michael. And somehow, someway, the days started to grow longer again, and the snow finally began to melt, and I hoped life would return to normal again.

The *new* normal, anyway.

* * * *

"What is this?"

Michael's voice was a bellow, a foghorn in the murky, cloudy dawn. It came from the barn, near where the skeletal remains of what was once a fenced-off jail stood amid the thawing snow as a constant reminder of our failed attempt at keeping justice in the zombie world. His voice emanated fury, and it sent a shiver down my arms. All the little hairs stood at sudden attention, even though the room in which I sat, braiding Sadie's hair, was almost uncomfortably warm. Sadie jerked beneath my hands, and the braid slipped from my fingers, undoing itself as it fell around her shoulders.

"Jenna," Sadie said, her voice soft and tentative.

"I don't know," I murmured, but then Michael's voice boomed again.

"Jenna! Sam! I said, what is this?"

God, he's going to wake the neighborhood, I thought, and then I remembered there was no neighborhood to wake. Or was there? The snow had all but stopped the constant passage of the undead, giving us the faintest of hopes that maybe *this* winter would have finally killed them all, but with the slightly warming days and less snow blanketing the fields and forests, we'd seen a slow but steady resurgence of danger at the mouths of zombies. The last thing we needed was to cause a ruckus and, quite literally, awaken the dead.

"Stay here, baby," I said as I stood to go. "I'll send Auntie Allie or Rosie up to hang out with you."

Sadie nodded, her eyes big and wide. "I don't like the sound of this," she said in the solemn little way she'd had since her mother's death a few months earlier.

I kissed her forehead. "It'll be fine. It's just Michael. You know him, he gets dramatic sometimes."

I almost choked on the lie, and found myself unable to meet her eyes. Michael was the least dramatic person I knew, and Sadie was smart enough to know the difference. As I reached the door, Rosie appeared in the hall, and she gave me the same look of confusion as

Michael bawled my name again. I only shrugged and pointed back to the room. "Stay with Sadie?"

"Of course."

"Maybe take her down to the basement, okay? Just to be safe. I'll feel better knowing you girls are down there."

"Okay."

I left them there, hoping nothing would happen to put either of them in danger.

Out of habit more than anything else, I paused by the door to pull my Louisville Slugger out of its home in a rusted old umbrella rack. Slinging it over my shoulder, I pushed the front door. Michael howled again. "*Jenna! Sam!*"

I paused, and called over my shoulder, "Chicken! C'mere!" and waited until my dog appeared by my side, which he did, a moment later, with the bleary look of a dog who'd been lying contentedly in a sunbeam. He nipped at my hand and I stroked his ears.

"You ready?" I said.

"I am," replied a voice over my shoulder.

I jumped. "Sam. God, you scared me." We started walking, falling easily into step with each other. "Do you know what this is about?"

"No," he said, but he didn't look me in the eye. Not that I exactly wanted him to. Where things with Michael and me were non-existent, and we avoided each other like the plague, things with Sam were awkward. Weird. Gone was the comfortable relationship of adopted big brother/little sister we'd had as kids, replaced by this new thing. This other thing. He'd kissed me once, before Michael and I split, and though I'd replayed the kiss in my head dozens—no, hundreds of times since then, he'd never once tried again. Which was better, I guessed, given that I'd once been married to his brother, and probably, technically, still was. Only now I wore the emerald ring Michael gave me on a string around my neck, tucked under my shirt at all times. I was too embarrassed to let Michael—or Sam—see how much I still cared. Better to let them both think I'd forgotten.

"He's out by the barn," I said. "Why would he be out there?"

Sam walked beside me with a bit of a swagger. I'd only ever seen him walk like that when he was hiding something, as though his ultra-confident walk could mask the discomfort he so obviously felt. "Don't know," he said, and he scratched his beard.

Our pace was fast, but it was still a bit of a trek to the barn. I hated the silence. "Why'd you grow that stupid thing back out again anyway? All you ever do is scratch at it like you have fleas."

He laughed, but it was forced. "Keeps my face warm. Like I've told you a million times already."

Michael called again, even louder and more insistent, putting emphasis on every syllable. "*Jen-na!*"

Sam sighed. "He's going to wake the neighborhood."

"That's just what I thought, too. What's this about, Sam?"

The barn loomed larger as we neared it. Michael stood out front, holding something in his hands. Behind him I saw Simon, arms crossed. Even from a distance, they both looked furious.

"Don't know."

"Sam! Tell me before we get there."

He groaned. "No."

"Fine. Chicken, c'mon, bud. Let's go."

I started to jog, leaving Sam behind. If he wasn't going to tell me what was going on, I'd have to find out for myself.

I swallowed back the fear, the discomfort, that bubbled up in the face of Simon and Michael's joint anger, which grew almost palpable as I crossed the final dozen yards and finally saw what Michael held.

It was a leg. A human leg, detached at the knee. Under normal circumstances, that would have been distressing enough, but that was only the beginning. I slowed to a walk, squinting, wanting not to believe what I was seeing.

For there, in Michael's hands, as the sun began to break through the morning clouds, I saw the strips cut from the muscled flesh of the leg's calf, each about a foot long, and maybe an inch wide. They looked like…

"Jerky," I whispered, and I ground to a halt, inches from Michael, Simon, and the cannibalized leg. "Someone's been making human jerky."

Chicken sat back on his haunches beside my legs, and he began to growl.

Chapter 2: Sam

The jig's up. I couldn't keep the smile from spreading across my face. *At least now it's out in the open.*

Of course, I'd have to deal with my brother, the fucking save-the-children-boy, who stood there, glaring, his eyes shifting from Jenna to me and back to Jenna. Michael could hold a grudge unlike anyone I'd ever seen, and he for sure had a grudge against Jenna. Stupid kid. She was only trying to survive, just like the rest of us.

That said, she had nothing to do with the jerky, though it was already obvious Michael thought otherwise. I couldn't see Jenna's face, but I could tell by the way she stopped dead in her tracks that she was less than thrilled to be facing Michael, especially as she put two and two together and came up with the right answer.

"Michael," she said, her voice cracking. "Is that…"

"Like you don't already know," he spat. "I heard what you said to Sam that day. You all but gave him permission to do it."

"Hey," I said, breaking in. "How d'you know it was me? I'm innocent until proven guilty." Again, I was smiling. I guess I never did like keeping secrets, and this one had been a pain to keep. Sneaking off with a couple of like-minded survivors, carving up dead people, and trying out different methods of drying out the meat. It wasn't pleasant work, but we'd done it. We knew we had to hide what it was, disguise it, in order to get people to eat it. Handing a big cut of thigh meat over to

Allie, the house cook, didn't seem like the best plan. Jerky would be easier to stomach.

Our first successful batch was almost ready to try.

Jenna turned to me. "*Are* you innocent?"

"Of course not. I did this. You knew I was going to." Behind her, Michael's eyes widened with that "I knew it" face, so I corrected myself. "I mean, you didn't *know,* at least not like that, but are you surprised? We need protein. Like I said, meat's meat. Doesn't matter where it came from."

"Are you serious?" In her fury, Jenna grew shrill, as always, and I winced. Her voice was far more piercing—and downright annoying—than Michael's. "How could you do this?" Beside her, Chicken growled a last time, then darted into the recesses of the open barn.

"Come *on*, Jenna." Michael's voice raised another chunk of decibels. "Do you expect me to believe you didn't know about this? I heard you that day. You were in on it from the get-go. You two disgust me."

"Jenna. Michael. You two should really keep it down," I said, keeping my voice purposely calm and even. "The zombies are on the prowl again. You don't want to attract any attention, do you?"

"Sam's right." It was Simon's turn to chime in. He stepped forward as though to separate Michael from Jenna, thought he'd have been hard pressed to actually do so. They stood almost forehead-to-forehead, nothing but a dismembered leg separating them. The space between them sparked like it was electric. I had to hand it to them—they really did have some chemistry. Simon reached out a hand but Jenna knocked it down.

"I don't care if Sam's right." She was still shrill, but now it was a shrill whisper. I laughed. "I had nothing to do with this, Michael! You have to believe me! And Sam, how could you?"

"How could I what? Eat? Try to survive? Try to find a source of protein to keep you all alive?" I shrugged. "Actually, it was pretty easy."

"Oh God." Jenna finally turned away from Michael. "Did you actually….eat it?"

I shrugged. "No. Not yet. We had some trouble getting it to turn to jerky without rotting first, and then we had some trouble with it freezing and turning pretty rancid, too. So we've got the first batch, and it's almost ready, but no. I'm not a cannibal. Yet."

Jenna's shoulders sank, I think with relief, but then Michael shovel-passed the leg straight into her chest. I felt a little bad when I saw her light-gray coat smeared with muck from the places we removed the flesh (with the days getting warmer, refrigeration was quickly becoming a problem). But then she squealed and dropped it like a hot potato onto the swampy, slushy ground.

"Hey," I said. "That's food. Don't ruin it."

"Food? That's a human leg!" Simon boomed over the rest of us. "It is not, nor will it ever be, *food*. At least not while I'm in this camp."

"Well, then, maybe you should go ahead and leave," I said, before I could stop myself.

"Sam Silverman! No! Stop it right now." Jenna lifted her eyes from the now-contaminated leg and glared at me. She raised her bat as though to strike, but didn't actually make a fighting move. She never would start a fist-fight, not ever since we were kids. Michael glared at both of us. I'm sure we made an interesting tableaux, each of us chuffing vapor clouds in the chill morning air like a herd of angry bulls getting ready to stampede. My hands gripped my shotgun around the stock, not exactly in a fighting stance, but close enough so that one wrong move by any of them could have started something none of us wanted to finish.

And then, Simon started something.

Had we been inside a dream, time couldn't have moved slower in those moments as we three stood, ready to fight. We'd stood this way so many times in our earlier lives together, Jenna always ready to scrap with the boys, and us always ready to fight her right back down. All our lives, it had been the three of us, shaking with feigned fury at ridiculous childhood mishaps, only now we stood as adults, or near-adults anyway. Adults more suddenly created by the end of the world, but adults nonetheless. And at our fingertips, instead of sticks and stones, we held guns and baseball bats, tools that could actually be used to slaughter one another if any of us made the move.

Beside us, Simon raised his gun, a military-grade M16 he carried everywhere he went, though I'd never seen him use it against anything more alive than the undead. He pointed it straight at Jenna's face.

Oh my God, he's really going to kill her.

The thought almost knocked me over.

"Simon." Jenna's voice was low and steady. Calm. She sank into battle mode with the ease of a hardened soldier. "Simon, put that down. It doesn't have to be like this."

Michael stood frozen. His eyes grew wide as he stared at the gun with its barrel trained on Jenna's face. I looked from Jenna to Simon, and then back to Jenna. Simon swallowed, his jaw clenched.

It was a split-second. That's all. I barely had time to register as Michael also pulled his gun, and pointed it at me. His eyes had narrowed to slits.

This is how I die. At the hands of my little brother.

He had the draw on me. I didn't have a chance.

"Michael. No." Jenna's voice was barely a whisper.

Simon groaned. "For God's sake, would you two just *duck.*"

Jenna and I dropped like stones, crashing together to the ground. Michael and Simon each fired and the smell of gunpowder filled the air around us. In the silence following the gunshots, the soft thuds of bodies falling to the earth were like thunder. Without raising my head, I spoke. "How many?"

Jenna had already rolled to her belly. "Lots. Too many to count."

My stomach sank but I pushed myself to my knees. Simon and Michael fired again, and again. In battle they were all business. I grabbed my shotgun from the sludgy ground. "Damn. It's soaked."

"There are rifles in the barn, just beside the door. Get one from there." Jenna pulled out her pistol and was firing from on the ground, the *pat-pat-pat* barely audible beneath the constant fire of the rifles. "Get me one too. This thing's shit at this range."

I jerked to my feet, blood rushing to my face the way it always did in battle. My heart rate soared, as did my mood. *Just another day at the office, but damn, it's good to be back.* It had been a long, quiet, hungry winter, and the thrill of a firefight was just what I needed to get my blood moving again. I won't lie—I'd been waiting for this day.

The rifles were right where Jenna said, and a flash of black caught my eye against the graying wood of an old horse stall. "Stay there, Chicken," I called. "No need for you to get shot today." I picked an old submachine gun for myself, and a rifle for Jenna, and then I rushed out to battle.

It was bad. Dozens of undead lumbered toward us, drawn first by the shouts but now drawn to the firing weapons and the smell of our own musky adrenaline. Many had already fallen, but many more filled the empty space behind them, pouring out from the thick trees that lined the edges of our farmland property.

I pulled Jenna up to her feet by her belt as she continued shooting. Pressing the rifle to her side, I spoke into her ear. "Aim well, little girl."

She grinned, dropping the pistol to the ground and taking aim with the rifle. "Fuck you, Sam. I'm not a little girl."

For the first time since our lone kiss months before, something stirred in me, something I sometimes thought was dead. I was…excited. When her first shot nailed a zombie between the eyes, and the top of his head exploded in a black, bloody cloud, the excitement grew, and I had to step away from Jenna. Close enough to my brother that I could almost hear his heart pounding, I watched him reload before I remembered: I had to shoot too.

And then the business of killing zombies began, and I soon lost track of anything other than shooting and reloading, shooting and reloading.

In the corner of my consciousness at one point, I saw Jenna again. Her cheeks were flushed and she had mud in her hair, and I don't think I'd ever seen her look more beautiful. She turned and grinned again, but she was looking past me, to Michael, who glanced back with only a withering stare. Jenna's face fell, but then she was all business again.

The herd kept coming, but the cold kept them slow and sluggish. Easy shots for the four of us. None ever got close enough to smell their putrescence or to hear their individual cries, though their low, collective growl broke the morning calm as much as our gunfire. It seemed they would never let up, and I began to worry about ammunition, even as I continued firing.

From the depths of the barn came the high-pitched tone of Chicken's howl. Jenna made a face. "Shit. They must be back there now, too."

Michael turned to look. "Not surprising. We're making so much noise, any zombie for miles will be headed this way. Any bright ideas to stop it?"

I shrugged, then took out two nearing zombies with shots to the face. "Do we have any flame throwers?" The zombies fell. Two replaced them so I shot them too.

"Negative," said Simon, shouting to be heard over the gunfire. "But we do need reinforcements. Where is everybody?"

As if on cue, the far-off echoing of gunfire from the main house began. The battle had reached the home-front, but that was fine. There were able bodies up there, and lots more guns and ammo than we had down here at the barn. Unless there were some super-zombies up front, I had no doubt the people at the house could handle things, at least until we got our herd under control.

"I'm out," said Jenna, just as soon as I started to relax again. "No more bullets."

"There are more inside," I said. "Just inside the door."

"You mean these?" said a small voice between us.

Jenna jerked. "Rosie!" she said. "What are you doing here? You're supposed to be keeping Sadie safe in the basement! How'd you…wait, never mind, just give me those."

Rosie grinned, handing Jenna her booty. "I also brought more stuff from the house. Allie sent me when the fighting got loud. It just took me a while to work my way through all the monsters."

She was proud of herself, that much was for sure, but Jenna's face screwed up in anger as she slammed a magazine into her rifle. "You should have listened to me, not to Allie. I wanted you to stay safe."

I pulled my trigger a few more times; the herd was finally starting to thin a little. Rosie handed me a fresh round of ammo and then she turned back to Jenna.

"Safe?" she said. "I think I can handle it." From the back of her pants she pulled a pistol, and then, like she was Annie Oakley or something, she swung it out to the front of her. She took aim, and pulled the trigger.

Fifty yards away, a zombie fell to the ground, its head completely intact but for the tiny hole between its eyes. We all paused and stared at little Rosie. She was twelve, and tall, but thin as a reed, a complete waif. Her hair was wild and blonde and curly, and it blew about her face even as she took aim again, and fired, *again*. A zombie fell, *again*.

"Damn," I whispered. Even I wasn't that accurate a shot, not from the range at which she was aiming.

She didn't miss a beat. "You guys gonna stare at me all day, or are you going to help me get rid of the rest of them?" She fired again, and again.

Soon we all got back to the business of killing zombies.

* * * *

It took another twenty minutes or so for us to kill the remainder of the herd that had gathered, and then another ten to walk through the battle field with knives, killing those who had fallen but still refused to die. I showed Rosie how to aim for the soft spots like the eyes or the nostrils, and soon she was off and running, a cold-blooded killer in the body of a twelve-year-old kid.

As I watched her dart from body to body, stabbing downward with calculated precision, I tried not to think about the fact that the world we lived in created killers, just like Rosie. It was too close to thinking about other killers the zombies had created, myself included. Maybe eating human meat wasn't the answer, but neither was dying. Life was easier for me when I didn't have to think and instead acted, so I shook off the dark thoughts in my head and kept on killing.

Jenna appeared at my side a few minutes later. Her eyes were red and I wondered if she'd been crying. Her voice was strong, though. "We need to burn these as soon as we can. It's warming up. They're going to stink."

"Yeah, I'll get on that.The shooting up at the house seems like it's done, too. Are you going to go up there and help them clean up?"

"Yeah. I'm taking Rosie with me. You can deal with your brother and Simon."

"Oh, great. Just what I want." The memory of the argument that started the stampede flooded my brain and I groaned. "Can't you take them?"

"You started this mess, so you can finish it. Besides, it's not like Michael will even look at me. You deal with him."

She turned and stalked off, picking her way through the tangle of arms and legs that covered the ground. When a hand grasped her boot, she paused, leaned over, and stabbed its owner through the head with such cool and calculated precision that the thing that stirred in me, that thing I thought was dead, stirred again, and I felt myself wanting Jenna so badly it hurt. I had to turn away.

"Michael," I called as I, too, paused for a kill-shot. "Michael, come over here. We need to talk."

He only walked away, and I stabbed the next writhing zombie with much more force than I needed to.

Chapter 3: Will

The sound of Jenna's footsteps thundering down the stairs meant trouble. I turned up the lantern I kept barely lit on my desk so she wouldn't complain that I had the lights down too low, and I squinted as I waited for the approaching storm to start.

It wasn't that I didn't like Jenna—on the contrary, I loved her, but not in that way, though she was the prettiest girl I'd ever seen. To me, she was like a goddess on Mount Olympus, strong and beautiful and perfect. Too perfect to ever take notice of a kid like me, now that she'd already rescued me once. She was my protector, my Wonder Woman, and I wanted to help her back. I did. But too often, there was nothing I could do but be a sounding board for all her troubles, and since I wasn't able to solve the *one thing* I actually knew I *could* solve, it all got a little frustrating.

I mean, who cared if Michael wouldn't talk to her, when the fact of the matter was, I held in my notebook the formulas I was sure would create the first ever vaccination against the virus that created the zombies, one that would keep the living from ever displaying the symptoms of zombie-hood, as I liked to call it. But there was nothing I could do with my data. It was all theoretical, at least as long as I stayed in the house in my old hometown. I had no tools, no equipment, and most of all, no samples.

In short, I was dead in the water, and even though Jenna knew it, there was nothing she could do to change things.

Her boots appeared near the bottom of the steps, and I drew the curtain around my bed back further and turned the lamp up even more. She hopped down the final two steps, waving a hand in front of her face to clear away the dust that always seemed to float around in the musty basement. She stared at me, hard.

"You're squinting. Did you just turn the light up, just now? Just for me?"

I sighed, leaning back against the wall, kicking both my feet out straight to create some semblance of a barrier between us. She ignored them and sat beside me, never seeming to wonder if I'd do anything other than welcome her frequent visits.

"No, Jenna. I leave the light turned up all the time, wasting copious amounts of kerosene just so I'm not sitting here in the dark all by my lonesome."

Her sharp elbow dug into my side. "Now I know you're lying. You're going to destroy your eyes, you know, reading and working in the dark like that."

"I was sleeping."

"No you weren't. You never sleep. Rosie fills me in on all your nocturnal activities. I know you come upstairs to hang out with her at night."

"Which is why I sleep during the day."

She rolled her eyes and shrugged, her shoulders moving up and down beside mine. "I wish you'd come up during the day. It's not healthy, living in the dark like you do."

"Can't help it. It's how I'm most comfortable. Anyway, did you need something, or did you just come down here to give me a hard time? Because suddenly I feel like I'm talking to my mother."

A laugh played on her lips, but instead of letting it out she stood and yanked the cord of the overhead light, which burst into brightness with so much force I had to shield my eyes. "There," she said. "That's better, isn't it?"

"God, Jenna, couldn't you give a guy some notice? I mean, you don't give me anything else I need. Could you at least give me that?"

My eyes adjusted to the light quickly enough to catch the tail end of the withering look she tried to give me—the one that never looked natural on her face. She was too pretty to look evil, and she knew it. I laughed outright, but then she stopped me.

"It's time to go," she said. "I need to get out of this place."

This was exactly the moment I'd been waiting for. I shot up from the wall, still sitting, but now leaning forward with my elbows on my knees in a position I hoped made me look completely engaged in every word she said. "Tell me more," I said. "What's the catalyst? The zombies today? Rosie said they were bad."

She sighed, then turned and walked to the small desk where she sometimes sat and tried to understand the formulas I'd show her. She leaned against it, and tucked a stray piece of hair behind her ear. She looked so young—younger even than me, though she had me by a handful of years and lots of life experiences. In her faded jeans, flannel shirt, and biker boots, holding a baseball bat so worn down with time and blood it looked almost black, she allowed a tear to slip from her eye. It glistened in the swinging bulb's light, tracing a path down her face.

"It wasn't that. They were nothing. Still slow and sluggish from the cold. I mean, there were more than I expected to see at once, and the cleanup was hell, but we were never in any real danger. Not from them."

"Then why now? What's changed?"

Another tear, this one bigger and faster-traveling. Chased by another, soon they were a flood. I tossed her a box of tissues from my bed, but she threw it back at me.

"I just can't stay here anymore. Not with them." She gestured vaguely toward the upstairs. "I'm done. I think maybe the three of us can go somewhere and finally get you the stuff you need to end this thing. Then we can come back and move everyone out and, I don't know. Maybe we can all live happily ever after or something."

I laughed, I couldn't help it. "Is that your scientific plan? Getting me the *stuff* I need to end this *thing?*"

Behind the tears, a small smile turned up the corners of her mouth, and I tossed her the tissue box again. As she leaned against the desk and wiped her eyes, a shower of dust fell from overhead, and more footsteps sounded on the stairs above.

"Dammit," she said. "Now what?"

It was odd to me how I'd come to recognize the whole of the refugee family based solely on the sounds of their footsteps. Rosie's, of course, I'd known my whole life. They were light and airy, and usually involved some form of stumbling, particularly on the tricky third-from-the-bottom step. Jenna's were more thudding, since she always wore her heavy boots, especially during the cold winter months. She, too, often missed that stair, and more than once came crashing to the ground.

Simon's were near silent; Allie's were accompanied by the cracking of ankle and knee joints; Sadie's were quick and reckless; Chicken's were the sound of dozens of toenails rat-a-tatting on the wood; Michael's were slow and steady—he took his time doing everything.

Sam's were the loudest, always the loudest. He wore combat boots, picked up during his months on the road, he said, and they were even heavier than Jenna's. The clash of each boot against each individual step was a deep boom, the sound of a kick-drum without the inherent rhythm of song.

It was Sam's steps I heard just then, and he'd obviously been listening for a while. As he neared the bottom, first his boots then his tattered cargo pants, and then his bushy beard grew visible in the fierce light. His voice thundered into the gaping basement, echoing back from the concrete walls. "You're not going anywhere, not without me."

A statement. Not a request. With all the positive confidence of a man with no expectation of being denied.

I leaned back against the wall to watch the show. This was going to be good.

"Like hell we're not," said Jenna, jabbing her bat into the ground, wincing in pain as it ricocheted back up at her. "Cannibal."

Her voice was cold, but it only made Sam grin.

"I didn't eat any. Not yet. Right, kid?" He looked at me, and suddenly I was part of the show. "I told you that you could have some of the first batch, and have you had any yet?"

I grimaced as Jenna's jaw fell, but there was nothing to do but go along for the ride. "Nope, not yet. And I hate it when you call me kid. You're not *that* much older than me."

Jenna turned her glare on me. "You knew? You knew all along?"

"Who do you think taught me how to do it? You know this kid knows everything there is to know." Sam laughed.

I sighed. "Protein is protein," I said. "No matter how unappealing the idea may be, it's a step toward surviving in this stupid world. But that's not what you came here to discuss, Jenna. So don't change the subject."

"I didn't. I only said I'm not going anywhere with that cannibal. Now I guess I'm not going anywhere with you, either." She let the bat fall to the ground with a clatter and crossed her arms before her chest, hugging herself a little. She looked as though she might fall apart at any minute.

Sam noticed. He crossed the distance between them with a few long steps and slid an arm around her shoulder. Though she stood stiff, she didn't pull away. "Where are you two planning on going, anyway?"

She shrugged, lifting his arm with the rise and fall of her shoulders. "Don't know. Don't care, really. Any place is better than here."

"You're so right," said my sister's voice from the top of the stairs. "It smells awful outside. Barbecue zombie isn't the meat of the future." She tripped her way down to the bottom, laughing at her own lame joke.

Jenna giggled, too, but it was weak at best. "Neither is calf-muscle jerky."

"Ew, gross," said Rosie. Guilty, but not really knowing why, I had to look away. Something in her wide-open face made me feel ashamed of myself, like I'd been caught with my hand in the cookie jar. Who knows? Maybe I had...well, the jerky jar at least.

"Okay," said Sam as Rosie flopped onto the bed beside me. "So you don't want to try my latest concoction. I get it. But seriously, what's this you're saying about leaving? Because you know I want in."

The brightness of the un-shaded bulb had begun doing a number on my eyes. "Jenna, can you?" I nodded to it, and she flicked it off, leaving us in the steadily waving glow of lantern-light. "Thanks."

"Sure thing. Sam, we're talking about going away, anywhere. Preferably somewhere with someone who's still alive who can make use of all of Will's knowledge, and all that he's cobbled together from Dr. Schwartz's notebook."

Sam laughed again, but it was a more gentle sound. "So you want to save the world."

I grinned. "Right. That's the plan."

"Count me in," said Rosie, snuggling against my arm. I slid it around her shoulders and squeezed her tight. We were both so skinny—just flesh and bone, really—that it wasn't exactly comfortable, but it was *comforting* to have her there. It almost cauterized the gaping hole left by our parents' absence.

"Are you thinking about heading east?"

Jenna's eyes closed. "Sam. I know what you want, but there's no way —"

"There *is* a way, Jenna. You didn't see them. You don't know for sure. You guys cut and ran and left my parents behind. I want to go find them."

"We *didn't* cut and run, and I can't believe you're still saying that. Sam! They were on the same train as my parents. No way did anyone walk off that thing alive. And we called and called and called. How many times do we need to go through this with you?"

"I guess at least once more," he said, dropping his arm and stepping away to lean against a post.

Jenna moved closer to him and leaned a head on his shoulder. Even mired in anger, they were tight. From everything I'd heard about their growing up together in the suburbs of New Jersey, it made sense. When the world ends, you hang on to the few things you can, as tight as you can. As if she read my mind, Rosie took hold of my hand and squeezed. An image of my father, dead on the top floor of our house, flashed in my mind, and I understood Sam's need to know.

"So why *don't* we go east?" I blurted. "It makes the most sense anyway. Jenna, you and Michael came from there, right? You too, Sam. You guys know what roads are passable, right?"

Jenna sighed. "That was months ago, Will. Even if they *were* passable then, there's no telling what's happened to them since."

"So we find other roads. It doesn't matter. But east is right. I know it. I mean, east is where you have the biggest cities in the country…"

"…and cities are where the zombies did the most damage," finished Jenna. "More people equals more zombies."

"But so what. It also probably means more survivors. More likelihood of finding people with connections. More hospitals, more labs, more everything. On the east coast."

"I've always wanted to see New York!" Beside me, Rosie was suddenly leaning forward, excited.

"Not like this, you don't."

"Jenna, don't be a dooms-dayer. It makes sense. Plus, we could look for Sam's parents while we're out there."

Jenna's face was a mess of emotions, tight with anger and frustration, even excitement. She was an open book, and we were winning her over. Beside her, though, Sam's face was suddenly empty. Blank. Borderline scary, the way his mouth was closed so tight it looked as though it disappeared behind his beard. Though Jenna leaned against him, he stayed stiff, his visible hand clenched into a hammy fist.

"Um, Sam?" I said. "You there? I thought that was what you wanted. East coast. Your parents. All that jazz?"

His eyes cleared as suddenly as his face had clouded over. "What? Yeah." He shook his head, his hair shaggy around him. "Right. East coast. I was just remembering…some other things that may be out there."

Jenna turned to him and gave him a sharp look. "Sam. Spill. What are you thinking? I hate when you close up like that."

He shook again, and it was like the previous few moments had never existed. "Sorry. I was just thinking about Ty, and wondering if that Captain guy ever succeeded in doing…whatever it was he hoped to do out there."

"The Captain." Jenna breathed the word, and Rosie and I stared. This was all new territory for us.

"But never mind," Sam continued. "It doesn't matter. Yes. East. That's the way we should go. I mean, it'll be dangerous, but if anything's survived, it'll be out east. I mean, what's our other choice? California? I, for one, am not messing with the Rockies, even in summer."

"I always wanted to see California," said Rosie.

I laughed. "Maybe one day. But for now, if we're all in agreement, let's make a plan. When can we go? What do we do next?"

Jenna grinned. "We'll figure it out. But the sooner the better. Any place has to be better than here."

Chapter 4: Jenna

"No, no, no, no, no!" Sadie's screams echoed down the hallway. I don't know how exactly I expected her to take the news of our leaving, but that wasn't it. She'd locked herself into the upstairs bathroom, and though Allie hovered outside the door, begging to be let in, it was to no avail. Outside she remained.

"Jenna, don't you have a key?" she called, her voice shaking and barely audible over Sadie's cries. "I need to get in to her."

I stared at the door that trembled from the three-year-old fury behind it. The knob was ancient, probably original to the house, built back in the twenties, and I'd never found any keys to the interior doors. We'd replaced all the outside locks ages before, for all the good they'd do against a full-on zombie invasion, but we left the inside ones alone.

I knocked. "Baby, you need to settle down and let Auntie Allie and me in. This is silly."

"No, no, no, no, no! You can't go! You can't!" Her voice rose into a piercing wail, and I looked over my shoulder toward the window at the end of the hall. If our argument out by the barn had brought the zombies running days earlier, surely this tantrum would do the same.

Clearly, I wasn't the only one with that concern. Michael appeared from the room he shared with Sam, looking surly. "Can't you get her to stop?" He was almost as loud as she was.

I shot him a look. "You know, I was just thinking how much I wanted you to come yell at me. How much that would improve this situation. So thanks. Thanks for reading my mind, Michael. You're the best."

He glared at me before going back into his room and closing the door.

I sighed again. It was amazing how much stress one small child could inflict on an already-tense household. Allie and I stared at each other, all-but paralyzed with indecision, until it came to me.

My hair was long and unruly; in truth, I hadn't had it cut since the zombies made their first appearance, and it had grown almost to my butt. I kept it out of my face with a never-ending series of rubber bands, braids, and a massive amount of bobby pins, filched long ago from a drugstore that had seen better days. I reached up and pulled one from my hair.

"I've seen this in movies," I said, opening it slightly and sliding it into the lock. "Maybe it'll work."

I jiggled the pin and shook the handle while a white-faced Allie looked on. The lock of hair that had been held in place by the pin fell forward, so I blew it out of my eyes, and continued jiggling. After a couple tense seconds, there was a small click, and the door popped open.

We rushed in.

Sadie sat in the bathtub, legs crossed, hands balled into tiny little inefficient fists with which she beat against the porcelain. Two of the knuckles on her right hand were split, and dark red blood glowed bright against the stark white tiles. Her face flushed and screwed up with rage. Her hair was soaked, and the whole room smelled like sweaty kid.

"Sadie!" Allie exclaimed. "Your hand! You poor baby!"

"No, no, no," she shouted in return. She reared up her left hand—the non-bloody one—to smash into the bathtub again, but I was quicker. I slid a hand beneath hers, and she slammed it into the tub, jarring my arm but not hurting herself. Her eyes opened in surprise.

"Stop it," I said, holding her right hand too. "Stop it right now. This is *not* how we expect you to behave."

My touch was an off-switch. Sadie stopped shouting, melting into my arms like ice cream left too long in the sun. I scooped her out of the tub and pressed her head to my shoulder, where she cried in the sudden silence. Allie gave me a look—slightly accusing, as if to reprimand me for leaving—and left the room in silence. I nudged the door closed again behind her.

"That's better," I whispered into Sadie's hair. "Much better."

She was limp in my arms, worn out from her tantrum. My sleeve soon soaked through with her tears. "Don't go," she said, her mouth against my clavicle.

"I have to," I said.

"But you're mine."

"Always. But I still have to go."

She sobbed a little before pausing to catch her breath. "But why?"

"To see what's out there. To help Sam and Will find the things they need to find. But I'll come back for you, little ladybug. I always will."

"But I love you."

Tears filled my eyes and spilled out, raining down on her damp head. "I love you too. I always will. But I have to go."

"Take me with you then."

"No. It's too far of a walk for your little legs. And anyway, I need you to take care of Chicken for me."

Sadie pulled away, looking up with wet, wide, red eyes. "You mean Chicken is staying?" Her face was suddenly hopeful.

It was my turn to sob. "Yes," I said through thick, shaking vocal chords. "His place is here, with you. I wouldn't separate you two for anything."

"Really?"

"Yes, really."

Sadie clutched at my neck and kissed my face four times before standing up and darting from the bathroom. "Chicken," she screeched, in her tiny little-girl voice. "Chicken, come here! You get to stay! I can't believe you get to stay!"

Just like that, the tempest had passed. I pulled myself up from my spot on the floor and leaned my head against the windowpane, letting it cool my cheeks as I gazed out at the brilliant blue sky, filled at the horizon with the pastel green of what promised to be a beautiful spring. In the distance, fluffy clouds danced and the sun shone, and it looked as though nothing in the world could ever go wrong again.

But then I looked down, and saw the tree line rustling with activity. I started counting. Before I got to ten, the first zombie appeared, looking small and insignificant against the beautiful day. Soon, though, it was trailed by at least a dozen others.

"Michael! Sam! Simon! Get your stuff! Zombies are coming! The zombies are coming!"

* * * *

The afternoon grew chilly, the final icy grip of winter not yet willing to relinquish its grasp, but the bonfire churning beside the barn tainted the crisp air with the sour-sweet smell of rotten, burning flesh. Bodies were still being added to the pyre as I slipped silently away and walked around the corner of the house, where a small stone marker, so natural-looking you'd almost think it just another boulder, sat beside a weather-beaten pasture fence.

I knelt beside it, the cool damp of the ground seeping instantly through my jeans, nudging out a shiver. Etched on the stone were two words: Beloved Gwen. I'd carved them myself, months earlier, though her body had only recently been interred beneath the thawing ground and grass had not yet begun to insinuate itself through the thick mud blanket of her resting spot.

I ran my fingers across the words. Beloved Gwen. The fiery, feisty woman who survived zombies only to be beaten by a cancer so vicious and malignant her final days were little more than a pain-fueled blur, when she cried out through the night in the shrillest of voices, voices that at once sounded less human and more…zombie. Voices that needed to be silenced, if only to end her suffering.

Billy, once her oncologist but, by the end, also her trusted friend and companion, ended her plight with a triple-dose of morphine and a kiss to her forehead. Her eyes fluttered open only once, but we, the two who remained by her side at the end, later agreed that she mouthed the words *thank you* before they fell back to where they would remain forever shut.

I carved her name in the stone later that day, and left it beside what had been her bed until the frozen ground finally opened enough to bury her. Now the stone sat silent vigil. I kissed it.

"You were my friend, Gwen," I whispered, still fingering the words I'd carved so carefully. Tears filled my eyes at the mention of her name, the pain of losing a woman who'd become a mother to me in our months together still too close to the surface to keep hidden for more than a moment when sitting beside her grave. "You were my friend and I loved you and I wish you were still here to come with us. I think you'd be brave enough and strong enough to help us know that we're making the right decision, and I think you'd enjoy one last adventure."

"Death was her last adventure," said a gruff, deep voice beside me, making me jump.

"Michael!" I said, my breaths coming in raspy puffs. "Why'd you sneak up on me like that?"

Without thinking, I turned to face him, wincing at the expectation that something terrible was about to happen, that he was there for one last fight before I left. What met my gaze, though, was far different, and far worse. He looked defeated. Deflated. Like a child whose balloon slipped off his wrist and floated off into the sunset. Just another lonely child missing a lonely balloon in a lonely world. A tear sneaked out the corner of my eye and trailed down my cheek. Neither of us made a move to wipe it away.

He sat beside me, wincing as he made contact with the damp, chilly ground. Our knees touched. It was the closest together we'd sat in months. A deer in a shotgun's sights, I was afraid to move, afraid any movement would end it all, frighten him away. Quickly I realized we were both deer, shy and skittish and terrified of one another. I exhaled a soft breath, and another tear followed the first.

"Were you going to leave without saying goodbye?" he said. He jabbed the business end of his hunting knife into the soft earth atop Gwen's grave, trailing it through in a swirling pattern. I was reminded of the hours he used to spend painting, and of his desire to one day be a graphic novelist. He hadn't picked up a pencil, let alone a paintbrush, in months. No, years. Had it been years already? I swallowed. It had.

I watched his hand pull the knife tip through the ground with smooth grace. It was hypnotizing, and it took me a few breaths to remember it was my turn to talk. "I didn't think you'd want me to."

"After all we've been through, I guess I deserve at least that much." He stopped swirling through the dirt, and drew back and stabbed the knife into the ground to the hilt. "Or do you disagree?"

And suddenly there he was, looking straight at me, eyes wide and his lips inches from my face. It was all I could do to keep from tackling him straight to the ground. The only thing stopping me: I didn't know if I wanted to kiss him or punch him. So I sat tight and met his look with as much strength and steadiness as I could muster.

"I don't," I said, ignoring the quake in my voice. "Disagree, I mean. I can say goodbye. See? Goodbye."

Half his mouth turned up in a smile, but the other half stayed flat. "You always have been a smart ass."

"I know. I'm sorry."

"Don't be."

"But I am," I said, all confusion melting in the face of his unwavering eyes. "I'm sorry for everything. For the way everything's gone down since we got here. For lying. For making you so angry. I'm even sorry for the zombies. I never have given up the feeling that they're our fault."

"Don't be a…"

"Whatever. We had sex, and then the zombies came. It was almost scientific. So I'm sorry for that, and I'm sorry that you hate me."

"I don't hate you. I just…can't be what you want me to be."

"What?" I said, almost choking. "When did I ever want you to be something you're not?"

As quickly as he appeared beside me, he was gone again, in spirit anyway, our knees separated by an insurmountable chasm of dirt and baby grass. "When you lied. When you hid things from me. You asked me to be the kind of guy who'd be okay with that, and I'm sorry I couldn't be."

So that was that. "You came over here just to say that?"

"Yes."

"Just to make me feel like garbage one last time?"

"Well…"

"Yes. It's a yes. I know it. And since it is, goodbye, Michael. Thanks for making this easier, and for letting me know it was time to give this back to you."

I slid a hand up to my neck and dug beneath my flannel shirt. From the nook between my breasts I pulled the tiny emerald ring that hung from a thin chain. I was a strong girl, and the chain was a weak, delicate thing. One quick tug was all it took. The chain snapped and fell away to the dirt, leaving the ring wrapped in the palm of my hand. I stood, and dropped it in Michael's lap. "Goodbye," I said again. It had the ring of finality to it.

"Wait," he said, and I paused. He reached up and took my hand. Into it, he pressed something small and round. His ring.

Without another word I slipped it into my pocket and walked away, refusing to turn back. This time it was for good. Some things can't be fixed, I thought.

* * * *

The sun hung low in the sky, and the air was still bright with the night's leftover cold as we stood on the gravel driveway beside Michael's old hatchback. It was a silent memorial to a prior life, standing there, reminding me of where we'd once been, and how far we'd gone in that little car. For now, the car was useless, what little gas we could salvage and purify from nearby homes and vehicles put to use in the generators powering the electricity for the house. We gathered beside the car—Will, Rosie, Sam and me—but we would leave it behind, a dead, silent creature whose value for scrap metal didn't yet outweigh its symbolic hope.

Beside us stood those we would also leave behind: Allie and Simon, Sadie and Chicken, and Mrs. Hanson, the woman who'd cared for Rosie in their shared captivity. Michael was nowhere to be seen, having already said his goodbyes to his brother, and to me. I tried not to hope he'd appear on the front porch and give me my ring back. I tried not to hope we'd suddenly mend all our broken bridges. I tried to focus on who *was* there, and not who wasn't.

"Now, Rosie, are you sure you're doing the right thing?" Mrs. Hanson fussed with Rosie's jacket. She pulled the zipper up, then down, then back up again, alternately choking and releasing poor Rosie, who stood still, enduring the onslaught. "I don't think your parents would approve. Will, tell her. Even if you have to go, she should stay here."

Rosie closed her small hand around Mrs. Hanson's fidgeting ones. "Yes, ma'am. I'm sure of it. And I think our parents would rather Will and I stay together, don't you think?"

"Well, yes, but…"

Rosie stood firm for such a little kid. "Will needs me. I need him. We can't survive without each other. And he's going to save the world. While he does, Jenna and Sam will keep us safe. So go ahead and hug me goodbye, then go inside before you make me cry. Please. I love you, but I have to go."

Mrs. Hanson's jaw clenched as she dropped Rosie's zipper. Her eyes filled with tears, but she nodded. Pulling Rosie's frail, lanky body into a tight, quick hug, Mrs. Hanson held her breath. She let Rosie go and, after a quick kiss on Will's forehead, she turned and rushed in silence back to the house.

"That was cold, Rose," said Will, his eyes wide.

"Not cold. Just true. She *was* going to make me cry, and that wouldn't have helped anyone."

Allie nodded and slid an arm around Rosie's shoulders. "You're right. You did the right thing. Clean breaks are always better."

Simon stepped closer to her and squeezed her free hand. I don't know how I knew, but I had no doubt they were both remembering a particularly clean break in their lives, and how easy it hadn't been. Their daughter, Del, had been my friend, and we hadn't been able to save her when we left New Orleans. I knew as I watched them that they were picturing Del's final moments. The bite on her neck. The way Allie cradled her head. The way the pistol sounded as Allie pulled the trigger, ending Del's life before the zombie virus could turn their daughter into a monster. I knew they smelled the smoke in the air, heard the screams that pierced the night.

I knew this because I remembered, too. I stared at them, and suddenly I was shocked by the way Simon had aged. He looked feeble, almost, as though he had no reason left to live. His face was gaunt beneath his beard, his eyes hollow. I suddenly saw the way Del's loss had left him a broken man, that he was barely holding himself together with his home improvement projects and his work on an old generator that would never run. I saw that the world had destroyed him, and I was suddenly afraid I would never see him again.

I rushed forward and wrapped my arms around his neck, standing up on the tips of my toes and burying my face in his neck. It was scratchy, full of bristly beard, and he smelled of old leather and charred wood. I closed my eyes and inhaled. "I'll miss you, Simon," I whispered. "I'm so sorry for everything I've done. For all the ways I've let you down."

Simon let go of Allie's hand and held me tight around the waist. He drew in a shuddering breath. "You never disappointed me, Jenna Price. Never once. You saved my daughter, and I never will be able to thank you properly."

"But I…"

"Yes, you did. You saved her, and her mom and me, in so many ways. I wish you'd stay, but I understand why you have to go. But there'll always be a place for you here. You know that, right? So come back to us. Even if it's ten years from now, come back."

I spoke into his beard, the wiry hair tickling my nose. "Thank you, Simon.

He let go, and I blinked back tears. Allie grabbed Will and Rosie, and Simon shook hands with Sam, the two of them talking quietly together, while I knelt before Sadie and Chicken. My two loves.

"I know I'll miss you two most of all," I said, my voice cracking.

Sadie stared at me, nodding, her eyes flying saucers in her small, round face. I touched her cheek, and let my other hand fall to Chicken's head. He nuzzled and nipped at my fingers. For a dog who always seemed to understand things—he'd appear from nowhere when I needed a hug on a rainy day, and more than once he'd saved me from an approaching undead creature while we walked our night patrols—he didn't seem to grasp that I was leaving. That he—a dog with a lifespan much shorter than mine—would probably never see me again. As he licked my hand, his eyes were bright and happy, like he didn't have a care in the world. And maybe he didn't, but I knew I did. I started to cry in earnest.

"So you two just take care of each other," I said as Sadie leaned into my side and Chicken jumped up to lap away the salty tears on both our faces. "And keep watch for me, over the south hill. I *will* come back to you, Sadie. I promise you. I promise you harder than I've ever promised anything. I *will* come back to you."

All too soon, Sam's hand fell heavy on my shoulder. "Jenna? We should really get going. Make the most of the day's light."

Still holding Sadie tight, I nodded. Allie reached down for the little girl, and I handed her over with a choking sob. Then I stood, and shouldered the backpack I'd packed and repacked dozens of times over the prior two days. Between the four of us we carried maps, tents, food, canteens, blankets, pots and pans. We hoped it was enough to help us survive, because from there we went on foot. We hoped to make it to the east coast before the end of summer.

Deep in the bottom of my bag was the one item I'd decided I couldn't live without: the small, silver ring I'd given Michael on a sun-drenched afternoon a lifetime before.

"Yes, let's go, you guys."

Rosie took my hand and Will's. I took Sam's. As we shuffled down the gravel driveway, headed southeast, weighted down by our physical burdens as well as our emotional ones, I risked one more glance back at the house that had been our home for so many months. The porch was empty, and I knew Allie would have ushered everyone else inside so as not to prolong the sadness of goodbye. Good old Allie, I thought, though I regretted not seeing Sadie one more time.

A flicker of movement in an upstairs window caught my eye. It was the window to Sam and Michael's room. For a moment I hoped against hope that it was Michael, seeking one last sight of me before I left, but then I remembered what Sam had told me earlier that day: as soon as he was gone, Michael was turning the room over to Dana and Allesandro, a young refugee couple who'd been living in the common room for months. It was probably just them, opening windows to air the room out from its boy-smell. It wasn't Michael. Michael and I were over.

Chapter 5: Sam

My head hurt. We'd been walking for about eight hours, down winding country roads torn up by the rough winter and littered with rusting cars and the occasional dead body, but already the whining had begun. The sun burned warm, flies flew thick, and vultures circled overhead, too high for us to know if they were alive or undead. Not that I cared. A single shot was all it took to kill a vulture, no matter what.

I'd been looking forward to walking, to getting back out into the world, away from the confines of the farmhouse and into something more productive, but it just went to show: I was better off on my own. I should have known.

Jenna couldn't stop crying, hadn't stopped crying since we left the day before. At least she did it quietly. Goodbyes had always been hard on her. I remember Michael saying she'd cried for three hours the day I left for college, and I also remembered ignoring the note of bitter jealousy in his voice as he reported the fact on our web chat that night. Her tears, however quiet, were grating, each one a silent accusation, making me feel like I was the one pulling her away from the little life she'd created for herself in rural Nebraska.

Rosie was too small to go on a journey like the one on which we were embarking, and I'd told Jenna and Will that dozens of times. They'd ignored me, of course, and now, though she tried to hide it with jokes and laughter, every word out of her mouth was a thinly veiled complaint. "Are we there yet," she said, joking of course, but also so serious. She had no idea what she was facing, that girl, and dancing and hopping around wasn't going to help.

And Will wouldn't stop talking. I'd never seen him like it. Normally he was quiet. Introspective. Withdrawn. But now he was babbling, on and on, about genetics and viruses mutating and Dr. Schwartz's notebook, and if I heard the word chromosome one more time I was really going to lose my mind completely.

"Guys," I said. "Can we walk quietly for a while?"

But they ignored me. Rosie kept laughing. Will kept talking. And Jenna kept crying.

The backpack on my shoulders wasn't too heavy, but it pulled at my neck and chafed raw the skin beneath my thin flannel shirt. I shrugged, the movement releasing the pressure but not for long enough. I tried to focus on my feet as they moved across the dark asphalt road, and I squinted my eyes, trying to blur the meadows surrounding us, to hide the fact that we were sitting ducks for anybody to swoop in and kill us. It wasn't working.

"Guys," I said again. No one responded.

I stared at my feet. Left moved, then right, then left, then right again. I was walking. I was moving. Life was better when I was moving, I knew that, but everything around me was suddenly so *loud*. Intoxicatingly loud, but not in a good way. More like in the way it used to feel when I'd go to a particular fraternity's party, back in the days when life was normal and the dead stayed dead. They were a decent group of guys, those brothers in the frat whose Greek letters had long since escaped my memory, and their parties were epic. The basement of their house would be full of people, of loud, thumping bass, and of beer and the fog of perpetual marijuana. If you went downstairs, there was no *not* inhaling, if you know what I mean, and so we'd go down and never even have to take a hit off any of the joints making the rounds. I'd nurse a beer and close my eyes and listen to the music and let it all carry me away and think it was the best moment of my life. But then would come the inevitable crash and burn; the room would close in, the smoke would choke me, and suddenly I'd find myself so wasted with alcohol and contact-weed that I'd need to escape.

Every time. I always thought the next time would be different, the next time I could handle it all, because I loved those first few moments when the kickdrum bass sounded like an old African beat and I could pretend to be anywhere in time, anyplace but there. But the next time was always the same, and I'd push through the crowd toward the stairs to the street-level of the house, and the arms and hands of the people in my way would reach for me, ripping at my clothes and at my face and eyes, and I wouldn't be able to breathe until I reached the top of the stairs or, better yet, the front door of the house.

That's what I felt, all at once, walking with Will and Jenna and Rosie. My crashing heartbeat became the thump-thump-thump of the bass, and their words became the arms and hands reaching for me, clawing at me, scratching my eyes out. I wanted to run. I wanted to hide. I wanted to be anyplace but there, but there were no stairs. No escape paths. There was only more meadow, more road, and more Jenna, Will, and Rosie. Jenna was crying, and Will was laughing, and Rosie was capering. It was too much. Way too much.

"*Oh my God, will you please shut the fuck up?*"

The words came out of me and before I really understood what was going on I found myself on my knees on the asphalt, my hands clasped over my ears and my eyes squeezed tight against the noise and the sunshine and the terrible clawing hands. I let loose a mighty warrior's yell and leaned my head against the warmth of the road, and lay for a minute as silence finally closed its comforting cool breeze around me, and my heart returned to its normal rhythm.

The danger was past.

I pulled myself up to sitting and opened my eyes.

Jenna stood in front of me, maybe five or six steps away. She held out her arms as though holding back the two smaller ones. Will and Rosie let her keep them away. They looked confused. Lost. And maybe even afraid.

What are they so scared of, I thought, but the answer was there in a flash. Me. *They're afraid of me. I did something bad. I lost my shit.*

I forced a smile. "Hi," I said, leaning back on my hands. Though the air was still cool, the sun had warmed the dark pavement until it was hot to the touch, but I left my hands there, soaking up the burn. The pain forced the spinning sensation in my head to slow. "I, um…wow. Thanks for quieting down finally, you guys."

Jenna squinted down at me, shielding her eyes from the sun with one hand, while the other hand kept what I knew was a killer's grip on the handle of her blood-stained Slugger. "Are you okay, Sam?"

I started to get up, noting with surprise the way my knees bled from two giant scrapes torn into them like the road rash of a kid who's fallen from his bike. I must have fallen harder than I thought, I realized with a start. I honestly didn't remember falling. But I kept that smile on my face. "Sure. I'm fine. It was just…you guys were being so loud, and it made me worry that we might attract some attention."

Jenna's voice was low and deadly calm. It was the way she talked to people she didn't trust. "We weren't being loud, Sam, until you screamed loud enough to attract any creature in a three mile span. And you scared the kids."

"We're not kids, and we're not scared." Rosie spoke from behind Jenna, making no move to step forward.

Jenna didn't move her eyes from me. I felt as trapped in her stare as I would have had she tied me with a thick rope. She spoke to Rosie, but also to me. "No, you're right, but you're still younger, and Sam and I are still supposed to be taking care of you. Not losing our minds and freaking out and being all kinds of crazy." Her eyes narrowed, and I flinched.

I'm not all kinds of crazy.

But maybe I was.

"You *were* being loud," I said, but it even sounded lame to me. Lame and weak. I cleared my throat, and reached a hand out to Jenna as though I needed help getting up. "You wouldn't stop crying."

She stayed frozen, standing there, lit up by the sun like a girl on fire. Her eyes were on fire, too. "I haven't cried for hours, Sam. Not since we left. Ask Will or Rosie if you don't believe me. And Rosie's been walking along beside me, quiet as a mouse. What's going on in your head?"

What? This was news to me, and it couldn't be true. Or could it? I shook my head and let my arm fall. I brushed the blood from my knee and shins, wincing in silence at the pain as my fingertips ground tiny pebbles of gravel deeper into the flesh. Blood dripped down my leg, the crimson startling against the pale, dirt-smudged skin. I squeezed my eyes shut for a second, and then I tried again. "But you were *crying*. I heard you." Opening my eyes again, I looked up, accusing.

Jenna's face was filled with something unidentifiable at first. I stared, trying to make sense of the way her eyebrows knit together with the little crease I used to love. Her eyes were big and round and blue, like she'd swallowed the whole sky and was letting it show in those two little spots. I flinched at the way they narrowed, the way her jaw clenched so tight I could see the muscles working by her ears, flexing and tightening as she worked hard to keep something inside.

Fear, I realized. It was fear. Jenna was afraid of something.

Of me.

"I wasn't crying, Sam," she said, her voice small. Beside her, Will took her arm and made to pull her away. He was giving me wide berth.

Shit. Damn. Fuck. I am losing control. I can't do this.

Balling my hands into tight fists by my side, I grimaced as I pulled myself up, the pain in my knee a foghorn reminder of whatever had transpired. Jenna, Will and Rosie all stepped back, further from me. From the monster they thought I was.

I let them, stepping back myself. If I was losing control, better to do it on my own, away from them. I turned my head. The woods on the other side of the road beckoned. It would be a homecoming of sorts, diving back into the wilds. Being on my own. Alone. No one to worry about, no one to regret losing. Just me and my knife and the wilds. I'd survived that way for so long, I couldn't help it. Suddenly, I salivated at the idea of leaving.

I took a step, turning away from the life I'd been living, the life that had tied me down with nightmares and anger. In the wild, that all melted away, I knew. I knew because I'd been there before, and out there, it was me and survival. I understood life out there.

Do it, whispered a voice, and it sounded like my old friend Ty. *Leave them here. You don't need them.*

And I did it. I took another step.

"Sam?"

This time it was Rosie's voice, but I took another step away. They didn't need me, and I didn't need them. I was a lone wolf, and the world out there was my home. I took another step.

But then a sound stopped me, a snapping of branches, a shuffling of steps, not far into the forest. A breeze wafted across my nose, teasing itself up into my nostrils, injecting the scent of decay up into my brain. I sniffed, pulling the scent closer, letting it in, following it like a Bassett hound on the prowl. It was coming from the east, and the north, and the west, and it was getting stronger.

I froze. Across from me I saw Jenna's gaze leave me for the first time. Her eyes darted to the treeline. She set down her Slugger and pulled forward her rifle.

"Company," she breathed.

"A lot," I said.

"Too much," she agreed. She reached out to Rosie and to Will. "Get behind me."

"Yeah right," said Rosie. From her backpack she produced a small pistol with a big barrel, pulling it forward and slapping in an ammo clip like a pro.

Will nodded, and reached over to Jenna, pulling her extra rifle from around her shoulder. "Mind if I borrow?"

Jenna's eyes widened—though I wouldn't have thought it possible minutes before, they were so big and round already—and she shook her head. "Don't." It occurred to me then just how terrified she actually was, though I had no idea exactly why.

"Let him," I cut in. "We need the help."

And just like that, we were a "we" again, without question. The pull of the wilds relinquished its grip, leaving me free to help, though not without a vague promise of returning, probably when I least expected it. But for the moment, I was me, Sam, and I could help.

Jenna swallowed—hard—but said nothing. As if in a dream, she faded back to the middle of the road, gesturing for the three of us to follow. We did, converging as a well-armed unit in the center of the road, our shoulders all pressed together as we circled up. The approaching footsteps grew louder, less defined, the shuffling of masses of creatures, the likes of which we couldn't yet tell. Human? Zombie? Animal? There were too many choices, but now they came from everywhere, all around us. Running wouldn't be an option, not yet.

"Wait," said Jenna. She darted out from our tight-knit group of child-soldiers, retrieved her Slugger, only to rejoin us, shrugging sheepishly. "I don't like it being so far away from me. Feels too much like abandonment."

I snorted. "Abandoned by a bat. Only you, Jenna. Only you."

A closer, sharper cracking sound silenced me. The trees before us parted. A tremendous groan filled the air, along with the overwhelming stench of the undead. I sighed. They were far away still, at least this group, and I had a moment to observe.

They were human zombies, this first group breaching the tree line, and they were traveling in a pack. A pack of undead. It was almost comical. The first zombie in the group was huge, as though in life he'd been a linebacker, at least two heads taller than me, and seemingly twice as long around his monstrously broad shoulders. He wore some kind of homemade armor on his upper half; it covered his torso almost completely, but it looked as though it was made of flattened out pots and pans.

Not bullet proof, not in the least.

But on his head he wore a helmet, strapped on and Army-issue, something I was willing to bet he picked up on his travels in the undead world, back when he was still alive. A translucent riot mask covered most of his upper face, though it was cracked and missing a chunk near his chin.

You were resourceful. I wonder how they got you.

My eyes trailed down, taking in the way his jaw hung slack from hinges rotting with age and decay. The way his left hand was a mangle of mottled red and black flesh, black blood oozing between his fingers as he fought the weight of his armor to raise his hand to reach for us.

Maybe it was the hand, then. His hands weren't covered.

I looked at my own hands, bare to the world, and made a note to seek out some kind of gloves at the next place we stopped. Thick leather gloves would work, and the idea of chain mail floated in my head like I was headed to a renaissance fair of the doomed. I laughed at myself, but only a little. Then I raised my gun to shoot.

All around us by then the trees were birthing a legion of zombies. Jenna's shoulders pressed against mine as we stood back-to-back, the younger kids to our sides.

"Are you ready?" Jenna whispered.

I aimed for the chunk of broken riot mask on the big guy before me. He'd be the hardest to take down; I was glad to be the one to face him.

"Ready," said Rosie and Will, together.

"Jinx," I whispered, still laughing. Ever since I'd become a soldier in the zombie world, I found battles exhilarating.

"Fire!" Jenna's voice rang out over the din of rotting, walking corpses. It was followed by the thunder of her rifle, and the pat-pat-pat of Rosie's pistol.

"Save your ammo, Rosie," I said, my voice sharp as my bullet ripped through the massive zombie's lower face. "They're not close enough for you to be accurate yet."

The big guy didn't fall. I'd missed the important part: his brain. I wasn't sure why I thought I could get him that way. I lowered my aim, but not before taking out the two creatures right on either side of him. They didn't have riot gear. They were easy kills.

"Oh yeah?" came Rosie's voice as the pat-pat-pat continued. "You sure about that?"

I turned, taking my eyes briefly off the big oaf who still lumbered toward me to check on Rosie's progress. Sure enough, she'd already taken down six. I counted shots in my head. "Damn, girl, you're good!"

"Would you two shut up and shoot?" said Jenna. "They're everywhere!"

And so they were. Filtering out of the trees on either side of us, appearing from around a curve in the road nearby. There was one clear path, just to my left. A huge tree lay uprooted, blocking the zombies who couldn't figure out how to get around it.

"Should we run for it?" I shouted.

"Not yet," she said. "We'll never make it."

I nodded, though I knew she couldn't see me, and turned my attention back to the matter at hand: the approaching beast of an undead man.

"Shit."

He'd begun to move quicker as he zoned in on me for the kill. He was less than five yards away, and I was his intended target. His stink was powerful enough to knock me over. Raw, rotten meat, paired with human excrement.

He must've shit himself before he died.

I retched, but only a little.

I pulled my shotgun tighter into my shoulder. The chin wouldn't work; I knew that. I aimed for the knees.

As soon as I pulled the trigger, the creature's legs exploded in a wash of black zombie blood. It sprayed my lower legs, the chill of dead blood sending a shudder through my body. The beast before me fell, collapsing atop his now-shattered legs, the weight of his massive body shaking the ground beneath my feet. Or maybe it was all in my head, the shaking. Or all in my knees. There was no way to tell.

But still he came, that massive monster that wanted to eat me. The scrape of his homegrown armor against the blacktop permeated the sounds of battle around me, cutting through my eardrums with a splitting, shrill agony. I had to stop it.

"I'm stepping out," I shouted, as though in some strange world I was headed to the store to buy a loaf of bread or maybe some milk. "I gotta handle this one."

"No," said Jenna, but she didn't move. There was too much for her to do, too many creatures for her to kill, and she knew it. "Don't leave your wingman!"

"I have to!"

I reached down and picked up her Slugger—she never minded loaning it out—and took the first step away from the warmth and companionship of my partners in battle. The screech of metal against pavement was enough to make me wince. I walked to it.

The zombie's wasted hand reached out for me, desperate and hungry. I let him grasp my foot, his fingers closing in a vice-grip that would, I knew, leave a bruise for me to deal with after the battle. He pulled himself closer to me, his mouth gaping wide behind the riot mask, revealing rotted teeth and a tongue barely hanging on by several stretching, dripping tendons. I let him come.

The mask hit my first foot, and the zombie smashed his face against it, his tongue making wet, sloshing noises as it slurped against the bulletproof shield. My foot was safe, blocked by the very piece of industrial-strength plastic that had kept me from being able to kill him. The helmet, held in place by a chin-strap that was giving way with age, moved off kilter, exposing the back of the zombie's neck.

That was all the space I needed.

I raised Jenna's Slugger, graying with age, black in part with ancient zombie blood, and brought it down on the exposed flesh with all the strength I could muster. It was, I must admit, considerable. The creature's head detached from it's body, the hand suddenly going slack around my foot. I flexed my toes with appreciation, even as the mouth below me continued to slurp and stretch, trying to bite me. I nudged it away with the toe of my boot, and it rolled end over end, the neck encrusting itself with debris from the road, before coming to a rest a few feet away. The opening of the neck pointed at me, wet and sparkling with glass shards and pebbles. The zombie's jaw flapped, open and closed, open and closed. I aimed at the wet spot.

That should work.

I pulled the trigger.

The mask, once filthy but still transparent, was instantly covered with sticky black muck. The jaw could no longer open and close, because the jaw was no longer there. The beast of a zombie was dead.

Sorry, friend. I admired your preparation. Wish you could've held out. I probably would've liked traveling with you.

But the thought was fleeting. Jenna's voice cut through the noise around me. "Sam! Quit fucking around with that thing. We've got to go."

A hand gripped me from behind—warm, this time, and small, Rosie's hand—and pulled me along toward the closing gap in the herd of zombies. Soon, all I knew was running and running and running.

Chapter 6: Jenna

We'd been running forever. Branches grabbed at me from all sides, tangling in my hair, my hood, my backpack, as my thick biker boots pounded against the solid, not-entirely-thawed mat of dead leaves and rotted forest debris. I focused on the sight of Will and Rosie, running steadily before me on legs strengthened during their months with us in the farmhouse—Will never could have run this far when we first met him—and the sound of Sam, crashing along behind me. We made enough noise, I'm sure, to keep the zombies' attention zeroed in on us for decades, but I had to hope we were stronger and faster and more determined even than the hungriest of the undead. Because if I lost hope, I'd stop running, and if I stopped running, we'd be zombiefied.

In the distance, I heard the moaning and groaning, the snarling and growling, of the herd of zombies in hot pursuit of us, their prey. I hated being prey. I very much preferred being the hunter, but their numbers would have overwhelmed us even if we'd still been on the farm. A horde the size of the one that continued chasing us long after my legs had turned to jelly would have overtaken just about any of the settlements I'd encountered on all of my travels. The outstretched tree limbs and gnarled roots of the dense forest were no match even for the zombies, so I kept running. And so did the others.

As we ran, the shadows in the forest lengthened and deepened, and I was aware of the passage of time as a dangerous thing. A deadly thing. If we were still running past dark, I knew, the fight would be over. We couldn't run in the dark without hurting ourselves, and in the dark our aim would be grim at best. Any hope of survival had to stay hinged on the lights staying on overhead, and that battle was being lost as each minute flew by and we continued to run.

Suddenly, Rosie and Will stopped dead in their tracks in front of me, and I reeled myself in to keep from crashing into them. I had no such consideration from Sam, who wasn't able to stop in time.

"Oof," I said as he smashed into my back. I feel to my knees, the breath that burned in my lungs exhaling in that one breathy sound. I hopped up as soon as the woozy, whirly feeling from the sudden halt began to dissipate, pulling myself out from under Sam's heavy body. He seemed content to lay there, panting.

"Why'd you stop?"

I spoke to Will, but Rosie answered. "Look," she said, beckoning for me to follow her. She and Will were a few steps ahead of where I'd fallen. "We have to."

I approached, slowly and with caution, though every part of me, every nerve-ending and hair follicle, every piece of muscle and sinew, screamed for me to run, run, *run* from the ceaseless beasties in the forest behind us. What I saw when I reached Rosie took my breath away. Again.

It was a field, stretching further than I could comprehend, opening out with a sinister emptiness for miles and miles without end. The sky above it looked bigger than I'd ever seen, spreading in its deepening hues of midnight blue and grey as the sun continued setting and the minutes kept on ticking. I stared, my mouth falling open, my hands opening and closing into tight fists, then opening again to let the blood back into my fingertips. On the road, we'd been partially protected from view by the forest on either side, but in the field, we'd be vulnerable. Naked. Visible for miles by anyone or any*thing* that didn't want us around. The field represented danger, on many levels, and for a moment I couldn't even imagine what it was doing there.

"What is it?" I said. I was from Jersey, and even though I'd spent time in country ever since the zombies, I was still used to cities and suburbs and buildings so close you could barely walk between them. This field, stretching so far and wide, was incomprehensible to me, especially after the closeness of the forest through which we'd run.

"Cornfields," whispered Will. There was reverence in his voice, the respect of a Midwestern farm-boy who knew from hoeing and planting and reaping, things I'd never even considered in my comfortable suburban upbringing. "Gone fallow. No one to harvest, no one to plant. It kind of breaks my heart."

"We can't cross it. Not right now," I said, and Will nodded. "But we can't stop, either."

"Why not?" Sam's voice startled me. He stood at my shoulder, still panting, but silently.

I turned and slapped his shoulder. "Don't sneak up on me like that, you creeper! Last I saw you, you were collapsed on the ground!"

"Ow, don't hit me!" he said, but he had that manic grin on his face like he sometimes did during battle or whenever I tried to argue with him. I slapped him again, and the grin widened.

"Stop it," I said. "Stop smiling. We have to go. We have to keep moving."

Rosie took my hand, maybe to keep me from hitting Sam again. But Sam only shrugged.

"I think we're safe," he said. "I've been listening, while you crazy people kept running. I haven't heard a zombie-groan in ages. And…" he paused and sniffed the air like a dog. "I can't smell them anymore either. We left them far behind us."

"But they can smell…"

He gave me a look. "Jenna, don't you think my sense of smell is better than a zombie's? If I can't smell them, they definitely can't smell us. And I agree with Rosie. We can't cross this field right now, not with the sun setting and us not knowing what's on the other side. We can stop here for the night."

"But," I said again, but he pressed a hand over my mouth.

"But nothing. Don't freak out. I know I may have freaked out back there, but you're our rock. Don't you freak out over having to stop. The kids have to stop anyway. They can't keep running like that. Not all night."

"We're not kids," said Rosie. She jutted out her lower lip and squared her shoulders for a fight with Sam. "We can keep going if we need to."

He laughed and patted her cheek, the ultimate move of patronization. "Yes, dear, but why? They're gone, and we could use the rest."

Sam dropped his pack to the ground and slowly removed his shotgun from the strap around his shoulders. He pulled out a bottle of greyish water and took a long swig, then offered it to Rosie. She accepted gratefully, took a drink, and passed it to Will, who still stared out at the destroyed cornfield. He drank, never moving other than to swallow.

I sighed. So much of me still wanted to run, to hide, but I had to agree with Sam. I couldn't hear or smell anything. I wondered how long we'd run after we no longer needed to, but it didn't matter. We'd covered more miles in our panic than we ever would have had we continued our slow and steady march. Only one thing remained a problem. As I peeled my own backpack and rifles from my shoulders, I raised my head. "Anyone know where we are?"

Sam continued unpacking. He pulled out the small tent from his pack and started clearing a place for it. "No clue," he said without looking up. "We'll figure it out in the morning. For now, we camp, here in the trees. I don't think we can have a fire tonight, but we should be warm enough in our tents." He was slow and methodical, and I turned to watch. His face was set in a strange, blank expression, as though he was hiding something.

I shrugged, and continued unhooking and unstrapping all my hiking gear and weaponry from around my tired body. One by one I placed items on the ground next to one another. My pack. My canteen. My gun belt. My extra ammo clips. My rifle. My…

A shock went through me. It felt like lightning.

"Has anyone seen my Slugger? Sam! You had it. I saw you with it back when we were fighting. Where did you put it?"

His shoulders slumped. I'd found what he'd been hiding. My heart beat faster. "I'm sorry, Jenna. I must have put it down…"

"What? You can't. That's impossible."

I barely noticed when I tripped on my path to reach Sam in three long strides. My heart, which had only begun to slow after our long run, raced off again. My hands clenched and my jaw ached, and even my lower back got in on the action, screaming out with a sudden, tense pain that made me almost fall. My Slugger was a part of me. An extension of my body. I found it the first night of the zombies, and it was the weapon of last resort that had saved me from hundreds of close encounters of the zombie kind.

Sam's face scrunched up as he withstood my onslaught. I took hold of his shoulders and shook him, hard. His head bobbled atop his neck, but other than that he never even flinched. "I'm sorry, Jenna," he said again. "I only just realized I didn't have it. I don't remember putting it down after I killed that big guy. I just…don't have it."

"But it's my Slugger," I said. "I need it." I swallowed. My throat felt like sandpaper. Tears burned in my eyes. "I have to go get it."

Now Sam winced. "Are you crazy? You can't. It's in the middle of that…those…you just *can't*."

A tear spilled over. It coursed down my cheek, cold and wet, and settled in the corner of my lips. I tasted it as I spoke. "But it's a part of me."

Sam's eyes turned cold. "I'll get you a new bat." He pulled away. "You can't be crazy about a stupid baseball bat."

"Yes I can," I shouted. He'd stepped away, but not far enough, and I reached out and shoved him. He backpedalled, then tripped over his pack, laid so carefully on the ground behind him. He tumbled to the ground.

"Hey!"

"Hey nothing. You lost my bat. I'm going to go get it back. Asshole."

I turned to go, and saw Will and Rosie, standing and watching, like two kids watching their parents argue. "What are you looking at?" I said, and I walked away.

* * * *

I didn't make it very far. The Slugger was a part of me, sure, but as the sun continued to set and darkness shrouded the woods, it became impossible to follow even a trail so carelessly created as the one we'd made crashing through the trees. As I walked back to camp, I mourned the loss of that stupid piece of stained, solid, deadly wood.

"I'm sorry, Slugger," I said to no one but myself, following the faint flicker of lights made by flashlights held by Sam, Will and Rosie. It hurt almost as much to lose that bat as it had to say goodbye to Sadie and Chicken. My heart ached. I shivered.

Soon I reached the camp, where our two small tents had been set up in my absence. That was good; I never had been very good at tent building, never having joined the Girl Scouts or anything. I'd set them up in my days with Michael on the road, but mine were always lopsided.

Sam sat outside, reclining against a tree trunk. He held a flashlight, pointing it at a tattered paperback resting open on his lap. He looked up and smiled at the sounds of my footsteps. "Oh good. You're back."

I nodded, and sank to the ground beside him, sniffling as I did.

He sighed. "I'm so sorry, Jenna. I'd never hurt you on purpose. You know that, right?"

He sounded so contrite, so gentle, my anger melted away like last winter's snow. Unable to speak around the stupid lump in my throat, I nodded again, and then lay my head against his shoulder. He shifted his weight and his arm until it rested around my shoulders, and then he kissed my forehead. His lips were warm and wet, and they lingered perhaps a bit longer than they needed to, but I found I didn't mind. Not on that night. Not when I needed a little bit of comfort after a long, grueling day.

"Forgive me?"

I nodded again. And again. I'd never in my life been able to stay mad at Sam.

"Love you," he said, his voice suddenly playful again.

I laughed. "Shut up." Then I yawned. "Where are Will and Rosie?"

"Gone to bed. They were beat."

"Me, too. Which tent's Rosie in?"

He pointed to the one further from us. "That one. With Will. Guess it's you and me together tonight." The flashlight illuminated the evil grin that curled his lips.

"Wait, what?" That was unexpected. I had counted on bunking down with Rosie, and the boys sleeping in the other tent. That felt more… proper, considering I hadn't fully divorced myself from Michael. But then I reconsidered. It made sense for the brother and sister to want to be together, and hadn't I always said Sam was just like my big brother? If only he wasn't so much like Michael—it made me ache.

But I could handle it.

I hadn't noticed Sam was talking, so lost in thought was I, and so the next thing I heard was, "And so if you'll take your shirt off, I'll take off mine, and we can check."

"Wait, what?" I said it again. I couldn't help it, even though I knew I probably sounded ridiculous. "I spaced out for a sec. *Why* am I taking off my shirt? Because you're a perv?"

He laughed, but it was soft. Still gentle. I shivered again. The nights cooled off quickly.

"It's a safety thing, doofus. We're checking for bites, scratches. Rosie and Will checked each other, but I figured I'd wait for you. It's not like I'm asking you to strip. I've seen you in a bikini hundreds of times…a bra and underwear are no different, right?"

Well, it's kind of different. But I guess not really.

I stood. What he said made sense, and I tried to ignore the inherent weirdness, and the part of me that thought I wouldn't mind being topless around Sam. That thought felt disloyal, and I tried to squelch it with all my strength.

Sam stood too. I grinned. "On three then?" I said. "One…two…"

Sam's shirt was off before I said three, but he was a guy and things were always different for guys. Before I could lose my courage, I quickly jerked my sweater and t-shirt up and off, dropping them on the ground beside me. I crossed my arms over my chest, as much to hide the tattered, filthy condition of my bra as to hide my breasts. Though it was dark, enough moonlight filtered through the trees to allow our eyes to adjust, and Sam still held the flashlight.

Goosebumps covered my skin as he got to work, inspecting me for the signs of a bite or scratch that would have meant my life was ending. Though I'd not been bitten, I could have as easily been infected by a scratch, one I maybe wouldn't have felt in the heat of battle.

Sam trailed the flashlight across my stomach and arms, tracing a finger along my skin as he went, checking for bumps or lumps that might feel suspicious. Suddenly the goosebumps weren't only caused by the cold. Without meaning to, I leaned into his touch.

He worked in silence, pressing a hand against my shoulder to guide me to turn around so he could check my back. Though he was flirty beforehand, while checking he was all business, like a doctor examining a patient.

Soon he was done. "All clear so far," he whispered. "Now you check me."

I took the flashlight, and began my own inspection, tracing the lines of his body with the flashlight and my fingertips. Always thin, now he was skinny, but wiry, with muscles stretched taut and lean across his shoulders, his chest, his abdomen. I lingered longest on the area just above where his shorts ended, the slow, sloping curve of his thin hips, the place where his stomach curved in and down, where a small trail of hair led into his pants. It was over too soon.

"All clear so far."

He stared at me, but I didn't feel embarrassed.

"Pants now," he said, and I nodded.

"One…two…"

We were both undressed before three.

I could have put my shirt on first. I probably should have. But it didn't feel necessary as we stood there, just the two of us, alone in the dark.

Again, Sam looked first, taking the flashlight from my hand, squatting down to check my legs. His breath was warm against my thighs, and I tried not to squirm.

It was over too soon.

He stood. "All clear."

He loomed over me, disarmingly close. Our hips touched. He pressed the flashlight into my hand. "Check me please?"

Sam's boxers were loose, hanging from his hips, as I knelt beside him. I trailed my fingers down his legs, where dark hairs curled and glistened in the beam of light. I stayed low, afraid to go too high. Afraid of what I might find. I stood quickly. "All clear."

Our eyes locked. I was afraid to move. Afraid of what I might find. Sam nodded.

"They say it's warmer, on a night like this, to sleep without clothes, so our body heat can keep each other warm."

I nodded. I didn't want to get dressed. I wanted to be close to him. To someone. And so I nodded.

We left our clothes outside the tent. I unzipped the flap, and spread out my sleeping bag on the ground. His would be our blanket. We slipped into the tent, me first, and then him. He zipped us in.

As we lay down together, naked but for some thin cotton and a bent underwire bra, he pulled me close, wrapping his body around me in a way not unlike the way Michael once did. He was close, so close, and it was so comfortable, so soothing. But it wasn't right. Not quite. And as his hands found a resting place against my stomach and his legs relaxed into sleep, I lay, stiff and confused, wanting things I didn't want to want, and knowing I couldn't have them. It was a long time before sleep found me that night, and a long time before a voice woke us in the night.

"Jenna? Sam?"

It was Michael.

Chapter 7: Will

I awoke to the sound of an agonized cry. An angry cry. The cry a creature makes when it's pinned back into a corner and its life is on the line.

My heart went into immediate hyper-drive, and Rosie bolted to sitting upright beside me in the blackness, struggling against the tangle of her sleeping bag's zipper. "What was that?"

I could only shake my head and run a hand through my hair. I was shaking, my voice failing, and I hated those things so much in that moment it completely washed away the terror I felt at that *sound*. That wounded animal, trapped in a cage with a claw around its foot *sound*.

And then came Jenna's voice, cutting through the darkness. "It's not what you think. Michael. Please, settle down. The zombies will find us again if you keep making that racket."

"How could it be anything but what I think? Jesus, Jenna! Were you just waiting till I was out of the way? Or did you even wait? Have you two been sleeping together this whole time?"

Beside me, I heard the slap of a hand hitting skin. In my mind, I saw Rosie's frustrated face, the irritated forehead smack. I almost smiled as I reached out and found her wrist in the darkness, pulling it back down. She squeezed my hand. We'd been here before; our parents used to fight sometimes, whisper-shouting when they thought we were asleep. Of course, they usually fought over money, not…

"We're not doing anything! I swear to God." There came a rustling sound, and Rosie and I wiggled our way to the front of our tent, peeking out through an opening in the flap. The moonlight illuminated plainly enough the sight of Jenna, in her underwear, casting about on the ground for her pants, as Michael stood over her in a posture of pure, broken despair. Sam stood beside his tent, also in his underwear, shaking his head and covering up a smile.

"Shows you what happens when we go to bed early," Rosie whispered, giggling. She didn't fool me, though. She always was a nervous giggler, her frenetic need to laugh punctuating most of the tense memories in my life.

Something pressed against our tent, against my leg, and I shifted my gaze down. "Oh, hey, Chicken," I said to Jenna's little dog, who cowered in fear from the shouts of his owners. "What are you doing here?" As if he could answer. "Never mind. Come on in. Scoot over, Rosie."

I unzipped the flap further and Chicken climbed way in, saying hello in his panting, slurping, tongue-ish way. Rosie squeezed him around the neck and buried her face in his fur while, outside, the drama continued.

"Nothing? Right. Then why were you naked in the tent with my brother?"

"For God's sake, it was cold, and we thought it would be warmer. You know, body heat?"

"That's a lame excuse," whispered Rosie.

I started to laugh, quietly at first, until Rosie joined in. Here we were, in the middle of nowhere Nebraska, surrounded by a horde of hungry undead creatures, and Jenna and Michael were arguing. Again.

"If you were cold you should have brought an extra blanket! Here! I brought some! Take mine! That way you won't be so goddamn *cold!*"

I peeked out just in time to see Michael hurl a blanket at Jenna's head. His breath puffed in front of his mouth in angry clouds, like a bull protecting his cows on a winter morning. Even his nostrils flared. The image of horns growing from his head made me laugh harder, and I collapsed backward. Chicken jumped atop my chest and started licking my face.

"Stop, stop," I whispered, choking and sputtering. Rosie grabbed him by the collar and hauled him off me, but she could barely keep a grasp on him.

"And I came here because I couldn't stand to be without you, even after everything! I find you in bed with my *brother!* God fucking dammit! What else can you do to me? How else are you going to break my heart?"

"Michael needs to grow a pair!"

"Rosie! Hush! Don't talk like that, Mom wouldn't like it. Chicken, stop!"

"For God's sake Michael, shut *up!"* Sam's voice was a roar, cutting through the night, and Chicken, Rosie and I froze. "There are zombies everywhere out there, nothing happened, and you're acting like a spoiled little asshole."

I sat up again, peeking. Jenna had given up on getting dressed, instead wrapping herself in the tattered old blanket Michael had weaponized. Michael still looked ready to fight, as did Sam in his torn and sagging boxers. The three faced off in the moonlight.

They're going to kill each other.

The thought was sudden and heavy with gravity. Michael was armed; his guns remained at his sides, for the moment, but I was afraid that at any point that could change. *Would* change, if something didn't stop the raging hormones in front of us.

"Stay down, Rosie," I whispered, my heart racing. Something was about to happen. I sniffed the air, and it was like I could actually smell the pheromones emitted by the angry threesome. If the noise didn't bring the zombies, the smells certainly would. I clenched my fists.

Jenna stepped forward, closer to Michael. He flinched, and so did she. But she kept walking until she was right in front of him, and from beneath the blanket she reached out a hand and placed it on his cheek.

"Nothing happened," she said, her voice quiet but firm. "But even if it had, you have no right to be angry. Not here, not now. Not after *you* left *me*, a long time ago. *You* left our room. *You* moved out. *You* decided you couldn't forgive me. It's been months, Michael. Months. And no matter what, I love *you.*"

Sam winced at that. I saw him. And I wondered, fleetingly, what *did* happen inside their tent that night. Or outside, based on the clothes littering the ground between the tents.

"So can we please stop fighting, just for a second? And get through the night so we can figure out what to do in the morning? There's a giant herd of zombies out there, in case you somehow managed to avoid then, and I, for one, don't relish the thought of fighting them, now, in the dark, in my underwear."

"What's happening?" whispered Rosie.

"Shh. Something."

Michael looked behind him, pulling away from Jenna's hand. "No, there's not," he said, his voice flattened like a stale pancake. "They're all dead."

That was interesting to me. "Dead?" I said, blowing our cover. "Dead how?" They'd been so alive, or at least *sounded* alive, hours earlier when they'd chased us through the forest. Surely Michael had come across a smaller group of dead zombies. It couldn't be the ones who'd pursued us. They were so *lively*.

Jenna started, and the three of them turned to me with my head poking out of the tent. I resisted the urge to shrink back inside, to continue being the unseen observer, which had kind of always been my role in life. I forced myself to emerge from my cocoon, from the tent, to face them.

"You must've seen a different group," I said. "Zombies don't just *die* like that."

"No, they don't," said Michael. "They were burned. Intentionally and systematically burned. Jenna, it was like that time…"

"…in New Orleans." She finished his sentence.

"Burned?" Sam said, for the first time looking invested in the conversation in a way that didn't involve pummeling his brother. "Burned how? What could have burned them?"

"More like who." Michael was calm. He scratched his head, then reached behind him and pulled something out from where it leaned behind a bush. "Here, I found this."

Jenna sucked in a breath, and let it out in a choked squeal. "My Slugger!"

I pointed my flashlight at it. It was charred, still solid but covered with a layer of black carbon. Jenna ran her hand down the shaft, and dusty ash rained down to the ground, glittering like black snow in the beam of light. She dropped her blanket, and even from far away I saw the goosebumps on her skin. I tried not to look, not to notice her near-nakedness. It was too violating.

From behind me burst a flash of black lightning, and Chicken bounded across the small space between the tents and where Jenna stood, his tongue lolling out as he leaped at her. She dropped her bat to catch the dog, and she hugged him close. Then she looked at Michael.

"You brought Chicken? I thought he was going to stay with Sadie?"

"He was miserable without you." Michael wouldn't return Jenna's stare.

She sighed, and set the dog down. He sat on her foot.

"Back to the subject at hand, though," I said. "Are you sure it was the same zombies you saw? Who could have burned them?"

Michael shrugged, and he filled us in. He left less than five hours after us, an impulse decision based on the fact that the last time he and Jenna were separated he almost died…and so did she. Chicken kept sneaking out anyway, that morning, so in the end he took the dog with. They made great time, following our trail, and came to the scene of our battle. But it was different from what we described. It was burnt, scorched, the ground littered with smoldering zombies. They were all dead.

He found Chicken midway through the scarred battlefield, sniffing and pawing at a stick on the ground. "That was your Slugger," said Michael to Jenna. "When I found it, I thought you were dead."

He pressed on anyway, hoping to find Sam or Will or Rosie. After picking his way through the gruesome piles of dead bodies, he had little hope of finding any of us alive, but Chicken ran faster and faster, as though hot on our trail. And if there was one thing Michael knew, it was to trust Chicken's nose.

"But there were hundreds of zombies," said Sam. "How'd they all get dead?"

He'd finally pulled on his shorts, so at least I didn't have to worry about Rosie seeing his stuff falling out of his boxers. I breathed a small sigh of relief, especially when I realized Rosie was standing beside me, all still and silent. She was good like that, especially for a kid.

Michael shrugged. "It must've been someone who really knew what they were doing, and had something like…"

"Napalm."

The Jenna and Michael finishing each other's sentences thing was going to get old fast, but at least the topic remained interesting.

"Napalm's easy to make," I said. "From household chemicals and all. Someone could have made some, right?"

"But they'd need a plane to fly it." Sam's voice was full of wonder. "To drop it on so many at once."

I couldn't help but echo it. "A plane," I said. "You're right. Michael, did it look like napalm? Was it totally scorched earth, like the end of a battle? And far-reaching? Not just a couple yards?"

Michael nodded. "We're talking about half a football field, burned to ash. I mean, trees still standing, but everything smoking. All the new growth gone. Burnt. Done."

"A plane," I said. Rosie took my hand. I looked down to see her staring up at me, her face eager and excited. "That means maybe they could fly us out of here. Maybe they can take us to where the survivors are!"

She squeezed my hand so hard it hurt. I couldn't believe it. A plane meant we were so much closer to me taking my notes—Dr. Schwartz's notes—to someone with a lab. With facilities to test what I knew would be a working vaccination against the zombie disease. "We have to find them."

"No!"

This time it was Jenna, Michael *and* Sam talking in unison. Shouting in unison. Shutting me down, just like they had for months. Rosie's face fell, and my free hand balled into a fist.

"Why….not…" I barely got the words out.

They talked over each other. It was hard to make out.

"Because…Russell…"

"The Captain…"

"Chase Franklin…"

"Nasty…"

"Angry…"

"Brutal…"

I held up a hand. "I get it. I get it. But we have to do this. We have to find them."

Jenna pulled her bare foot from beneath Chicken's rear end and she walked over to me. I tried not to flinch. She was still in her underwear.

"Not tonight," she said. "For tonight, now that the drama's over, I think it's time to get some sleep. We'll figure out the rest of it in the morning."

She turned and headed back into her tent. Sam and Michael exchanged a look, shrugged, and then both followed her, along with Chicken, leaving Rosie and me alone outside, wondering how three people and a dog would fit inside a tent built for one…and how the three people who moments earlier wanted to kill each other would ever find rest together in the end.

But that wasn't for us to worry about, and eventually we headed back inside our own tent. It was late, and Rosie's breathing steadied quickly, but I lay awake a long time, daydreaming of planes and escape and an end to the zombie apocalypse.

* * * *

Sunrise came quickly, the shortening of the nights both a blessing and a curse to sleep-deprived, weary travelers like us. The first rays of sun pierced through the trees like daggers, cutting through the tent in which I dozed fitfully after last night's chaos. They were a painful wake-up call to the realities of our world: for one, it was time to get moving, and for two, we had no idea what we were going to find as soon as we left the safety of the trees and crossed into the great, fallow cornfield beyond.

I tried to hide beneath the balled-up sweatshirt I used as a pillow, but it was no use. I was awake, and with a crick in my neck and an ache in my lower back and left knee, I felt a heck of a lot older than fifteen years.

Rosie, on the other hand, was still sound asleep beside me. I wished I had her ability to close my eyes and shut out the world, but that had never been the case. Mine was a brain not easily turned off, and much more easily awakened.

I slid my arm out from beneath her head (*that explains the sore wrist)*, and she barely moved, so I slipped out of the tent before pulling on the sneakers I'd outgrown at least six months earlier. My toes hit the end with a sharp stab of pain, but I ignored them. My cramped toes were the least of my worries. I had a world to save, didn't I?

Though I'd made the assumption that I'd be the first one up, I was wrong. Jenna knelt nearby, poking at some sticks and kindling as she tried to light a small fire with the old "spinning stick" trick with which I'd succeeded only once, back in the days when my parents forced me to be a Boy Scout. "You're only eight," they'd say, then nine, then, ten, then eleven, before they finally let me quit. "Your *research* can wait." And I hated the way they'd italicize research when they spoke, like my interests and pursuits weren't good enough since I was just a kid. And maybe that was true, since most of the time back then I was researching things like how to make a car fly or how to make an airplane transform into a submarine upon crash landing in water. But they seemed like noble pursuits at the time, and clearly my interest in research back then had prepared me for the leaps and bounds I'd been able to make with Dr. Schwartz's notes…if only I was able to test my theories on real people…

"Um, you just gonna stand there, or are you gonna come down here and help me?" Jenna's teasing cut through my thoughts, and for a split second I wondered how long I'd been standing there, watching the way her shoulders moved as she spun the stick back and forth, back and forth.

It didn't matter. "Sorry," I said, moving to sit beside her. From my pocket I pulled a pack of matches—I always had matches on me, even now, what with "be prepared" having been drilled into my head for four years of my childhood—and tossed them into her lap. "Will this help?"

"Yes!" Her face lit up. "It will, thanks. I have some, too, buried in my backpack, but I didn't want to have to run the gauntlet of that tent again." She fake-shuddered, then grinned. "Those boys are a mess."

I'm not sure what my face looked like, but it must've been ugly because she lost her grin quickly when I looked at her. "What?"

"You're laughing about them? After last night? I honestly thought Michael was going to kill you, and then there you all went, into the tent together. Like a bad late night movie or something." It was my turn to shudder.

Jenna shrugged. "We've been together our whole lives. Even when we hate each other, we still love each other. Nothing can really change that, I guess. And what else were we going to do? Michael didn't pack a tent, and it's still too cold at night to sleep outside."

"At least you're dressed now."

I blushed, but Jenna only laughed again. "Yeah, that. I don't know. It's all weird. But I swear, nothing happened with Sam. But why am I telling you that. It's not like you care."

As she spoke, Jenna lit the fire, which caught slowly and smoldered as she blew on the sparking moss. Smoke blew into my face. It smelled good, like s'mores and hot chocolate. My stomach rumbled. "What's for breakfast," I said, half-joking.

Jenna closed her eyes and grinned. "Pancakes. Bacon. Can't you smell it cooking?"

And I could. But not in my mind. Like, I really could. I jumped to my feet. "Jenna, get up. Do you smell that?"

Her eyes flew open and she leaped to her feet beside me. "Bacon," she breathed, as though having a religious experience. Which I understood completely. Though my parents had stocked our underground storage room with all kinds of canned foods and dried goods, we hadn't thought of meat. It had been well over a year since I'd eaten meat of any kind, and the smell of bacon was enough to almost bring me to my knees. Almost. Jenna caught me before I fell, and we stood there, holding each other, sniffing the air as though we could inhale the salted, bacon-y protein straight from the ether around us.

Quickly the rest of our group emerged from the tent, including Chicken, who leaped and bounded around the fire, nipping at the air with his tongue lolling loose from his wide-hanging mouth. He yipped and yelped as though it was his best day ever.

Rosie was the last to make her appearance, her hair tousled and sticking out in all directions. "Is that bacon?" she said as she rubbed her eyes and stretched. "Where'd you get that?" She stopped and stared at the barely-rumbling fire. "And where are you hiding it?" Her lower lip stuck out in her angry-pout, and she turned to glare at me.

"Don't look at me like that," I said. "If I knew where it was, trust me, I'd be eating it."

Sam looked around at the edge of the trees, a few crowded yards away from us. The cornfield was barely visible through the lush forest foliage. He looked back at the pitiful fire before kicking a shower of damp soil on top of it. "Someone knows we're here," he said. "They're fucking with us. So Chicken, stop that. We need to be quiet. We should get out of here."

Jenna nodded in silence, then turned her glance to Michael. "You're sure they're managing back at the house?"

"Yeah. Simon's started a new council already. It's all the older guys. They'll be safe. Boring, but safe."

"So you're sticking with us?"

"Yes, just not with…"

"I don't care what you think about me. At this point, you're either in or you're not. It's your call. But if you're in, you need to quit being a jack-ass to me. Is that a deal?"

Jenna's eyes, always a light blue, could be downright icy when she wanted them to be. In that moment, they were frozen. Clear, pure, like the sky on a day in February when snow is coming but the clouds aren't there yet. I wouldn't have dared to challenge them.

Neither did Michael. Instead, he looked down, digging in the dirt with the toe of his boot. "I'm in. Just not…"

"Shut up."

"Right."

"Great. Now that's settled. Fabulous. Now can we get the hell out of here? I don't like this." Sam's voice was low and gravely. He was worried. Even I could see that.

"Sir, yes, sir," said Rosie, and she turned and dove back into our tent. Soon the sounds of zippering and packing filled the air, along with the gut-wrenching smell of bacon, and within seven minutes we were ready to go.

As the final arrangements of weapons across chests and backs were settled, and the final knife slid into its scabbard in someone's boot, and as Jenna picked up her Louisville Slugger, ready to go, the morning stillness was cut by the sound of a motor, approaching—fast—from the east.

Chapter 8: Jenna

"Holy shit," said Rosie. Will clamped a hand over her mouth.

The thing was, I didn't blame her a second for what she said. I would have said the same thing, had she not beat me to it. Because even through the thick trees I could see the cloud of dirt and debris raised by the approaching vehicle, and I could smell the diesel cutting through the heady, cloying bacon that had, moments earlier, filled our mouths with saliva and longing.

Michael and Sam stepped closer to me. I could barely breathe, with the two of them sandwiching me as though I was the only person there, but I also liked it. It was nice to feel protected, after spending so long as the farmhouse's protector. But I couldn't tell them that. They didn't need that power over me.

So I shoved Sam toward Rosie, hard. "You stay with them. Michael, you come with me." And I walked away, toward the break in the trees, to see what I could see without a half dozen yards of branches and leaves clouding my view.

They may have bickered behind me—they probably did, in fact—but I didn't care. I kept on walking, aware of footsteps flanking me. From the way they crashed I knew it was Michael. I didn't need to see.

I tripped over a root that stuck up in the air like a giant F-U to the world, and cracked my shoulder against a tree trunk. Michael's hand stopped me from falling the final few feet, out into the clearing.

"Thanks."

"Don't mention it."

He'd gripped too hard, and his fingers left my arm stinging almost as badly as the shoulder that hit the tree. It didn't matter, though. The motor was louder, the diesel was stronger, and over everything I could still smell that damn bacon.

"I hope they don't want to kill us," I whispered. "I'd rather they invite us over for bacon."

"Yeah, but what are the chances of that?"

"Slim to none, I'd say."

"Exactly."

As we spoke, I hunkered down behind the massive root bed of a tree that had overturned probably months—if not years—before. It lay at the edge of the clearing, a perfect hiding spot. Michael squatted beside me at the same time, our breaths falling effortlessly into the same rhythm like they always had. We poked our heads up, prairie-dog style.

"Shiiiiiittt…" he breathed.

He was right.

The truck closed in on us at a breakneck pace: the huge, beat-up old pick-up, flying across the field. We were lucky the field was so large. We had thirty seconds to watch him before he'd be right on top of us.

The truck itself was an impressive thing, decked out in camouflage paint and dark brown netting. It stood much taller than a normal recreational pickup, and the dual wheels in the back told me it was ready for much heavier-duty as well. There was a winch in the front, and some kind of protective armor hanging down over the windshield, but even those things weren't what *really* got to me.

What bothered me—the most, actually, because there was a lot there to bother me—was the oversized gun mounted in the bed of the truck, and the way it pointed directly at us.

"That's an M2 Browning," whispered Michael, who'd taken to studying old copies of Guns & Ammo that we picked up on some of our journeys. Ever since New Orleans, he wanted to know what weapons could do, and what we would be facing in the event of any sort of attack. Looked like that knowledge was about to come in handy. "That sucker could cut us in two if it hit us."

Or not. "Do I need to know that right now?" I hissed. "Or are you just trying to scare me?"

"Just saying…"

"Well, don't. I don't even see anyone on the truck bed to fire it."

This was more to make myself feel better, of course. In the day and age in which we lived, nothing surprised me, and it wouldn't have been a shocker for a truck to have some sort of automated weapon mounted on the back. I figured the driver could probably fire the gun at us from his little cocoon in the front seat if he wanted. Could…and would.

"Stay down!"

Michael crouched, and I followed him behind the tree as the truck roared to a halt ten feet from where we cowered.

"Oh, shit."

"Michael. This isn't the time to…"

"I want y'all to freeze where you are. I know you're behind that tree trunk. You didn't exactly do a great job of hiding yourselves while I was driving up. So freeze now. I can kill you from where I sit."

It *was* the time to panic. The voice was deep and gruff. Masculine. Angry. Michael and I exchanged a glance. Without speaking, at the same time, we asked, "Run?"

We shook our heads. We wouldn't stand a chance in the field, and in the forest we'd lead him right back to the kids. With a shaking hand I shoved Michael to keep him down. "Let me," I said in silence, and in silence, he nodded. It was just like old times: whenever there was a potential threat from a man, he let me do the talking. I was cute. Men liked me. Even the nasty ones.

Especially the nasty ones.

I looked around for something white to raise, but saw nothing other than my shirt. I knew how Michael felt about me taking off my shirt for strangers, so instead I raised both my hands. "Don't shoot!" I called, hoping my voice sounded loud and clear, and maybe a little sexy. That would help. "We're frozen."

"You're armed," came the masculine voice.

"Yes." No sense denying that. "But we don't want any trouble."

"Girlie, it's been a long time since I met anyone who *didn't* want any trouble. So tell me, how'm I s'posed to believe you?" With his thick accent, "time" sounded more like "taaaaam," so I knew we were dealing with a good old boy.

I paused, thinking before speaking for one of the few times in my life. *What next? Stalemate?* That didn't seem likely. He had the jump on us, he had the truck, and he had the Browning. We had a bunch of trees to trip us up, and a lot to lose. There was only one thing to do, so I did it. I threw all caution to the wind, and, pressing my hand harder against Michael's shoulder and ignoring the look of horror that crossed his face, I pushed myself up to standing. I turned to face our latest captor.

"I'm Jenna Price," I said. "And you have no reason to believe me. But if you let me live, at least for a little while, maybe we can work out a deal."

His voice echoed across the field, deep and gruff and sounding more surprised than I'd heard in ages. "Jenna Price. Well, I'll be damned. That's not a name I expected to ever hear, at least not from the girl herself. And you're such a little thing, too. I'll be *damned*."

My knees almost buckled, and for once I was completely at a loss for what to say. Me? He knew my name? How? Why? Before I could ask, the man began to pull himself out from the truck.

He emerged a piece at a time. First came a boot, all thick, heavy leather and scarred from what looked like years of blue-collar working and living. Next came the pants—Dickies for sure, I thought—ragged at the edges and stained with dirt and oil. His body was massive—*Of course he's huge. Why can't we ever run into the smaller crazy people?* —though nowhere near as thick around as he was tall. His face was mostly hidden behind a busy beard and a tangle of long hair, as well as a pair of mirrored aviator sunglasses. His workman's ensemble was topped with a baseball cap.

"Museum of Modern Art?" I said, reading the words emblazoned on the hat. It wasn't quite what I was expecting, though neither had I expected him to *know my name.* Still, it was easier to deal with a question of a hat than a question of my infamy.

Michael and I walked to the front of the tree stump. We still carried all our weapons. But with the M2 Browning trained right on us, and with the memory of Michael's reverential respect for the gun, as well as the possibility of a remote control, neither one of us was at any pains to point or shoot a gun at the giant before us.

The giant's face broke out into a grin. "What? Why shouldn't I wear a MoMA hat? It's my favorite museum!"

"But that's in New York! And we're in Nebraska!"

"Yeah, and I'm a hick who never travels, right? Shows what y'all know."

Michael elbowed me. "How's about you don't antagonize the man with a gun pointed at us? Ever think of that?"

But the man was still smiling. "Jenna Price. Well then. This day's just taken quite a turn, hasn't it?"

I was less thrilled by the day's "turn," but I still had a sense of humor. And curiosity. "Yes. Yes it has, hasn't it? Unexpected in so many ways. How do you know me? I don't think we've met."

The giant man leaned against the truck, at ease even in the face of our supposed "threat," while I white-knuckled the grip on my Slugger. My hands shook. The man cracked his own knuckles against his thigh. "No. No, of course we haven't met. But….how should I say this…let's just say I've heard about your reputation for trouble."

"My reputation?"

"Word gets out, even at the end of the world." He shrugged, his massive shoulders rising and falling like the tide. "I'm not sure what to do, seeing you right here before me. I'll be honest. I'm a little… conflicted."

I looked from Michael to the man, to the gun, and back to the man. Michael, who'd been hanging back, letting me take charge, stepped forward, pressing his hand against the small of my back. *Don't worry,* his touch said. *I've got this.*

"Sir," he said, lowering his rifle. "You've obviously got the upper hand here. You've got a giant gun, you outweigh us both together, and is it just me or did I smell bacon cooking earlier?"

"You sure did."

Michael nodded. "So you're probably working on a full stomach, while we haven't eaten real food in ages. I mean, seriously, we're about to pass out here. So whatever you've heard about Jenna, do you think you could maybe give us the benefit of the doubt?"

The man raised one of his massive hands and pushed the hat up further on his head, revealing a face reddened with sunburn and maybe also thought. My heart raced and my palms sweat as I waited for the burst of gunfire that would spell our final doom, but it didn't come. Instead, the man stared, and stared some more, as though by looking me over, up and down, left and right, the correct answer would be revealed to him. It would never be that simple, though. Even I knew that. *I* wasn't that simple.

"Look," I said. "Let me put it to you straight. Like I said earlier, we don't want any trouble. I mean that. We're trying to make our way east, looking for his parents. Whatever you've heard about me, I promise you it's exaggerated, or completely untrue." My voice broke. It had been so long since I had to defend myself, my actions, that I'd forgotten how hard it was to remember New Orleans. "If you heard about New Orleans, I can also let you know there's lots more to the story than you probably know. So please. Let us be. We've got a couple kids back there. They don't deserve trouble just because I'm less than perfect."

The man snorted. "You're just a kid yourself. I just can't believe it. Jenna Price."

Not being able to see his eyes behind the mirrored glasses was enough to make me crazy. I couldn't tell if he was kind or cruel, teasing or simply stringing us along before he cut us in half with that terrible gun. But I had no choice. I was cornered. It was either fight, flight, or… flirt.

I stuck out my hand and took another, tentative step closer. His belt was heavy with a few different knifes, and now that I could see the inside of the cab of his truck, I saw the small arsenal within. I swallowed hard, and forced a smile. "Be that as it may, we'd like to make a deal. We didn't mean to cause trouble here, didn't mean to trespass, which I'm assuming is why you're out here so early in the morning. So we'll happily be on our way, if only you'll point that gun elsewhere so we can leave quietly."

He didn't move to take my hand. I refused to let it fall.

"What's in it for me?"

"I'm sorry, what?"

He all-but growled. "I said, what's in it for me? You said we could make a deal. You get something—getting off my property without getting killed—but what do I get?"

"I…I…" While I was thinking, a different voice came from within the trees.

"You get to not get killed by us," it said. Sam. It was Sam. "How's that for getting something? We've got you surrounded."

Behind me, I heard the slap of Michael's palm slapping his forehead, and I'll be honest: had I not been frozen in terror before this mountain of a man, I'd probably have done the same thing. As it stood, I wanted to scream, so certain was I that Sam had just signed my death warrant. It seemed that, even as I stared, the M2 Browning curved on its stand to point even more directly at me. It pinned me, straight through the heart.

But the giant man began to rumble, deep in the back of his throat. It was a laugh, and as the rumble burst forth it was loud and infectious, shocking in its volume and intensity. I jumped back, crashing into Michael, knocking us both to the ground. *Please don't start shooting. Please don't start shooting.* I prayed as I lay in the dirt, painfully aware that we had enough guns and ammo pointing in both directions to kill everyone who stood.

The man laughed harder. "Now that's more like what I expected from Jenna Price and her entourage." He practically howled the words. "Balls. Lots of balls."

"What the fuck," whispered Michael into my ear. "What's so funny?"

"I don't know," I said, shaking my head, refusing to let my eye leave the man's face as tears spilled from beneath his glasses, driven out by the force of his laughter. "Should we run? Now? While he's distracted?"

"I don't know."

Rosie appeared from around the fallen tree's stumpy roots. "C'mon you guys," she hissed in her high-pitched, shrill voice. "What are you waiting for? Let's go!"

The laughter stopped as though someone flicked an off switch. We froze, watching, our eyes trained on mountain of a man who held our fates in his hands. His mouth dropped open to form an O. "Well, I'll be damned. Again. You *do* have a kid with you. A real kid. A kid in this day and age. I never would've dreamed."

Rosie's face scrunched up and she pulled herself up to standing. She had the face of a child, but the attitude of a much bigger person. "Yeah? So? All you want to do is kill us anyway, so don't act like it's so exciting to see a child. I'm probably more of a grown up than you'll ever be, because I don't kill kids!"

The man peeled off his sunglasses as though he was peeling back bits of his own flesh. Behind the darkened glass, his eyes were wide, and a dark, kind brown. He looked surprised, even hurt, at the venom in Rosie's accusations. "I'd never kill a kid," he said. "Especially not now. But never. Ever. I couldn't do that. Especially not one who looks like…" He paused, letting his voice trail off into nothing, and then sighed. "Is that all y'all? Or do you have more hiding out there? I don't think I want to hurt any of you—not even you, Miss Price, even though some people'd prob'ly say I'm crazy for that. Eh, screw 'em, I always say. Talk's big, and I'm bigger than talk."

He spoke to himself more than to us. Considering. Rationalizing. He wiped beads of sweat from his forehead, from the edge of his beard. As he seemingly came to a decision, his hands dropped to his hips, nearer to his gun's holster. "I need to know I can trust you. Really trust you. If I can, I'll take you back to my house. If not, I'm gonna have to go against ever' thing I believe, just to protect myself. So I'm askin'. Again. Can I trust you?"

"How do *we* know we can trust *you?*" I said.

"Do you really have a choice?"

"No," I said, standing back up. Once again, I stepped forward, holding out my hand. "Let's try this again. I'm Jenna Price, but I guess you already know that. I promise you can trust us."

"Dave," he said, taking hold of my hand. His grip was strong and his skin papery-dry. "Dave Mason. I'll give you kids a lift back to my house. But you've gotta leave the guns up front."

* * * *

Sam took some convincing in a heated, whispered conversation before he finally relinquished his guns. In fact, I think he wouldn't have, had Chicken not slipped the lead Will had hastily tied around his neck and gone bounding over to Dave and leaping up to lick his hand. At the sight, Dave's eyes went liquid all over again. He knelt down. "A kid and a mutt," he said. "I never woulda thought…"

We piled our weapons into the front seat, and climbed into the truck bed, beside the M2 Browning. I shuddered as I sat beside it, but then I couldn't help myself. I reached out and touched the stand, running my hand up to the top, letting my fingers lightly graze the well-oiled black metal. The sun was warm already, and the gun hot to the touch. I jerked my hand away, looking around with a guilty feeling in my gut.

"I don't think there's anything controlling this, Michael. I think we could've run."

He nodded. "Probably. But I think rolling with this is probably the best thing."

Beside him, Sam glowered. "Yeah, unless he's taking us back to his secret lair to kill us."

"Shut up," said Michael. "Besides, we need to know what he knows—or thinks he does—about Jenna. And how the hell he came to know it. Because what the fuck? There's a post-apocalypse rumor-mill now? Are we back in high school?"

Rosie and Will sat a bit apart from the three of us, whispering to each other. I knew they were worried—I was worried—but Michael had a point. Rolling with things had for the most part worked out for us in the past. Why wouldn't it work now?

Right?

As the truck took off, Dave shouted, "Hang on, kids. We travel fast 'round here." The truck bolted away, jerking around in a three point turn that would've spilled at least Chicken and me onto the ground beside us had Michael not grabbed me, and I not grabbed my dog. We all settled quickly into the rhythm of the bumpy ride, tossed and thrown about the back of the truck like so much baggage as we sped across the retired corn field.

The ride wasn't long, and it was as fast as Dave promised. The field gave way after about a quarter of a mile to a dirt road that we followed back into the woods. Squinting my eyes against the dust thrown by the tires, I saw a compound appear in a clearing, with a huge fence topped with razor-wire surrounding a small bungalow and a clearing on which sat a little bi-plane.

"Holy shit," said Sam. "I didn't believe it was possible. But there it is. Hard to deny it when the truth is staring you right in the face."

But I wasn't looking at the plane. My eyes were stuck on the fence. The gate. The lock. I'd sworn to myself when we left New Orleans under cover of darkness and flames that I'd never again enter any sort of compound with locked gates and barbed wire. I felt transported back in time, to a day as hot as the sun and as stormy as the seas in a Melville novel, when I was separated from Michael and I ran through empty streets on a mission to find and rescue the love of my life. The love who sat beside me now in the back of a truck that passed through the locked gates and the barbed wire, and suddenly we were in danger. I was sure of it.

I swallowed back a flood of bile and turned to look at Michael. His eyes reflected what I'd already felt myself. "I've got a bad feeling about this," I said, my voice drowned by the roaring of the truck's diesel engine.

Michael nodded. "Me, too. But we're in it together again, aren't we?"

He took my hand, and I squeezed his. Then, pulling Chicken tighter to me so I could grip him between my thighs, I reached out and took

Sam's as well. Across the way I saw the firm set of Rosie's shoulders, and Will's chin. We were in this together.

* * * *

Once, when Michael and I rode into a compound surrounded by razor wire, we were met with men in riot gear wielding syringes full of drugs that almost killed us. This time we were met with sweet tea and bacon.

As Dave pulled the truck to a halt before the aging bungalow, he called through the open window, "You kids thirsty? Hungry? I think y'all look famished."

He hopped down from the cab, surprisingly light on his feet for such a big man, and offered Rosie a lift down from the bed. He seemed taken with her, his eyes lingering on her cheeks, her hair, her long, coltish legs. She gave him a wary stare as she pointedly walked to the other side of the bed and climbed down like a gecko. Will watched her all the way, and made sure she stood by me before he turned to get down from the truck himself.

Meanwhile, Dave kept up a constant chatter like a nervous little girl. "I know it looks intimidating, but it's not bad around here. I had to put up the fence to keep the crazies out, you know?"

"The crazies?" said Will. Despite his reluctance, I could see his curiosity winning, pulling him into the discussion about this little compound in the middle of nowhere.

Dave gave him a curt nod. "The crazies. The ones who eat people. *Those* crazies. Y'all look like a bunch of normal kids, not apt to eat anything b'sides some tea and meat. Now, come on in. Sit a minute and I'll bring y'all somethin' to eat."

We crossed the threshold into Dave's house, into a world where the zombies were "crazies" and there was bacon. It was insane, or at least it felt that way. I wondered how long he'd been out here by himself. I wondered why he was by himself. I wondered so many things, including whether or not I'd be able to eat while surrounded by…well, by the little bungalow surrounding us.

The living room in which we stood was clearly a piece of a man's world. Nothing but a tattered old couch and a few scattered magazines covered the floor, and the décor was hunting cabin chic. Guns stood silent sentry in each corner, and the floor-to-ceiling windows were boarded up on the bottom, allowing only a little light to filter in from above, far above where a normal person's head would reach. In the far corner, a lamp glowed with a warm, yellow light.

"You have power?" called Sam. "Where's the generator? How do you have enough gas to keep it running?"

From a nearby room came the sound of sizzling, and my stomach lurched. Dave's voice rose over the sound. "Two words. Solar power. The whole compound uses it. But I have gasoline, too. Lots of gasoline."

"But how?" I couldn't help myself. I walked toward the sizzle, toward the smell, trailing my fingers along the rough wooden panel walls. "How did you just happen to have all this stuff?"

I reached the kitchen, where the scent of frying bacon was overwhelming. I hadn't seen meat in so long, I'd forgotten how heavenly the smell could be. My head swam with memories of Sunday morning brunches and secret sips of my mother's mimosas when she and my dad were engaged in conversation, and I had to lean against the wall to keep from falling over. I steadied myself by looking around, seeing what else there was to see in the kitchen. It was much like the living room—ill-equipped, functional, and well-armed. A machete sat near the sink, and a rifle hung over the door. As the bacon sizzled cheerfully in a pan atop a small gas range, and a kettle puffed on a second burner, I counted on two hands the many ways a person could be killed here in the kitchen. I hoped against hope not to need to resort to needing the weapons surrounding me, and again I wondered how this had all come to be.

"How?" I repeated, and Dave looked over his shoulder at me and grinned.

"Girl, I've been ready for the end of the world for most of my life. Haven't you ever heard of us preppers? We were all over the place, at least before the crazies came out. I keep in touch with some, still, but…" His grin faded. "Even I have to admit, some of us didn't make it through the onslaught. But still. This is home. Do you like it?"

"I…I…" I didn't know what to say. After so many months of fighting for each bite we ate, living on soups of dried beans, canned beans, and out-of-date grocery-store-brand chicken broth, the smell of meat frying on the stove was too good to believe. Surely he was hiding something. Surely this wasn't pig, but was well-butchered human meat or cat or dog. At that point, I wasn't sure I cared. I'd have eaten whatever was frying in that pan, based solely on the smell. My hands shook. My knees again threatened to give way.

Dave noticed. He reached out and grabbed my arm. I flinched, a reflex reaction that I tried to cover up, but he held tighter until he pulled out a chair and gently lowered me into it. Then he handed me a bottle of water. A bottle! My hands closed around the old, familiar plastic bottle, with its bright blue label. My eyes burned with stinging tears. We'd run out of bottled water after just a few months on the road, and had been living on boiled well or stream water ever since. Water was, in fact, one of our biggest challenges; never had I imagined someone would hand me a bottle of water once again, like it was nothing out of the ordinary.

I cracked it open, my lips parting in an absurd grin at the familiarity of the sound of plastic snapping. I raised the bottle to my mouth, allowing just a few drops to trickle in. The sweetness of the water, the way it tasted so clean and fresh—it was shocking. I tried to wait, to savor it and enjoy it, but instead I closed my eyes. I chugged the whole thing in three gulps.

When I opened my eyes, the whole group stood in a tight circle around me: Sam, Michael, Will, Rosie, Chicken, and Dave, too. They stared at me.

"What? Apparently I was thirsty."

Will laughed. "Can I have a sip?"

My mouth dropped. "I'm sorry. It's empty."

Dave opened his mouth and let out a hoot of laughter. "Don't worry. I have enough for all of you," he said. "I have more than I know what to do with, most of the time. Here. It's in this cabinet."

He opened a door and it was like seeing God. Bottles filled it; water, soda, juice. I hadn't seen so much liquid concentrated in one spot since the zombies came. I cast my eyes around the room; the walls were full of cabinets. Were they all full? Was he really willing to share? And if so, why? What did he want from us?

As always, Sam read my mind. "But wait," he said. "We don't take handouts. At least not without knowing why. Why are you being so nice to us? What do you want?"

Dave, who moments earlier wore a look of delight at the sight of our thrill, crumbled. It was slight, and if you blinked you'd have missed the transition, but he did. Sam had wounded him. He turned to face the stove. "Well, I don't want anything," he said as he flipped the bacon and, miracles never ceasing, cracked a couple eggs into the pan beside the bacon. "Just a little companionship, maybe. It's been a long time since I've had anyone to talk to."

Michael elbowed me and shrugged. He spoke with his eyes. *Maybe it's okay?*

Me? I didn't know what to think. So, in doubt, I kept him talking. "We can do that," I said. "Why don't you tell us how you got here? And we can tell you our story, too."

Dave began talking, pausing only briefly to fill our plates with proteins we hadn't imagined still existed in the world, and then pausing again to fill our plates when they were empty. We ate, and we listened, and we tried to hope.

* * * *

Dave's tale was unlike so many we'd heard. There was death, sure, and fear, of course, but Dave had prepared. He'd planned ahead. This house, deep in the woods of Nebraska, amid fields gone long fallow from years of not being used, was his "bug-out spot", where he and his wife and twin teenage daughters would meet in the event that something bad happened, any sort of disaster, man-made or otherwise.

He'd prepared for everything, here in the house ten miles from where he grew up, and where his daughters were born. Solar panels on the tin roof meant electricity wasn't a problem. A shed out back was filled with bottled water and juices and canned and dried goods. To that day he didn't know what all his wife had crammed in there. They'd put in a chicken coop and a deep freezer, stocked with meats and cheeses and milk, anything they could think of to keep their girls healthy and happy and safe.

Dave had been in charge of the weapons. Surrounding their compound were mines that he could arm remotely in the event of an attack of any sort. He had a small garage stocked full of guns and ammo and knives and a crossbow and all sorts of other sundry items. He had a satellite phone, as did his wife and daughters, and even a small airplane, since he'd once, back in the day, kept bills paid by crop dusting. The business had gone under with the advent of organic farming, but the plane had stayed at the bug-out house.

When the first zombies hit their small town, well ahead of the reports that would soon flood the airways from the surrounding big cities, Dave had been walking his daily rounds at the compound, feeding the chickens and checking a broken solar panel to see if he needed to order some replacement parts online. His satellite phone rang, and his heart leaped into high-gear. He'd drilled it into the heads of his family: the satellite phone was for emergencies only. Never use it unless the end-times had begun. And there it was: ringing.

It was his wife. "What's going on," he asked, bracing for the answer that would change everything.

But the connection was bad. He'd spent hundreds of dollars on that phone, and the one time he needed it to work, it wasn't. It was almost as if something was jamming the signals.

"They probably were," Sam interjected there. "The government was trying to keep it quiet at first, to avoid mass panics. I bet they shut off those signals." Dave dismissed him with a curt nod.

He hopped into his truck—his bug-out truck, the one with the M2 Browning in the back, not his normal Tacoma he drove every day—and headed for the town, avoiding the main roads, not having any idea what he'd find. It took him almost thirty minutes to cover the ten miles, with dusty dirt roads clouding his vision, and a few cars scrambling in opposite directions. By the time he got to Main Street, the zombies had already won. They were everywhere, like flies around a trashcan on a hot summer's day. He saw things that day he'd never forget: people eating people; blood and guts littering the sidewalk in front of the old five-and-dime; a little girl in a purple hat, crying in the midst of the chaos, carried off by a snarling man-creature before Dave could reach her. His windows rolled up, the bullet-proof glass protecting him, he rolled over zombie bodies, crushing heads beneath the thick, heavy-treaded tires.

He reached the school, but found only devastation. A fire burned in the courtyard, consuming the building that surrounded it. Burnt bodies strewn on the ground were feasted upon by the undead. He saw the boyfriend of one of his daughters, his eye gauged out and mouth hanging slack. Dave moved to action. He had a gun, a rifle, and he rolled down the window and shot the boy in the chest, hoping for a kill shot.

The bullet hit him right in the heart, but aside from the jolt of impact, it had no effect on him. He turned and walked toward the truck, along with a dozen of his closest undead friends. Dave aimed again, higher this time. A shot to the head took out the boy, and Dave pulled away in a panic, hands grabbing at his truck's door handles, slapping at the windows. He rolled over more bodies, more living and dying and undead, as he accelerated, but then he saw them.

Two girls, walking together, holding hands in the surrounding pandemonium. Two beautiful girls, marred only by bite wounds—one in the neck, the other in the gut, both as clear as day and twice as devastating as anything he'd ever imagined, even in his most terrifying nightmares. Together they walked, lurching and lunging, and at the sound of the truck, together they turned, their lips pulled back in identical smiles. For even in death his daughters, the twin daughters he'd been able to hold in the crook of his arm, two babies in one arm, together, were identical. From the distance even he, their father, could not tell them apart, and he cried. He howled. With rage, with anguish, and all the creatures in the area, his two beautiful daughters included, turned and ran to the truck, toward him. He couldn't help himself. He floored it, roaring out of the remains of the school parking lot, barely able to see and certainly not able to think.

His wife's office—she was a lawyer—was his next stop, but the roads were too thick with crashed cars and the undead for him to make it. He tried calling her again, but the line was still dead. He turned around, hoping against hope that she'd appear at their meeting place, the bug-out house they'd taken so much time to prepare. He dreaded telling her about the girls. In fact, he couldn't even begin to know how to tell her. So even though he'd held out hope she'd be there, waiting at the compound for him, it was almost a relief when he was met with silence when he pulled up to the house. Only the chickens were there to greet him.

He waited that day, hunkered down in the basement bunker, his eyes glued to the television screens hooked up to the cameras on the compound's perimeter. He waited to hear the hum of his wife's little Honda, or the ring of the satellite phone, letting him know she was fine, that she was hiding somewhere and would be at the compound within the hour. In time for dinner, even. But dinnertime came and went and he never heard a thing.

Nor did he have to use any of the compound's protective devices, at least not that first day. No, nothing came that first day. Not a single creature, though he'd corralled all the chickens into the basement with him, the sour scent of their droppings mixing with the musky smell of his own sweat and fear until the stench was too much to take. But the silence surrounding the compound, silence but for the low and steady thrum of the solar-powered generators and the freezers, was a blessing. Nothing found him, not on that first day. Not even his wife.

The days passed and still she didn't show, and still the phone didn't ring. He was sometimes in contact with other survivors via short wave radios, but soon they stopped calling. For a long time, it was radio silence, all the time.

One day he went back into town, back to the school, back to hopefully find his girls. He wasn't sure what he hoped to do when he found them, but he did. It had been a month, based on the days he tried to keep track of on the calendar but sometimes forgot, and they'd decayed significantly in that time. Their hair, once so impeccably kept, brushed and clean and flat-ironed to that glossy, near-black shine, hung in tangles around their faces, matted with dirt and mud and twigs. Their clothes were rags, nothing like the fancy jeans and sundresses they'd once loved. Their skin was torn and mangled.

And yet still they were together. Still they held hands like they had when they were young. And still, when they moved, they moved as one. When he pulled the truck over to the side of the road and called their names, they turned together toward the sound. And then, together, they attacked.

He cried as he put bullets through their foreheads. He was always a crack shot, even with shaking hands and shoulders, and Dave was only grateful that the area was quiet enough for long enough (he had to kill six more creatures while he worked) that he was able to pull their bodies up into the back of the truck so he could carry them home to the compound.

As he pulled away from the school something red caught his eye. It was down in a retention ditch beside the road, and he pulled over, disregarding the small swarm of crazies headed his way, to see what it was, the sinking feeling in his gut telling him more than his eyes ever needed to.

It was his wife's Honda. Of course it was. Because of course she, too, had gone to the school to try to find the girls, probably on that very first day. They'd probably just missed each other.

He didn't—couldn't—pull off to see if she was still inside. He knew she was gone. He didn't need to see her. Not that way. Not when his last memory of her was in her business suit, smelling of lavender lotion and a light, flowery perfume she favored, her hair and make-up done up because it was a court day and she liked to feel beautiful when she had to go before a judge with a client. And what she never realized was that she was always beautiful, at least to him, no matter what she wore or how her hair was done, but he knew whatever he'd find in that car—

rotted remains, or living, breathing crazy—it wouldn't be her. It wouldn't be his wife. And now that the twins were resting, he couldn't face another bit of living dead, at least not then.

He drove away, never to return, and he buried the girls later that day, out back by the short runway he used for his little airplane.

Since then he'd used plenty of mines to ward off visitors—both living and undead—but we'd been the first kids he'd seen on the road. He'd been tracking us, warm bodies among the cold crazies, while we walked the day before, using some gadgets and gizmos he'd perfected in all his post-apocalypse free time. When the swarm of crazies he'd also been tracking found us, he acted quickly, taking off to take them out to give us a fighting chance, hoping we'd leave him alone. That we'd never get close enough to his compound for him to have to kill us, too. Because he hated killing the living, but he would, if he had to.

When we stopped for the night, so close to the compound, he thought all night about what to do, not knowing if we were friend or foe. He never *wanted* to hurt us. But he'd only survived so long by being tough, and he knew that to keep on surviving, he couldn't change his ways.

Until he saw Rosie, anyway. Sweet Rosie. She looked so much like his girls did at that age, it almost hurt to look at her. He could never kill a girl who looked so much like his twins.

So there we sat, eating his eggs and his bacon, and he couldn't have been more thrilled to have found us.

* * * *

As Dave spoke, he pulled out a sketchbook and a pencil and he worked, his pencil flying over the paper in short, delicate strokes. I couldn't see what he was drawing, as his eyes focused on paper, and then us, glazing over entirely as he spoke of his wife and daughters. Though I assumed he filled the paper with absent-minded doodles, as the story came to an end, he tore the sheet out from the notebook and held the paper out to Rosie. She reached out for it, but then snapped her hand back to her side, gaping at the paper.

I gaped, too, as my eyes settled on a likeness of Rosie as real as any photograph. It was idealized, her cheeks fleshed out rather than hollowed, her eyes not shrouded in black, and, somehow, it was loving and gentle.

"You have a real talent," said Sam, taking the picture from Dave's hand. Rosie made no move to take it from him, so Sam folded it up and pocketed it.

"Thanks," said Dave. "It's not hard to make a pretty picture when there's a pretty girl in front of you."

And I suddenly wished, based on the way Rosie cringed and the slight darkness that passed across Dave's eyes, that he'd drawn a picture of Chicken instead. Drawing a dog felt so much more harmless than drawing a picture of a beautiful, defenseless little girl.

Chapter 9: Sam

For the first time in what felt like forever, I pushed my chair back from a table, my belly fat and satiated, full of meat and eggs and even a giant helping of frozen hash browns that tasted like college. All I needed was a breakfast beer to wash it down, but I figured beer was probably asking for too much. I counted back the months; nope. I still wasn't twenty-one, not that it mattered. I was sure there was beer somewhere in the compound, though, and I planned to find it, if we stuck around for a day or two. Whether or not I believed his "oh, just sit here and talk to me and we're square" story, Dave had definitely prepared for the apocalypse, and he'd prepared well. A few days of living in the lap of luxury sounded like something I was ready to experience, regardless of his secret motives.

I opened my mouth and ripped out a huge belch. Rosie howled with laughter. Jenna shot us both looks, like a mom reminding her kids to use their table manners in front of company. I burped again. After the night before, the return of Michael to our little party, and the destruction of what *almost* happened between Jenna and me, alone in the dark with our clothes pooled on the ground around us, I didn't care what she thought. I'd probably be sleeping alone that night and for the rest of my life anyway.

Fuck manners.

I burped again.

Michael reached across the table with a silly grin on his face—drunk on food, obviously—and gave me a shove. I slapped his hand and he pulled it away, knocking into a full glass of OJ (frozen, thawed, but still sweet and good). It spilled across the table, running down into Dave's lap. We, the kids at the table, froze. The thing with life after the zombies is that there are rules that maybe didn't exist before. And one of those rules, weird as it may sound, is: no sudden movements when you're eating breakfast with a stranger, and definitely no spilling orange juice on that stranger, because you never know how they're going to react. Jenna stifled a cry with the back of her hand, and I held my breath. We stared at Dave, waiting to see if he would squall.

Dave…laughed. "You two are brothers, huh? It shows." He stood up and walked to the sink—*running water*—and grabbed a towel to mop up the mess. Jenna stood to help but he waved her away. "No big deal, no big deal. I spill stuff all the time." He shot Rosie a cross-eyed look that chased the fear from her eyes and almost made her laugh again.

Jenna sighed, exhaling her own anxiety and leaning back in her chair while Dave worked over the spillage. "Dave, I don't honestly know how we can thank you for your hospitality."

Dave's shoulders jerked in a quick shrug as he reached across the table to wipe up the final few drops. "Y'all don't hafta thank me. I see the thanks in your eyes. Even in that one's burps." He pointed at me. "There's a lesson here, though. I think I can't believe everything I hear over the shortwave. Gossip's still gossip, I guess, and whatever happened in New Orleans, I've got a feelin' you were maybe on the right side of wrong. So just sit a spell, maybe stay for a few days, and we'll call it square. I sure would love some company."

Jenna's eyes widened at the mention of New Orleans and the short wave. I watched her calculate the appropriate response—as if appropriate still existed—and come up empty. She wanted us on the road; Will wanted us on the road. Me? I was content to stay, but I knew she didn't want to hear that.

Beside me, Will sat up straighter in his chair, knocking it back an inch or two. The legs cried out as they crossed the tile floor, and we all winced.

Ever the observer, he'd sat in silence through most of breakfast, packing away more food than Michael and me combined. But now he was ready to participate. "We can't stay," he said. "I have to get east, as quickly as possible. It's the most important thing in the world." His hand trailed down to his side where he kept the journal from that crazy doctor in a small pouch he'd sewn from ancient leather before we left Nebraska. "And actually, if you have a radio, I'd like to get on it. As soon as possible. I need to find a hospital."

I'll be honest, I didn't think he could save the world. Even in all the time we'd spent together, planning our escape from the farmhouse, I never thought he really had a chance. He was just a kid, for God's sakes. His obsession was just that—the obsession of a kid, and though our goals of heading east matched up, I was starting to get concerned about his delusions of grandeur. Besides, I wanted more bacon. I wanted to see what else Dave had saved in the massive freezers. So I laughed at Will. It was rude and childish, but it's what I did. My laughter cut off whatever Dave had opened his mouth to say, so I spoke instead. "You're not going to save the world. You're just a kid. We can stay here a few days. Maybe even send some supplies back to the farm. Poor Dave could use the company."

Will's face fell. His mouth, which had only a second earlier been pulled upward with excitement at the thought of his "most important thing in the world," drooped way down at the corners. He stood, and left the table in a rush, Rosie hot on his heels.

Jenna glared at me, but that was fine. If I had a nickel for every dirty look she'd ever shot me, I'd be able to swim in them. Ignoring her, and the fact that Dave stood statue-still holding a juice-soaked dishrag, looking like he had no idea what he'd gotten himself into, I stood, pushing my chair back until it hit the wall. I walked to the stove. Back in the day, my parents had a deal: whoever cooked didn't have to clean, and that always seemed fair to me. I picked up the bacon pan and carried it to the sink. "Hey, Dave, what do you want me to do with the bacon grease? Seems a shame to waste it."

****

It takes a while to clean a kitchen when everything but the hash browns have been cooked from scratch, and you don't have a dishwasher to handle the bulk of the washing, but an hour later, it was done. I'd shooed everyone else from the kitchen so I could work in peace—another luxury long gone from the days before the zombies. I'd barely had a moment to myself since…well, since the days I didn't like to think about, the days I hardly even remembered except for in my nightmares. So it was nice to wash dishes in warm water, my sleeves rolled up past my elbows, while everyone else kept busy doing God knew what else. I didn't care. I had a task to do, and the time with which to do it. Luxury, indeed. I even found myself humming from time to time, strains from a song I'd almost forgotten, from a life I used to live.

"You can check out any time you like…but you can never leave…"

My air guitar solo, complete with wet hands splattering the enamel backsplash behind the sink, was epic. I swear.

Later, I found Jenna and Michael huddled together outside, sitting on the front porch stairs. Though their body language was less than loving, with her arms crossed and his body turned completely from hers, an angst-ridden stance I remembered from Freshman Psych, at least they were talking. Their heads were closer together than I'd seen them in ages. Wonders never did cease in the age of the zombies.

"Hey buttheads," I said, sliding down on the other side of Jenna, probably a little bit closer than she would have liked, judging by the way she scooted aside. "I have a headache. Anyone have anything?"

Michael snorted. "Anything like what? Pot? Beer? I have a feeling Dave's got both of those inside somewhere."

"Now what makes you think I'd want that?" I said, grinning. "I just meant an aspirin."

"Right. Sure." Shaking her head with a fast-fading grin, Jenna handed me an aspirin.

"Thanks, *sis*," I said, and I laughed.

"Sis?" she said. "You haven't called me that in a while."

"Yeah, well, maybe it's time I started again. You *are* my little sister, aren't you?"

My little sister who stood in front of me in her underwear last night, and who probably would have…if only I'd….

I pushed *that* thought aside. It was too dangerous. My thoughts were too likely to carry me away to another world, another time, which wasn't great when I was the one who was supposed to be hyper-vigilant. Time to change the subject.

"So, what do you two kids think of our new friend Dave? Me, I'd like to stay a while. Fatten up on his bacon. I'm sure we can find a way to repay him, eh, Jenna?" I elbowed her with a laugh.

She shoved me off. "Shut up, you jerk. That's disgusting. I could never…would never…oh, just shut up." She exhaled, directing the air upward so it blew her bangs back on her forehead.

Beside her, Michael smirked, staring at the airplane in the yard. "I wonder if he could fly us east. I mean, we know it flies. That's how he took care of that horde, right? So why can't he? And as for repayment, well, we'll figure that out when we get there, right?"

"Michael, don't be silly. It's a two person plane." Jenna dropped her head into her hands and rubbed her eyes. "We don't all fit. And we can't ask him to fly there, back, there, back. No one has fuel like that. Not anymore."

"Then maybe he could just fly Will there. That's not asking too much, is it? I mean, Will's the one who wants to save the world and everything."

"I *am* going to save the world."

We all jumped. While we'd been talking, Rosie, Will and Chicken had come out from the house and were standing behind us, listening. As he spoke Will stepped to our front and then stood with his hands clenched in fists at his sides, daring me to challenge him again. I didn't want to, so I sat and stared back at him.

Will had grown a bit since we'd met him back at the farm. He was still skinny—so skinny it almost hurt to look at the way his elbows and knees jutted out at bizarre angles—but he looked stronger. More convinced of his ability to save the world. A wave of regret smacked me in the face. *Delusions of grandeur at least give him hope.*

"Yeah," I said. "Sorry about that. I didn't mean it. I know you've got something good going, something you're proud of. I shouldn't have said what I did."

He nodded, and Rosie smiled. Chicken crawled to Jenna, and she hugged him to her. "Are we all okay?" she said, though with her voice muffled by Chicken's fur it came out more like, "Awweahhohay?" Everyone laughed.

"Yes," said Michael, for once sounding friendly. "I think we are."

"Good," she said, lifting her head. "Because as much as I'd love to stay here and get fat again, I think it's time we move on. No one is this nice unless they want something, and I don't know what we really have to give. I don't trust this."

I shrugged. "Maybe he's really just a sad, lonely guy who just wants some company?" Not that I believed it, but it sounded good.

Michael laughed. "Yeah. Wants to *eat* some company. Soon we'll find the cookbook. To Serve Zombie, or some shit like that."

Giggling, Rosie glanced over her shoulder. "Shh. Don't let him hear you. I think we should at least stay a day or two, to make him feel better."

"No, no," said Jenna, thinking aloud. "Have you guys noticed there are no pictures anywhere in the house?"

I shrugged. "No. Why would I notice that?"

"I don't know, maybe because for a self-described family man, who's lost his family in this totally tragic way, it's a little creepy to have absolutely no mementos of them. Anywhere. Don't you think?"

"Huh," said Michael, rubbing at his ear. "That's an interesting point. You think he's making it up?"

"Not sure. Maybe."

Rosie looked appalled. It was kind of cute. "Oh, come on you guys. Maybe it's too hard for him to look at them. I mean, I don't exactly carry around pictures of our mom and dad, you know."

Jenna smiled indulgently. "I know, sweetie, but I don't think that's the best idea right now. I'm really afraid he wants something from us. From you or me especially. Think about that picture he drew. Think about what he could want."

"What?" Rosie was wide-eyed.

Jenna gave her a pointed look.

"No. Ew. I don't believe that. Not for a second."

But suddenly Rosie looked less sure of herself. Will stepped closer to her and took hold of her arm. He understood Jenna's implication.

"Maybe we should go," Michael said, turning an eye back to the house. Dave was nowhere to be seen.

"Yeah, maybe," I said. It was like the out-loud suggestion of something more sinister made it real. Suddenly even I didn't want any bacon. Because Jenna had a point. There weren't any pictures, any ways we could compare Dave's version of reality to the real one. Suddenly, that didn't make me feel so secure.

* * * *

We found Dave sitting at the kitchen table, surrounded by bottles of citronella and powdered sugar. Beside me, Will drew in a sharp breath. "So that's how you made it," he said.

Dave looked up, blinking, as the five of us entered the room. Chicken had opted to remain behind in the living room, basking in a ray of sun that filtered in through a tall window. Dave smiled. "Made what, son?"

"The napalm you used to fry the zombies. Um, I mean…the crazies. I'd been wondering what you had used to make it. According to Michael it was very effective."

"The only way to kill them en masse is to burn them," he said. "You kids should be grateful I did. That horde would've overtaken you last night if I hadn't. And then you'd be just another crazy. Think of it. We wouldn't all be friends."

He paused to pour the oil into a jug via a huge, red funnel. As he did, the fumes of the homemade chemical weapon wafted up and out, splashing across my face and nose. To me the smell was like…a blowtorch, on low, waiting to explode. A sick feeling burst in my stomach. When I'd been with the Roughnecks, back when my best friend

Ty and I had barely escaped the first weeks of the zombie plague with our lives, we used flame-throwers when fighting large groups of the undead. That's what it smelled like, there and then, the moment before battle. Cries of the undead hovered just out of hearing, but somehow, my ears picked them up, and the smell of chemicals began to change, to morph, into dead and dying flesh, burning in the nighttime.

"Sam? You okay? Sam? Sam?"

Now it was Jenna's voice that was far away, down a road and around a curve. The sunlight in the room darkened until all I could see were two pinpricks of light, barely visible in the blackness that suddenly engulfed me. Screams—terrible, dreadful, piercing screams—filled my ears, and gunfire pounded around me.

* * * *

"Sam? Sam?" Michael's voice was foggy, froggy. I tried to figure out where it was coming from, but around me was only darkness.

* * * *

"Sam? Sam!" Ty's voice came to me, and suddenly he was there, extending a hand. "Come on, Sam. It's time to go! We need to get out of here."

It was true. We were surrounded by undead, and they wanted to eat our flesh to replace the skin that melted from their bones and puddled around their feet—just like Jenna's clothes did—*in viscous, bubbling goo. They stood like islands in the midst of liquid rot, and they were hungry. They wouldn't be still for long.*

"Run, Sam! Run!" Ty's hand faced as he turned away, and suddenly he was gone, leaving me along in the middle of the monsters.

"No!" I screamed. "I don't want to lose you again!"

* * * *

"Who, Sam? Who don't you want to lose? Wake up! You're scaring me!"

Even in the darkness I could hear the tears in Jenna's voice, and I wanted to soothe her but I had no idea how.

* * * *

The next thing I heard was a ticking clock. It was loud, echoing like a ping pong ball through my head. I wanted to turn it off, like you would an alarm clock that went off twenty minutes before your 8 a.m. class, when you knew you'd have to skip because you were too hung over from far too many games of quarters at the party the night before.

It was dark, but for the first time I could sense motion around me, too. Real, solid motion, not fluid and melty like the zombies had been. My head throbbed in time with the ticking clock.

"It's never been this long," said Jenna from miles away. "Nothing like this."

"You're sure?" The second voice wasn't as familiar.

"Yes, we're sure." Michael spoke. "He's never been out this long."

"I've seen people black out before," said the other voice. "He'll come back around. I guess we all have our struggles, what with everything that's happened in the world lately."

Everything that's happened in the world lately? That made it sound like there was some faraway war, or a terrorist attack. Not like our entire world had been upside down for the past year and a half.

The realization that I couldn't see because my eyes were closed made me work to open them. They felt dry, heavy, crusted over like I hadn't opened them in years. Or like I'd been crying in my sleep. I peeled back one lid through sheer determination, and used my hand to pull back the other.

Jenna yelped. "He's waking up."

"Of course I'm waking up. Didn't even know I'd gone to sleep." My mouth felt thick and dry. "Does anyone have any water? I'm thirsty." My stomach roiled dangerously. "Ugh, I'd kill for a ginger ale."

I lay on the tattered old couch in Dave's living room. Jenna knelt beside me, her arm resting atop mine. It was her watch I heard ticking and ticking, and without thinking I shoved her off me.

"Hey," she said, but smiled. "Welcome back."

Dave pressed something cold into my hand. I pulled myself up to sitting. It was a can of ginger ale. "Ask and ye shall receive," he said. "How you feelin'?"

I cracked the can, barely able to believe my eyes, and tilted it back to take a long swig. It was sweet—almost too sweet—but so very good that I drank until half the can was gone. Then I burped, and from across the room Rosie giggled. "Never better," I said, groaning. "How long was I out? What happened?"

Michael sat in a chair near my feet. "You passed out. Like you do. What triggered it this time?"

I was a little surprised to hear him acknowledge something I knew but tried to keep hidden. My blackouts were concerning, but I figured they were part of life. I didn't know if it was a brain tumor or what, but the point was: we'd never discussed them. Since it was suddenly on the table, I answered, "The smell of chemicals. The thought of flames, and the zombies. You know, the usual. We used to carry flame throwers back in the Roughnecks."

Dave jumped. "The Roughnecks? You were part of the Roughnecks?"

"You've heard of them?" It was my turn to jump.

Dave nodded, and his face turned a bit grim. "Yes. They've taken over the east coast, it seems. Led by some captain fella. I don't gather they're the nicest of folks in the history of post-apocalyptic realms."

"No. They're not. I escaped."

"Escaped. Yes. Good to know. They've got control of the east coast, pretty much from Boston through Charleston. I think they've got some areas set up as refugee camps and such, with some kind of zombie-protection units or something. But again, it doesn't all sound square, I guess. Not like somewhere I'd want you kids to head."

"But that's where we have to go," said Will.

"Why?"

Will groaned. It was a long-suffering sound, full of drama and heartache, and even in my slightly-weakened state my own heart went out to the kid. He'd lost everything, just like the rest of us, and it sucked, plain and simple. "Because of this." He pulled the notebook from his pouch. "It has notes on the vaccine to stop the virus from taking hold. If I can just get it to people who have actual research equipment, they'll be able to stop this once and for all."

Dave gave him a sharp look. "Are you serious? You meant what you said earlier, about saving the world?"

Will nodded, all clear-eyed and earnest. "Yes."

"I don't know. You better spend the night here, at the very least. Looks like this one won't be up for travel any time soon." He jerked a thumb at me.

I tried to sit up straighter, to cover my sudden weakness. Jenna wanted to leave, but as soon as I got my feet under me the world went crosshatched again. The headache I had while waking up still hadn't faded in the least. I settled back onto the couch cushions. "I hit my head when I fell, didn't I?"

Michael looked sheepish. "Yup."

"And you didn't even try to catch me, did you?"

Even more sheepish. "Nope. It all happened so fast. And you're so heavy…"

"Guys, guys, knock it off? We need to make some plans." Jenna eyed Dave, who hovered like a mother hen over our group. He didn't notice.

I eased myself further down on the couch and patted the cushion beside me. "Then come sit, sweetheart, and let's make some plans."

The sound of her punching my arm was one of the nicest things I'd ever heard.

Dave stood over us, shaking his head. "I don't think that's the best idea…"

Jenna ignored him.

Chapter 10: Jenna

Sometimes, when the darkness fell and the air grew still and the nights grew cold, I lay down to sleep, exhausted from a day filled with travel or stress or terror. But as I lay, waiting for sleep to overtake me, it receded. It hid. It flew away from me so fast I couldn't imagine ever sleeping again. The weight of my eyelids remained insurmountable, but the speed of my thoughts and the echoes of the day kept sleep from ever finding me.

At times like those, I feared sleep. A part of my brain reasoned that, were I to fall asleep, there was a chance I'd never wake up. There was a chance that I'd die in my sleep or get caught in a dream so permanent I'd never see the sun again. I lay in bed, trembling in fear, exhausted, afraid to sleep, and afraid to stay awake. There was so much to fear in the world.

I couldn't fall asleep at Dave's house. It was dark and quiet—oh, so quiet—with even the chickens having turned in for the evening, when we gathered in the living room to get what rest we could manage before we got on the road the next day. Dave didn't want us to leave. Not really. His stores of supplies were available to us, he said, as long as we stayed, but he couldn't support the idea of us traveling straight into the lion's den, as he called the east coast. He didn't seem to understand that we, perhaps, were the true lions.

I lay on a mat on the ground in the living room, surrounded by the oily smell of guns and the sharp, pungent odor of un-showered men. The darkness was near complete, with barely a hint of moonlight filtering in through the cloudy, dusty windows, but I couldn't lay still anymore. The sounds of Michael and Sam's snores on either side of me were more than I could bear.

Whatever, I thought. I'll sleep when I'm dead.

And then I shuddered because the truth was: death never felt far away.

I stood as quietly as I could, taking care not to disturb the boys, nor Will and Rosie, each sleeping on a couple of chairs pushed together. I slipped from the living room, toward the kitchen, where the makings of napalm still littered the table and the smell of bacon still scented the air. I traced my hand along the wall, reaching, grasping for something, anything, to tell me what to do.

There, in the house, as fingertips traced the swoops and curves of the wood panel walls, were enough supplies to carry us comfortably to our final destination, wherever that happened to be. There, behind the house, were a couple of trucks that could take us there, sparing our feet and cutting months off our trip. But the owner of all those supplies wouldn't let us have them. Never mind that he had enough to sustain him for years and years; he could share, easily, and still be fine. But he wanted us to stay, or at least a reassurance that we'd go back home instead.

"Don't go east. You'll die there. And I'm not givin' you supplies just to have you go off and kill yourselves. I'm not that dumb. There's no need to tilt at windmills, you know? Don Quixote?"

Dave Mason. The man with the country voice, the art museum hat, and the literary references. The man who wouldn't help us, and who stared at Rosie non-stop whenever she was in the room. The man who had no pictures of his family, anywhere in the house, though he'd proven that afternoon he could draw a startlingly real likeness of a little girl he'd just met. Where was his family? Why had he hidden them away, not letting us see, not giving us the option to believe a word of his goddamn story?

The floor creaked beneath my feet, a sound that echoed, hollow and mournful, below. *Is there a basement? What's down there? More supplies? Or dead bodies? Lonely travelers like us, lured in only to be murdered in their sleep?*

Staying awake suddenly took on a new urgency. My eyes darted around in the dark. A door cried from down the hall. A latch clicked. *Dave's door.* I was filled with a sudden, intense urge to see where he slept. Maybe it held all the answers. Maybe it would tell me if I could trust him or not.

I held my breath.

If only there were pictures. I want to see his family. I want to know he didn't make it up.

My footsteps in the hall were light. I'd learned well through the years to travel soft, travel quiet. In silence, I moved toward the only door at the end of the hallway. A faint, dull light filtered out from under the door, reminding me of an exit sign at the end of another hallway from so very long ago. My stomach tightened as I reached my destination: the thin, composite door with the small, brass knob.

I pressed my ear to the wood, and from the other side I heard a low groan. It wasn't inhuman, wasn't zombie, but it was enough to raise my internal alert even higher. *Is he sick? Is he crying? What's going on?*

The doorknob was cold beneath my palm. I turned it slowly, gently, wincing as the faintest of clicks indicated it would open. I pushed slightly inward, opening the door the slightest of cracks. A panting sound rushed through the newly opened space.

Is he having a heart attack? Did we kill him?

I pushed the door open the rest of the way, marveling at the silent, well-oiled hinges that gave no sign of my trespass. I stepped into the room.

It was dark, but with the slight light cast from a small lantern in the corner I could see the room itself was fairly innocuous. Wood paneled walls gave way to a pale carpet floor. A bed sat in one corner, and a chair faced it.

In the chair sat Dave, his back to me. His breathing was quick and labored. His arm moved up and down before him. He groaned, and the realization set in.

I was interrupting.

Gross.

Of course I knew all men did it, but that didn't mean I wanted to see it. The pumping of his hand, the thrusting of his hips. I started to turn, the queasy feeling of being an unintentional voyeur settling fast in my gut. *It's time to go.*

By that I meant leave the room, of course. I didn't mean leave the entire compound. But then, just before I took my first step out the door, I saw.

In Dave's other hand—the hand that wasn't frantically jerking, up and down, up and down, with a wet, squishy sound—he held his sketchbook. My eyes fell upon it in my frantic need to look anywhere but at the frenetic movement of his elbow, and as soon as they did, I had to stifle a gag.

It was me. It was a picture of my face, my eyes, my hair, as skillfully rendered as the picture of Rosie handed to Sam earlier that day.

Oh God, he's jerking off to me.

Ew.

Now it's really fucking time to go.

I didn't bother being quiet. I stepped back, knocking the door into the wall behind me. Dave froze, sweat beading immediately on his neck. He turned. His eyes met mine and his lips moved as though to say *something*, but nothing came out. I turned. I ran.

I burst into the living room, Dave's footsteps following too close behind me. My Slugger lay on the ground beside Michael. I left it there, opting instead for my rifle. Sam appeared at my side as Michael jerked to his feet.

"What's happening?"

"It's time to go."

"Why?"

"I'll tell you later. Something happened. Trust me."

They did. In a millisecond Sam, Michael, Rosie and Will stood beside me, weapons trained on the door. I nodded. "We leave now. We take what we need. Fuck this place."

I couldn't shake the image of Dave's jerking arm, my face in his hand. What if we had stayed, and what if he'd tried something? What if he'd touched Rosie?

The sick fucking bastard.

My heart beat so fast I thought it might implode.

Michael spoke first. "We'll keep Dave under wraps. You and the kids raid the supplies. There's a truck out back, too. Keys still in it. Throw everything in that and we'll take it."

Before I could nod, Sam shouted, "Freeze!"

"We've got you surrounded, Dave," added Michael. "Don't make a move."

The bastard. No pictures of his daughters, his wife. Figments of his imagination. But there's a picture of me, and he used it to masturbate.

Bile worked its way up my throat. Dave had been nice and all, but he was *old*. My parents' age at least. And he was whacking off to a *kid!*

"But I took you in…"Dave stood in the doorway. His eyes were huge, his hair mussed and hanging down around his face. "I tried to help you. Jenna, I know what you think. It's not like that."

"Fuck you," I said, side-stepping him. "Kids, come with me. Let's pack up and go."

"Don't touch my stuff," he said. "That's mine. Don't steal from me. You're better than that."

I looked over my shoulder. "Consider it borrowing, then. Rosie, Will, come on. Boys, don't let him move. Shoot him if you have to."

Apparently I was good at bluffing. Dave began to cry, fat tears rolling from his eyes. "But I wanted to help you. I wanted to save you."

Fucking liar.

* * * *

From the garage we grabbed a cooler and we filled it with supplies from the freezer and refrigerator. Will helped me heft it into the bed of an old Toyota pickup. The keys were in the ignition, just like Michael had said.

Then we filled boxes and bags with canned goods and old military MREs, tossing them in the back too. For good measure, I grabbed a few of the rifles stacked in the corner of the living room, while Dave looked on in teary silence.

"You don't know what you're doing," he said once as I crossed through the room on my desperate hunt for supplies. "It's not safe out there."

"It's not safe in here," I said. "You proved that tonight."

"What did he do, Jenna?" Sam's whisper was sharp.

"I'll tell you later." Mine was sharper.

Dave's head fell. His shoulders slumped. He leaned against the wall and slid down to sitting, his legs collapsing in on themselves beneath his weight.

* * * *

We pulled the truck out into the night, bursting at the seams with supplies pilfered from Dave's stash. When I wouldn't immediately tell everyone what happened, they stopped asking, and we rode in a tight, uncomfortable silence. Eventually, as the miles of dirt road passed beneath the Toyota's tires, everyone fell asleep. Everyone, that is, except for Sam and me.

As the sun's rays breached the horizon, kissing the truck's hood and brightening the world around us, he took my hand. "Now will you tell me what happened? I'm worried about you. Did he touch you? You can tell me."

I sighed. I knew it was only fair, that he deserved to know why we left. I knew he, especially, had wanted to stay.

"No. No, he didn't touch me. But he was a liar and a creep. We know that, right?"

"Because you couldn't find pictures of his family?"

"Yes. Who wouldn't have had pictures of his family, Sam? He was hiding something. Besides. There's something else."

"What?"

I cringed. The memory made me nauseous. "I walked in on him tonight. He was holding a picture of me, and he was…um…"

Sam's head turned sharply to me. "He was what, Jenn? Spit it out."

I groaned, a sound not unlike the one made by Dave in his room. "He was jerking off. Okay? Now are you happy? He was holding my picture, and he was jerking off. And I'm sorry but no way would I ever trust him around Rosie, not for another minute."

"Jesus, Jenna!"

Sam's voice was sharper than I expected, and I flinched. "What?"

"That's why you cut and ran? Because you caught the dude whacking off?"

"With my picture! He's a perv!"

"Every guy whacks off, Jenn! Every goddamn one of 'em. If I had a dollar for every time I've whacked off to a picture of…oh, Jesus. Never mind. What the fuck, Jenna? I didn't know you were so damn squeamish."

From the backseat, Rosie stirred. "What are you guys talking about? Why's Jenna squeamish?"

Sam barked a sigh. In my lap, Chicken raised his head and licked Sam's elbow. If it was meant to be a comforting gesture, it wasn't. Sam glowered at the front windshield as he sped the truck up, leaving Dave's compound as far in the dust as he could.

"Nothing," I said to Rosie. "Go back to sleep."

She was tired, so she did.

Later, I reached into the truck's glove box, searching for nothing.

I found something.

From an old, tattered paperback I pulled an old, tattered photograph. It looked like it'd been well-looked at, the corners roughened and the front speckled with droplets of water. *Tears.* Looking at it brought immediate tears to my eyes as well.

It was Dave, younger and rounder, perhaps, but unmistakably him. Beside him, a woman, tall and elegant. An attorney in a business suit. In front of them stood two teenage girls, identical but for the looks on their faces—an impish smile on one, a quiet, thoughtful expression on the other.

Dave's family.

As a tear spilled from the corner of my eye, I offered the picture up for Sam to see. He didn't stop driving, but he saw at a glance what I held. For a second, he closed his eyes.

When he opened them again, his grip on the steering wheel was tighter, his knuckles white. He shook his head.

"Throw it out, Jenn. Throw it out. You screwed that guy over. You keep making decisions like that, one day you're gonna get us killed."

I rolled down my window and the cool breeze washed over my face as I dropped the picture out the window. A quick look in the side mirror told me Michael was awake, and he'd heard everything I said. He'd seen. He knew. *The damn spy. He's judging me, right now.* He said it with his eyes as he glared at my reflection. I had to look away.

Sam was right, and we all knew it. One day I was going to get us all killed.

* * * *

Now we were on the road again—*again*—but this time with wheels. It was familiar territory to Michael and me, bringing us back to the days right after we escaped New Jersey the first time, when we traveled the east coast in his little old hatchback. It was nice to have the miles pass quickly beneath our tires, without the trudging slog that would otherwise have marked our journey east.

We ate like kings and queens in the first days with the truck, knowing we should ration what supplies we'd pilfered from Dave's stores, but not quite able to stop ourselves from gorging on things like cheeses and milk that were perhaps a bit freezer-burnt, but were still so delicious we could hardly stand it. For the first time in ages I was able to pinch a bit of skin off my skeletal frame, and my pants fit tight. I don't think Michael disapproved; also for the first time in ages I felt his eyes on me as I went through my daily routine—washing, dressing, making sure Rosie and Will were fed and Chicken had eaten and our tents were folded properly. His eyes didn't quite look like Sam's did that one night, but it was close. I could tell he wanted me, and that was a coup.

The miles didn't fly by, though. Not on roads often jammed with other vehicles and dead bodies, swarms of flies thick in the warming spring air. Lucky for us the truck had four-wheel drive, and Michael and I were both adept at navigating tricky terrain. That got us out of a few tight spots as small herds of the undead often congregated around these jam-ups, almost as though they were setting traps. Who knows, but maybe they were. They certainly were the only zombies we saw, those converged upon a roadblock. And sometimes I'd even swear I saw them draw closer to us in something resembling attack patterns, similar to those we used in defending ourselves from them. Spreading out, watching perimeters. It was creepy, how aware the zombies seemed, but we told ourselves it was all in our heads, and that we were so used to them by then, we imagined seeing things that weren't there.

Sometimes that helped me sleep. Other times it added to my nightmares. Because if the zombies could think…if they could communicate and rationalize and apply brainpower to their unending thirst and hunger, well, that was too terrible to contemplate.

We ran into piles of dead zombies as well, sometimes around those roadblocks. Once I saw a "living" zombie feasting at one of these sites of the dead-undead, and a few minutes later, we had to pull the truck over so I could throw up. To think of those undead creatures, finally dying when the virus in their bodies ran out of food or whatever it needed to keep the dead animated and hungry, only to become sustenance for another zombie. It was too much.

We ambled onward, eastward, stopping whenever Will got carsick or Rosie and Chicken got too antsy to sit still any longer, but mostly we drove. East. Into the unknown.

Lesson 2: Death will find you in the end

Chapter 11: Will

"Jenna, pull over," I choked from the back seat.

She jerked the truck over to the road's narrow shoulder, the tires crunching on gravel on the side of the deserted highway. I barely made it out the door before it came, the sickening spasms and the flood of bile and other stomach acids that poured from my mouth, splattering in a puddle by my feet.

From behind me came a sigh. Rosie, probably, worried or annoyed at what had always been my downfall: car sickness.

As it turned out, that wasn't a disease that was cured by the toughening of hides brought about by the zombie apocalypse. When we were kids, road trips with our parents had always been hell for Rosie and me. For me, the sickness was awful, and for Rosie, who was phobic about vomit, seeing me about to hurl was as stressful as life got back then. And while she'd gotten tougher, sometimes even able to rub my back when the sickness overtook me, it seemed I hadn't.

"Sorry guys," I said, leaning back against the silent, immobile truck.

"No worries," said Jenna, from the driver's seat. "It's all good. You okay?"

"As okay as I ever am," I said. I'd have killed for some Dramamine to let me sleep through the days when the curving, bumpy roads unsettled me, but we still hadn't found any during our pilfering runs on drug stores and old groceries. Besides, as Jenna was always quick to point out, if I was asleep, I couldn't help out in the event that something happened on the road, which always seemed to be the case. Something *always* happened.

"Good," Jenna said. "Get back in. We need to go. I don't like the way that field is swaying. It's not from the wind."

We were deep into Kentucky by then, home of the red clay soil and as many farms as we'd seen in Nebraska and Missouri combined. We traveled southeast, hoping to avoid the population concentrations of Chicago and its suburbs, and were used to seeing fields long gone fallow, grown up with weeds taller than any cornfield back home. The fields were great for hiding things—other weary travelers, groups of whom we'd seen only once or twice, and lots of zombies.

Jenna was right. The wildflowers weren't swaying in the wind. They were only a hundred or so yards away, and they were being trampled.

"Shit," said Sam. "Get in! I don't care if you puke on your sister. We've gotta go."

"I care," said Rosie, but a nudge from Sam silenced her.

I shuddered, a final wave of stomach spasms passing over me, forcing me back to my knees over the puddle of half-digested food and bile that I'd already spewed. I dry heaved, trying like hell to force my stomach calm, to stop it from lurching in that dangerous way. My throat burned and my eyes teared but still I heaved. There was no way I could move, not yet, regardless of what the shifting wildflowers forecast.

Though my eyes squeezed shut, blocking the sight of the vomit-puddle, my ears were working fine as my stomach clenched and unclenched another time. And what I heard wasn't good.

"C'mon, Jenna, get it started." In a panic, Sam and Michael's voices were indistinguishable. I had no idea who was speaking.

"I'm trying! It won't go!"

Next came the sound of an engine trying to turn over, an engine that had seized and smoked. Burning oil filled my nose as my head swam with sickness.

"Jenna!"

That was Rosie, squealing. She saw something.

I forced myself up, ignoring the way my knees buckled beneath what I knew was a pretty slight weight—car sickness hadn't helped my big plans for weight gain—holding onto the side of the truck for support.

"Jenna! Start the fucking car!"

That was definitely Sam. I saw him reach across Michael to try to force the key or the steering wheel, but there was no forcing it. The smell of oil told me enough: we'd sprung an oil leak somewhere, and the truck's engine was done.

In the haze of chaos I remembered a day, a day long before, with my father. Long before the zombies came, long before he was forced to play gladiator in a losing battle with an undead killer, he used to work on cars. Sometimes, on weekends when my homework was done and my mother forced me out of my bedroom, away from the studies I deemed so important, I'd go out and help him.

On one such sunny Saturday afternoon, I found him outside the barn, an old Ford pickup up on blocks, the hood wide open. Ordinarily, Dad was calm when working on his cars. It was his therapy, his church. But on that day, as sweat beaded above his thick red beard, sweat he mopped away with his trusty blue bandana, he looked angry. Frustrated. I approached with caution.

"Hey, Dad," I said, leaning against the car's passenger door, poking my head through the window. It seemed the casual, laid back thing to do. I thought of the books in my room, books that were much less stormy than my father's face right then, and I considered fleeing. But he'd seen me.

The look on his face changed a little. It softened, smoothed, and he forced a bit of a smile. "Hi, Willie," he said, and I shuddered. I hated my childhood nickname, and everyone but my Dad had conceded to calling me Will by then—but oh, in that moment by our truck with Jenna screaming and the engine burning, how much would I have killed to hear him call me Willie—and he beckoned me over. "Smell that?"

I sniffed. "Sure do, Dad." It was burned metal, oil, and it smelled hot. I clapped a hand over my mouth and nose. "What is it?" My fingers muffled my words.

"It's the engine," he said, and the smile fell from his face. It was his favorite truck. "I had an oil leak, and I didn't catch it soon enough. The engine seized. Smells terrible, don't it?" He shook his head.

"Yeah, Dad. Sure does. How do we fix it?"

Dad's head hung just a little lower. "Thing is, Willie-Boy, we don't. You can't fix an engine that's burnt to a crisp. I'll have to save up to buy her a new engine. That's gonna cost a pretty penny."

I looked over my shoulder at our fields of corn that were nearly ready for harvest. In the coming weeks I'd break my back, neglect my schoolwork, all in an effort to help the family bring in our crops. I dreaded those months, but I also secretly loved the way Dad would look at me when I was working hard, the pride in his face. "Looks like a good harvest," I said. "Maybe we'll make enough…"

"…enough to survive the winter and pay the mortgage, sure." Dad nodded. "But not enough for a new engine. I'll have to find another way."

"What if we put new oil in it? Lube it up real good?" Dad liked when I talked like a normal kid; I always made sure to make a grammatical error or two when we had our chats.

"Nope. A seized engine, like I said, is done. Smell that smell, Willie. Any time you smell that smell, it's bad news."

Just like that, the memory was gone. Dad was gone. But the smell remained. "That smell's bad news," I said, but no one heard me.

"Jenna! Start the fucking car!"

"Jenna! They're coming!"

"Shut up you guys! It won't start! I'm not joking!"

I climbed into the car, the spasms having finally passed as a spike of adrenaline took the place of the carsickness. I slammed the door behind me. "That smell's bad news," I repeated, but louder. "Shut up and listen."

I scanned the field. There were no zombies or people visible, but something was happening, all around us. The field surrounded both sides of the road, and it was on both sides that the flowers—taller than the truck—swayed in such a bizarre, inorganic fashion. I rolled up the window to my door, the one that minutes earlier had been rolled way down to try to assuage my sickness.

Jenna, Michael and Sam whipped their heads around to look at me. Chicken cowered by Rosie's feet, and without thinking I took hold of my sister's hand, lacing our fingers together. She squeezed. Her face was flushed with fear. If I could have lived out the rest of my life without ever seeing her face like that, I still would have seen my baby sister terrified way too many times. My throat clenched.

"What do you mean?" said Sam, his voice dead calm all of a sudden.

"You smell that?"

As one, they nodded. Chicken sat up and growled.

"The engine seized. No oil. Must've sprung a leak somewhere. It's done."

"No," said Jenna. "No! We just checked the oil, like two days ago, and it was fine. Fine! It just needs to cool off for a second, and then we can get out of here."

But beside her the other boys were nodding. "That makes sense," said Michael. "The way it started and then stopped like that."

"Yeah. You know about cars, Will? How do we fix it?"

"We don't, Sam. It's done. My dad taught me." Rosie squeezed harder at the mention of our father.

But then she sucked in a breath. "I remember," she said. "He's right. Our dad's Ford died like that. He always said he was going to buy a new engine, but he never did."

Jenna's eyes went wild. "So how do we get another engine? And what the *hell* is going on out there? And what do we do now? Holy shit." Her voice dropped to a hiss. "What was *that*?"

That was a sharp banging on the roof of the now-silent truck. It echoed throughout the cabin. A stone tumbled from the roof, down the windshield. We all ducked.

It was followed by another stone, then another, until soon it was raining stones upon our truck.

"What the fuck," said Sam. "It's raining rocks!"

But the only stones that fell were right upon our truck.

"So it's people out there," said Rosie. "People throwing things at us to scare us?"

A chill settled at the base of my spine. "I have a really bad feeling about this," I whispered.

Jenna reached across the seat and grabbed my arm. "What, Will? Tell me about your bad feeling. Right now." Her jaw was clenched and her grip was firm.

I let go of Rosie's hand and pulled Schwartz's notebook from its leather pouch. From above, the stones continued to rain down, punctuating our words with a sharp bang. I flipped to a page near the back and read something real quick before I met Jenna's stare. "They're mutating. Again. Worse this time."

"Who?" she said, but I could tell: she knew. She squeezed my arm harder, and beside me Rosie clapped a hand to her mouth.

"No."

"Yes," I said to my sister. "Schwartz wrote about a bunch of the possibilities here. He'd mutated the virus enough to make it stronger; he worried what it would do if it was loosed on an uncontrolled population, and Jenna, didn't you say you let all the ones out from the New Orleans lab?"

She nodded. She got it. So'd Sam and Michael. I'd never seen the three of them so silent, especially considering the thunder of stones hitting the roof over our heads.

As if to emphasize the words I couldn't quite get out, a bigger rock flew overhead. It landed on the windshield. A spider web of cracks spread from the point of impact.

"So that explains everything we've seen. Why are the zombies surviving longer? Why do they seem to communicate? Jenna, they've been mutating. They *are* stronger. They *are* smarter. These aren't people around us. They're zombies. And they're using a coordinated attack."

"No," said Jenna. "They're undead. They're zombies. They have no brains left in their heads." But she ducked as another small boulder flew overhead. This one missed its mark and fell harmlessly beside the truck. "That can't be what's happening."

But it was. Michael and Sam each reached below their seat and sat up armed to the teeth. Michael pressed a shotgun into Jenna's hands. "Get ready," he said. And then, "I love you."

That's when I knew *he* knew how much trouble we were in, because he hadn't said that to Jenna in months. Not since before she killed Russell.

I gulped. Rosie took hold of Chicken's collar and helped him climb the seat to be by Jenna. Then she found her pistol. I hated seeing my sister armed. I pulled out my own gun.

"We stick together," said Jenna, her voice low and calm. She'd entered battle-mode. I wished to God that we could stay safe and I'd never have to hear that tone again. I wished to God I had my own battle-mode. I wished to God I believed in him.

"Open the doors and run north. Stay on the road, let me lead. We'll still be faster than them. If we sit here, this truck'll become a tomb. We can come back for supplies later, after they've moved on."

We nodded.

"On the count of three," she said.

"One…two…"

A shriek pierced the air, a sound unlike anything I'd heard. Shrill, like a bird's talons on a chalkboard, it ripped a hole through time and space. A dinosaur's death cry, perhaps. Or a god's. It wasn't human—no, no fully-human vocal chords could make a sound that loud, that piercing, that avian.

That it was an attack signal was clear. All at once, from the wildflower fields surrounding us, the zombies charged. They held sticks and rocks, swinging them as weapons. Within a single rapid, adrenaline-fueled heartbeat, the truck was surrounded.

The window beside me filled with a face, a near-fleshless one with bloody, sinewy muscle instead of a right cheek. The mouth peeled open to show rotten teeth and a shredded tongue. It licked the glass, but not with the desperation of the zombies we'd encountered before.

No. This creature was taking a moment to relish the kill. His eyes sparked intelligence, confidence that it would succeed. He stared at me as I winced, and then he licked some more.

The tongue left a sticky, clotted trail. Without thinking I reached up a finger and traced it.

Chapter 12: Jenna

Now I've seen it all, I thought. *Zombies with weapons.*

Then came the realization: *We're going to die.*

Two creatures wielding clubs staggered to my door, slow and cautious despite their obvious balance issues. They weren't frantic. They weren't hurried. They were calculating and careful. The difference between these creatures surrounding me and the original, slobbery, stupid zombies was like summer and winter. The old zombies were summer—hot and fast and burning. These were cold. Brutal. You could starve to death while surrounded by them, and then they'd eat you in the end. I shuddered.

Maybe it's time to give up?

No, I can't give up. I can't give up on Rosie. On Will. On Michael or Sam.

The one nearest me was a man, or had been, a lifetime earlier. Though he'd been slight—in his zombie state, he was skeletal—and though he walked with a limp thanks to a massive, gory bite on his leg, he didn't look all that inhuman. Only his eyes—cloudy, dark, dilated—told me he wasn't alive. Not in the traditional sense, anyway.

The rest of his movements, though? Super-human. His hands gripped a fallen tree branch, not unlike how I held my Slugger. He neither drooled nor snarled. He raised his branch and looked to his right, as though awaiting a signal.

Behind him stood a woman. Her face almost could have been called beautiful had the gaping hole in her neck not caused a bizarre-o death wobble of her entire head. Her hair hung, tangled with debris and clumped into dreadlocks, but the pale skin of her cheeks was flawless. Her body moved with a fluidity that approached grace. She seemed impossibly alive. Had I not been able to see her spine through the torn skin of her neck, I may have opened the door to let her in, to save her from the zombies surrounding her.

Then she nodded to the creature beside her. He nodded to another. As one, the creatures smashed their clubs down, crashing them into the truck.

The sound of metal creaking and glass shattering thundered in my eardrums. I suppressed the urge to drop my gun and cover my ears as the creatures pulled back their sticks and clubs and loosed them on our poor, defenseless truck again. Rosie shrieked. Michael cursed. Sam turned to me, his eyes wide. "They're working together!"

No shit, stupid, I wanted to say, but that would've been mean. Besides, I was just as surprised as he was. The truck canted to the left, then the right, with each impact of a dozen clubs brought down at the same time.

"We have to get out of here!" I could barely hear myself over the crashing and the shrieking. Down at my feet, Chicken went wild with rage, growling and snarling and leaping at the windows. I'd have to keep him close or he'd get himself killed. "Knock it off." I pushed him down to the floorboards.

"How? How do we get out? What do we do?"

They all shouted questions, a blend of high and low voices, looking to me for direction.

I don't fucking know. I wanted to say that, too, to make Sam or Michael make the decision, but I choked on the words. Outside, the creatures shifted tactics. Bashing their way in wasn't working—their clubs weren't all *that* solid, and some already littered the ground. Instead of continuing the frontal attack, they moved to one side of the truck. My side. The girl zombie, who seemed to be the leader, stepped in closer. Black-red fluid oozed from her neck wound. She shook her head as it wobbled unsteadily, splattering the window with gore. She reached out and pressed her hands to the window. Her fingernails were black. I remembered manicures in that moment, and spas. I missed those days desperately. I needed a vacation.

But at least their change in tactic was our salvation.

"They're going to push us over," said Sam. He was calm, more interested than afraid. In fact, all of us had silenced. We were watching, waiting.

Moments later, the girl-zombie shrieked. As one, the creatures pressed against the truck. It rocked, the wheels on my side lifting up from the ground. The zombies would succeed.

"We need to go. Out! Now! That way!" I pointed to the passenger side. Without another word we piled out. "Grab what you can," I added, but it was too late. We held the supplies attached to us—my rucksack, always attached to my shoulders, guns, and my Slugger—and that was it. Tumbling from the truck like clowns in a circus car, we tripped over each other, falling to the ground. In my arms I held my weapons; my fingers found Chicken's collar and held tight. Chicken wasn't such a chicken anymore, pulling and pawing at the ground, trying to get free to take on the zombies himself. I preferred his old cowering to the sudden recklessness.

It took the zombies half a second to realize we were out. *God, they're thinking! They're noticing things! They're fucking smart!*

The girl shrieked again, louder and more insistent. I half-expected the glass windows to shatter at her voice, but they held firm while we fell apart. As a unit and with military precision, the zombies turned and rushed the truck. Chicken escaped my grasp; Rosie tackled him, wrestling him into her arms and pulling him into a headlock as I pulled my shotgun to my shoulder and fired. The nearest creature's head exploded in a cloud of black-red gristle, and its body fell. Beside it, another zombie knelt, as though to check on it. The second creature hopped back to its feet and snarled, its eyes locking on me.

At least they still snarl. It was comforting, the zombie-ish behavior. I shot the snarling zombie, too. But there were too many.

"Run!" I shouted. "Run!"

The undead drew closer, far too fast for my comfort. Rocks fell like snow as other creatures, creatures we couldn't see in their hiding spots in the wildflowers, launched more and more projectiles in our direction. Dirt crunched beneath my boots as I struggled to take the first steps into the crowd.

"Run!"

Rosie and Will ran, Rosie staggering beneath Chicken's thrashing weight. From the corner of my eye I saw them reach the comparative safety of the wildflower field. I hoped no zombies were close enough to follow. "Sam, go with them," I shouted. "Keep them safe. Michael, to me. Let's see if we can get these fuckers."

Without comment, Sam was gone and Michael stood at my side. In battle, I was in charge, hands down. I was the leader. The general.

"Back to back," Michael said, but of course he didn't need to because I was already moving that way. Our backs pressed together, we began shooting, reloading, shooting, reloading. The zombies were strong, and they were fast, but we had guns.

One by one they fell, until only the girl with the dreadlocks, their apparent leader, was left. She ducked behind the truck, stalking from one end to the other, shrieking her shriek, calling out for her comrades, but they were dead. For a second I felt something like sympathy—her friends had once been human after all, as had she—but then, with bullet speed, she picked up a rock and launched it at Michael. He wasn't fast enough. The rock nailed him square in the temple. Blood burst around the point of impact, and Michael hit the deck with a dull, solid thud.

"You bitch!"

No one hits Michael! Blinded with anger, I tore around the truck. I wanted the zombie-girl. I wanted to feel her throat collapse inward when my fingers reached around it and squeezed. I wanted the simple pleasure of blowing her zombie-brains out with a single, point-blank shot to the face. *No one hurts my Michael.*

The zombie-girl ran the other way. Near the driver's side door, I slipped in a puddle of blood and vomit and flipped head-over-heels, landing on the ground with a jaw-wrenching thud. Only then did I realize my mistake.

The zombie-girl slid to a stop beside Michael, laying unconscious on the ground. With her gnarled, filthy hands, she took hold of his leg, bare below the hem of his shorts. She opened her mouth, sticky with saliva and full of rotting teeth that still gleamed in the sunshine. Her maw gaped wide, a shadowy cavern beneath eyes bright with hunger.

I shot her from my spot beside the truck, aiming my rifle beneath the chassis and praying for a direct hit as I lay in the vomit and the blood. But I was too late. Her head exploded, but not before the damage was done.

Not before her jaws snapped closed, tearing through the flesh of Michael's calf.

* * * *

No. No. No. No. No. No. No. No. No.

I dived beneath the truck, clawing my way toward Michael.

No. No. No. No. No. No. No. No. No.

It was a big truck—wide—and it was taking me too long to reach him. I was caught on something, and it was holding me in place while my hands and feet scrabbled in the dust.

No. No. No. No. No. No. No. No. No.

I reached behind me, untangling the rifle strap from where it hooked onto some part of the truck's underbelly, slicing my palm open on a piece of jagged, rusty metal.

Shit, I thought as warm blood spurted from the gash, pouring down over my jeans in a wet, sticky mess. It didn't matter. I crawled on.

As though in a dream the distance between Michael and me stretched and morphed. I blinked my eyes. At this rate it would take me a lifetime to reach him, and in that lifetime I'd relive the moment again and again. The moment where the zombie's mouth closed on his leg, delivering to him a death sentence I could never undo.

I crawled on.

Finally, my hand—my good hand, the one not spurting blood—landed in a pile of brains and skull bits, a cold, thick mess that insinuated itself under my nails and up my sleeve. I choked, the flood of stomach contents threatening to spew forth, but Michael's leg was there, right in front of me, right past the goo. The bite on his leg sparkled, slick with blood, reflecting the brilliant sunshine. The edges blackened quickly as the virus from the zombie took hold and began its dirty work.

No. No. No. No. No. No. No. No. No.

With a final tug, I pulled my body through the mess and emerged from beneath the truck. I pulled Michael's head into my lap. He was mine, for the moment. My Michael. But only when he was unconscious, with the angry bite wound on his leg, a scarlet badge of doom, did I remember exactly how mine he was.

* * * *

We sat in the backseat of our friend Diana's car, headed home from a movie. Diana called it a double-date, since she wanted it to be a date with Andy, who sat, drunk, in the front seat, but Michael and I laughed at that. We laughed at everything back then. Everything.

We laughed especially at the way Andy hung his head out the window, letting the fresh air wash over his face, most likely to quell the nausea induced by the pint of Southern Comfort he chugged while the rest of us ate popcorn and drank sodas. Michael and I were only sophomores, hanging out with the upper classmen that night, and we knew if we smelled of alcohol when we got home, we'd both be grounded for years.

Up front, Andy belched. It was warm and wet.

"Ew," I whispered, then dissolved into giggles when I saw Diana try to take Andy's hand, to pull him back inside the car. "He's gonna hurl in her car if she's not careful."

"Yeah, and I'm sure as shit not gonna clean it up," said Michael.

I laughed. Sure as shit. Like shit was ever sure. We loved cursing for the sake of cursing back then, the way the words rolled around our mouths, our tongues. We laughed whenever one of us said something ridiculous like that.

"What are you two laughing at?" Diana snapped, taking her eyes off the road and swerving the car to the right.

"Whoa," said Andy. "I don't feel so good. Can you pull over?"

This only made Michael and me laugh harder. Diana yanked the car over to the side of the deserted back road. Andy hustled out of the car and darted into the trees. I don't know if Diana glared at us or not, but she slammed the door hard when she left to go after him.

I couldn't stop laughing. Sure as shit I couldn't. It was getting hard to breathe. I leaned over to Michael's side and put my arm across his shoulder. We tilted our heads together. He poked my side, tickling me, and we started to wrestle, nearing hysteria as he tried to pin me in the back seat. He was my best friend, and this was what we did when we were together. We laughed. We fought. We wrestled. As long as we were together, it didn't matter where we were. We would have fun.

"Jenna," Michael said, and suddenly he sounded choked, like the laughter was overwhelming him.

"What?"

"You're choking me. Get off my throat!"

Turned out I'd pinned him, and had my forearm across his neck. As soon as I let off the pressure he grabbed my arm, about to twist it behind me.

The driver's door opened and Diana slipped in. Andy slid into the other seat, a sheepish grin on his face. "Sorry for interrupting," he said, with a bit of a laugh. "Looks like you two were having fun."

I sat up, jerking away from Michael, the smile quickly falling from my lips. Michael, however, didn't let my hand go. Not that night. He held it tight, stroking the back of it with his thumb, interlacing our fingers together.

He held my hand the whole way home, and I let him. We stayed silent, together, holding hands in a way that was new and foreign and not altogether unwelcome.

When Diana dropped us off in front of our houses, he let go. He barely looked at me as he mumbled goodbye and darted through his front door. I didn't blame him. I didn't know what to say either.

The next day at school we acted like nothing had ever happened, but it was a long time before I forgot the feeling of my small hand in his bigger one, and the way his thumb traced patterns on my wrist, almost as if he was trying to tell me something, but couldn't.

It was a long time before I forgot that night.

But I did. Until I saw Michael lying by the side of the truck.

* * * *

"Michael? Babe? Can you stand? Wake up!" I slapped his cheek, gently at first, but then harder. His head rolled back and forth on his neck, reminding me of the zombie who'd done this to him, the one who lay in the dirt beside him. "Babe!"

He wasn't waking up, and I couldn't just sit there, slapping him. I needed to find Sam and Will and Rosie. I knew there were more undead creatures waiting for us all in the fields. These zombies had shown some basic hunting tactics; who knew if there were even smarter ones nearby, waiting for the initial carnage to end so they could sneak in for easy pickings. By that point, not much was going to surprise me.

"Baby, we have to go."

I set my Slugger down, and my shotgun. Keeping the rifle slung across my back, I reached down and pulled up from beneath Michael's shoulders. I didn't know how long it would be before the virus took hold, but I had to hope it would be longer than a couple minutes. I had to hope I'd have a chance to say goodbye.

I wiggled and squirmed until I had Michael up over my shoulders in a fireman carry, and my legs beneath me in a deep squat.

"I don't know if I can lift you, babe. Let's do this together on three. One…two….three."

With a grunt and a heave and no small amount of cursing, I managed to get to standing, the top half of Michael's body holding secure across my shoulder, the tips of his toes dragging against the ground. Then I ran.

* * * *

Running on the road was easy, at least comparatively. But when I turned into the wildflower field at a place where living people had obviously crashed through, chasing after Sam and the rest of them, things got a little trickier. Plants taller than me with leaves broader than my thighs slapped at me and snarled my hair with their thistles and thorns. Flowers that had looked sweet from afar looked angry, glaring down at me with false cheeriness as, up above, the sun began to set. The air was perfumed heavily with floral scents, spicy and heady, but through it all I could smell putridity as Michael's leg began to rot.

No. No. No. No. No. No. No. No. No.

"Sam?" I hissed into the flowery abyss. "Will? Rosie? Chicken?"

No one responded.

Darkness was falling fast, and the path through the flowers that I thought had been left by Sam, Will and Rosie seemed to have dried up. Closed off. I must have taken a wrong turn. And worse, Michael still hadn't awoken. His dead weight was becoming more than I could handle.

"I can't quit. Michael needs me."

Needs you for what? The voice inside my head was vicious. Accusing. *He needed you back at the truck and you let him down. Now he only needs you to put a bullet in his brain. Might as well aim for the cut in his temple. It's a good target.*

"Not yet," I said, and then, because my voice sounded weak and timid, I repeated myself, louder and firmer. "Not yet."

"Not yet what?"

That voice came from behind me, and I jumped, suppressing a too-girlie squeal. "Who said that?"

"Me, Jenn. Who else?"

"Michael! You're awake! How do you feel?"

I slid to the ground, easing him down as best I could, which wasn't quite "easy." My shoulders burned beneath his weight, and my arms, to which circulation had long been cut off, were dead. He slipped from my shoulders and crashed to the dirt.

"Ow!"

"Sorry. Let me help you up. Are you okay? How's your head?"

I rolled to my side and pulled him up to sitting. He rubbed his head. The sun, as it slipped below the horizon, lit him up like he was an angel. Like he was already dead. Tears filled my eyes, but he didn't notice.

"My head's alright," he said. "But my leg's killing me. What the hell happened? Where are we?"

I sighed. "We were attacked, back at the truck."

"Yeah, I remember that. Those fuckers surrounded us. Did we make it? Where's Sam? Where are the kids?"

"I don't know. I was looking for them but couldn't find them. I was carrying you, so I guess that slowed me down. You got hit in the head."

He made a face as he pulled his hand away from his temple and it came away bloody. "By what?"

"A rock. A zombie bitch threw it at you. But that's not…"

Michael's eyes widened. "She did what?"

"She threw it. The rock."

"A zombie threw a rock?"

"Yes. But that's not the worst…"

"Zombies can throw rocks…use weapons…and you're telling me that's not the worst of it? What the fuck's worse than zombies using weapons?"

Michael pulled up to his knees and tried to stand. As soon as he put weight on his leg, he crashed back to the ground. "Ow."

"Yeah," I said. "Don't get up, buddy."

"Does the worse thing have to do with my leg?"

"Yes." I stared at the ground. It was dark, the soil rich.

"Do I want to look at my leg? Do you have a flashlight?"

"No. And no."

"Jenna. Tell me what's going on."

I started to cry big, wet tears. Choking tears. Oh, God, how I hated myself in that moment, how I despised my weakness. My inability to tell the love of my life—for even with all the past few months had brought, I knew then that he was the only love I'd ever find—that he was a dead man, marked with the plague, sure to be gone in an instant, only to rise again to wait for me to kill him a second time. But how could I not cry? How could I not be weak in the face of losing the one thing—the one person—who'd been a constant source of light in the darkness? For even when we fought, even when we yelled and screamed and pretended to hate each other, we were still there. Always there.

Soon he wouldn't be.

Suddenly, there was a hand on my face. Michael's hand. He wiped away my tears and pulled on my chin, forcing me to look at him.

"That cut on my leg. It's a zombie bite, isn't it?"

I nodded, and through my tears I managed, "How'd you know?"

My eyes blurred with saline and it was nearing full dark, without a moon to guide us, but even so I caught the tail end of his sad grin. "I touched it," he said. "I smelled it. And then, the final nail in the coffin. I found this."

He held out his hand, balled into a tight fist. Slowly he let his fingers fall open. There it sat, glittering in his palm like a jewel—a moist, wet, blood-splattered jewel. A tooth. She'd left behind a tooth, probably when I shot her in the head.

The look on his face said enough, but he said the next words anyway. "You're going to have to kill me now."

Chapter 13: Sam

Running. Again. All we ever fucking did was run.

First we ran down the road. I wanted to stay and help Jenna and Michael, but Jenna said go so I went. Like a good little soldier, taking care of the children and the dog. The fucking dog who was attached to Rosie by some leash she rigged on the run, and who kept darting between my feet like he was trying to trip me up. Like even *he* knew that sending me away was a bad idea. A very bad idea.

On we ran, down the road, me letting Will and Rosie lead the way and set the pace because, let's face it, had I been ahead I would've left them in the dust. Not that I'd have meant to, it's just what would have happened.

I was a *very* good soldier, wasn't I?

Rosie's ponytail bounced around her shoulders as she ran, up into the air and back down. It was hypnotic, almost, and I found myself watching the way her little body moved. She was fluid when she ran, steady and quick. She might have been a track star someday, had things gone different.

Beside her, Will seemed in danger of disappearing altogether. Like an elf from some Tolkiensien world, all wispy and flowing. But not graceful. No, Will wasn't a graceful runner. He was heavy-footed, for all his slightness, as though he ran in thick, heavy combat boots like me, instead of his old tennis shoes, relics from another time.

We covered about a mile with absolutely no sign of any other zombies before Chicken nipped at my hand. He was gentle, but I jerked my hand away reflexively, dragging my wrist across his canine tooth. I smelled blood almost immediately.

"Dammit, Chicken, stop!" I pushed him down. "Hey you guys, hold up a sec!"

They pulled themselves to a halt, then turned and trotted back. Will's eyes were wild and his face was flushed, but Rosie looked remarkably composed for a little kid. She spoke first. "What's up?" She saw my cut. "Oh, here, let me."

Without another word, other than to shoo an increasingly frantic Chicken away to the side of the road where he sat, staring back the way we'd come, she pulled a cloth out of her pocket and dabbed at my bloody wrist. Then she wrapped the cloth around the wound and tied it with the skilled touch of a seasoned doctor. My respect for the kid was on the rise. When she was done, she looked up at me. "That better?"

"Yeah, thanks."

Will touched her arm before turning his crazy eyes on me. "We have to keep going. They could be right behind us."

I shrugged. "Who? The zombies? Or Jenna and Michael?" Then I laughed. I wasn't sure which one scared me more sometimes.

But Will's breath was coming in short gasps. "The…zombies…." he said, as though some big realization was setting in. "They could be anywhere. Didn't you see them? They're changing! They're *evolving!*"

"Yeah, I got that. I saw it back there, and I heard you say it in the truck. Why are you freaking out now?"

"I'm…not…freaking…out…it's…just…bad…news…"

"Will." Rosie stepped in front of her brother and took both his hands in hers. She squeezed them, and it was like magic. His breathing slowed and his eyes got less crazy as she stared steadily into them. "Calm down."

He did. My respect for Rosie went even higher. She was pretty tough, that little cricket. And she'd given me time to hatch a plan.

"Alright, guys. We need to stop running. Let Jenna and Michael catch up."

In that steely voice, Rosie interrupted. "What if they're dead?"

"They're fine," I said. "They're tough. Nothing's gonna get them down. Not ever." I said it with a firmness I didn't necessarily believe, but both Rosie and Will smiled at my reassurance. "So what we need to do is hide out a bit. Get off the road. Leave a trail for them to find us, and then we wait. They'll catch up, probably in a few. Maybe even with the truck."

"The truck's dead."

"We don't know that for sure, Will. Don't be a doomsdayer." Like I was Mr. Fucking Sunshine all of a sudden. I turned to the side of the road, overgrown with tall, thick weeds laced with flowers and, I was sure, all kinds of hidden nastiness. I didn't want to get off the road, but the sun was getting ready to go down, and I felt vulnerable in the middle of the open.

So I did what I had to do. I stepped into the weeds. Sharp grasses and thistles scratched at my face, and wispy, reedy things tugged at my clothes. The smell was overwhelming with sweet, but I did it anyway. I stepped side-to-side a few times, tramping down a human-sized path in the weeds. "They'll see this," I said. "I mean, they're not exactly hunters or trackers, but this is pretty obvious, don't you think? Help me out, would you?"

Soon the three of us had made a path wide enough for two, as though we were inviting Michael and Jenna in, letting them know exactly where to find us. I wasn't worried about the undead finding us. Even if they were smart all of a sudden, I doubted they understood Tracking 101. We pushed ourselves back a little further into the field, tucking away in a small nook, a clearing surrounding what must have once been a massive tree but was now little more than a stump in the ground, with its outstretched roots blocking the copious growth that flourished everywhere else.

"Let's wait here," I said, sitting down on the stump. "Take a breather. Calm this shit down. Jenna and Michael will be along in a few."

Will sank to the ground and immediately pulled out his leather journal and a penlight. He opened the book, holding the light in his mouth for later, I assumed, as the sun was beginning to set. Chicken wandered off into the bramble, nose to the ground. I figured he was looking for Jenna, and I didn't worry. I knew he'd be back.

I didn't have my backpack—I'd left it in the truck—but I figured that would be fine. We'd double back for it come morning; we'd lose half a day, but at least we'd have our supplies, even if the truck was dead, which I still wasn't convinced it was. But my stomach growled, and I regretted not at least grabbing a snack on my way out the truck. You'd think I'd have learned to always grab food by then, having starved on my own for months on end, but I guess I'd never learn.

I was suddenly aware of Rosie's presence, hovering just outside my peripheral vision. I turned and smiled. "Come have a seat," I said.

"The tree is happy," she said as she obliged.

"What?"

"That old Shel Silverstein story. You know it? The Giving Tree? About the tree who gives everything to the boy she loves, until she's just a stump, and he uses the stump as a seat. That's what this reminds me of."

"Sounds like a nice tree."

She shrugged. "Sounds like a jerk of a boy to me. Always taking, never giving. What an ass."

I laughed, and she made a silly face. Then she whispered, "Will's really into what he's doing if he didn't just fuss at me for saying ass."

"You know we were just kicked out of our truck by zombies with battle formations, right?"

"Yes?"

"So I think you can say ass any time you want, as loud as you want. I'll back you up."

Rosie giggled. She was so young, and it was so nice to hear her laugh. She shot Will a look, and then gazed up at the darkening sky. "Ass!"

"Louder!"

"ASS!"

"Rosie," said Will, but he barely looked up. Rosie and I burst out laughing.

We calmed quickly, though, and in the ensuing silence my stomach seemed to howl out with its emptiness.

"Your stomach's rumbling," said Rosie.

"You think?"

"You should eat something."

"I left my pack in the truck."

"Oh," she said, and then she pulled her own from where she'd stashed it beside the trunk. "Here."

She tossed me a granola bar and a pack of crackers, pilfered from Dave's stash. Next she pulled out a bottle of water and offered it to Will, who pushed it away, too intent on his reading, before taking a sip herself. She offered it to me.

"Thanks, kid," I said, wolfing down the snacks and feeling a little ashamed for taking candy from a baby. I patted her shoulder.

"You're welcome, Sam." She leaned into my touch, and suddenly she was there, a kid who needed comfort, and for once I was able to offer it. It felt nice. I slid my arm around her shoulders and let my lips brush the top of her head.

"You're a good kid."

"I know."

* * * *

Less than five minutes passed before Chicken reappeared, carrying a severed human arm in his mouth. It still wore the sleeve of a ragged flannel shirt. He dropped it on the ground by my feet, smiling up at me with his goofy dog grin, as if to say, "Look at this yummy treat I found you!"

"Ew," said Rosie, pulling her legs up on the stump, away from the arm.

"Chicken! Where'd you get that? Ugh! *Why'd* you get that?" It stank, and I threw my own arm across my nose and mouth to block the stench.

I looked around, and something seemed to click. Will looked up, too, finally removed from his precious notes. It clicked for him too as he looked from the partially-decomposed arm to the overly, one could say freakishly, fertile field around us. He jumped to his feet, wiping loose dirt from his hands, and began digging about with his toe, amid the roots.

I did the same.

The dirt was very loose, and very dark. Very well fertilized.

Nothing more harmful than an old glass bottle appeared amid the roots during our initial search, but as we trailed off into the weeds, Chicken nipping at our heels, pointing us toward his discovery, our probing toes quickly turned up a mess. Arms, legs, torsos, all buried just a few inches beneath the soil. Some looked burned, some didn't, but soon we were surrounded, it seemed, by body parts, as though they heard us coming and were saying hello. Where moments earlier we'd seen only the darkness of the earth, now we saw burnt flesh, and the occasional raw, white bone.

"Oh Jesus," I said.

"I thought you were Jewish," Will hissed.

"I am. But I'll take all the help I can get here."

We stood in the middle of a mass burial site, bodies everywhere, and then, just as my heart began to return to a normal rate following our gruesome discovery, Chicken growled.

"Fuck," I said.

"Fuck," Rosie said.

"Fuck," Will said, and for a moment I was proud of them.

I pulled out my pistol and my hunting knife. "Stay close, both of you."

"Affirmative."

"Will, you too."

"You got it."

We tightened up into a clump, backs pressed together, each clutching our weapons, each regretting the arsenal we'd abandoned at the truck.

I heard the first zombie before I saw it as it moaned and crunched through the bramble.

Will sighed. "Oh God, I hope it's not a smart one."

It wasn't. When we saw it a moment later it was obviously one of the old school undead creatures, all lurching and uncoordinated. I breathed a sigh of relief and looked down at Chicken, who crouched beside me. "Get her, boy."

He complied. He leaped forward as though a floodgate opened, and lowered his head like a battering ram. In an instant he knocked the zombie to the ground. She barely resisted, so decomposed was her body. I stepped forward to slip my knife through her empty eye-socket, into her brain. The mouth, which gnashed its teeth at my approach, stilled.

By the time I looked up, three more creatures were on us. Rosie took one out with a shot straight through the forehead, and Will trained his handgun on another. The third was still a few steps away, tangled up in the tall thistles. I tried and failed to ignore the crunching of bones and old, decaying flesh beneath my boots as I covered the distance to the writhing creature that leaned and pulled as it tried to get to me, too. As the sun set and the light glared, I squinted and tried to focus. I didn't want to shoot him; we'd already been loud enough.

When I was close enough to smell the foul, rotten scent of bile and decay that spewed from his mouth, I dispatched him, fast, with an easy stab to the temple. Behind me was quiet. Stillness. The attack was over.

We'd wandered far into the weeds, far from our little clearing, and soon Rosie and Will joined me by the final zombie, who swayed with the flowers in the cool evening breeze. Chicken sat on my foot, and I reached out to touch Rosie and Will on the shoulders. "You two okay?"

They nodded.

"We should find our way back. It's getting dark."

Another joint nod.

As if he agreed, Chicken leaped back to his feet. Then he bowed his head to the ground, sniffing, his rear end jutting up into the air. Next, he sniffed up, the breeze around him. He growled. He yelped. And before I could stop him, he ran, back in the direction from which we came, back toward the clearing.

"Well, shit," I said, and then I took off running after him, trusting Will and Rosie to follow.

* * * *

Chicken reached the clearing first, and the next thing I heard was his low, mournful howl. He only howled when there was trouble.

"No, Chicken! Not now!"

Jenna! She's alright!

I ran the next few steps into the clearing, and skidded to a stop as I took in the scene before me.

First I saw Chicken, and the way he sat on his haunches, his head thrown up toward the sky as he wailed and howled and screamed in despair. I'd never seen him like that before.

But it wasn't the sight of Chicken that stopped me short. No. That was nothing compared to what I saw beyond him.

There, resting against the very stump on which Rosie and I had talked and laughed not thirty minutes before, lay Michael, spot lit by the moon, which had chosen that exact moment to burst through the evening clouds. His eyes squeezed closed, and his fists clenched tight at his sides.

Beside him sat Jenna.

She held a gun, point blank against his temple.

Jenna was about to kill my brother.

I raised my rifle to my shoulder. I pointed it to the sky. I fired. "Drop your weapon, Jenna Price!"

My cry mixed with Chicken's howl and I doubted there was anyone within a ten mile radius who couldn't hear us and wouldn't come running. I didn't care.

"Get the fuck away from my brother."

* * * *

We stood in the silence following gunfire. Even Chicken ceased his howling. Jenna turned and stared at me.

It was hard to say, with the lighting so weird, being from the moon and filtered by the clouds, but she looked hurt. Angry. Her cheeks looked shiny and wet, and as she lowered the gun she opened her mouth as if to speak, but no words came out. Instead, she let loose a choking, shuddering sob.

Michael's eyes popped open. "Don't let him stop you, Jenn. You have to. Please."

I lowered my own gun. "The fuck's going on?" My voice was a whisper.

Michael pushed himself up on his elbows, sliding up to a sitting position, his back to the tree stump. "Sam. I'm glad you're here. But please shut up and don't stop Jenna."

"What the fuck is going on?"

I tried to ignore the kernel of ice that settled in my stomach. I tried to pretend I wasn't seeing the one thing I'd dreaded for years. I tried to pretend I didn't know what was happening.

"Sam." Jenna could barely talk, but she stood, forcing herself calm. "Sam. I'm sorry. It's not what you think."

"I think you were just about to kill my brother."

"Well, yes, but I don't want to. He's making me."

"He's making you?"

Behind her, Michael struggled to his feet, and I noticed the way he didn't put weight on his left leg. The kernel of ice expanded, spider-webbing through my gut like the cracks in the truck's windshield. A trail of blood dripped down the side of his face. "Yes. I'm making her. I don't want to do it myself."

Jenna shuddered and lowered her head, until Michael took hold of her shoulders. She spun. He pulled her to his chest, where she buried her face. The sobs took over again as he held her.

To my surprise, I felt my own tears on my cheeks. *Why am I crying?*

But of course, I knew. The signs were all there, right in front of my face. "You're bit," I said. "On the leg, it looks like. You guys didn't get away safe."

"It's my fault," Jenna wailed against Michael's chest, and Chicken let loose his howl again. I nudged him. He was going to bring more creatures running. He stopped.

"It's not your fault. We underestimated them. It was just a matter of time. Stop crying."

Michael was calm, as though he'd already accepted his death. Well, I hadn't.

"How could you let this happen?" I leaped forward and pulled Jenna from Michael's arms. She didn't deserve to be there. "How could you do this to Michael? To me?"

Her head hung down as though she didn't have the strength to hold it up. "I'm sorry," she said, tears and snot raining down her face. "It's my fault. I chased the zombie. She tricked me."

"She *tricked* you? A zombie tricked you? A smart, *alive* girl like you? Oh, now I've heard it all!" I shook Jenna, back and forth, trying to shake the stupidity out of her, and though a million times before she'd have fought back, shoved me off, put me back in my place, this time she didn't. She stood and shook. Her head wobbled back and forth, back and forth, and I shook her harder. "You killed my brother." I screamed in her face, and she flinched and cried and sobbed.

A light flickered in the weeds beside us, but I barely noticed. I could only see Jenna's face, the way its tears admitted her guilt, her blame. It was her fault my brother was about to die.

"You bitch!"

Without thinking, without even knowing what I was doing, I raised up my hand, drawing it back, clenching it into a fist. My world, my vision, narrowed to Jenna. Her face, her tears, her guilt. Everything else was black. And the only sound was her wail.

A truck hit me.

Or at least that's what it felt like.

We fell to the ground, Jenna and I, but she was free and I was pinned. My vision suddenly cleared, and opened back up, and my hearing expanded beyond the sound of her wails, and then I could see him, hear him. Michael. He sat on top of me, his face inches from mine, his arms pinning my own to the ground.

He growled. He snarled. He spoke.

"I said, back the fuck off my wife."

Chapter 14: Jenna

I stopped crying. His wife. He hadn't called me that in ages. It only took a zombie bite to fully reconcile us.

Not that it mattered. He was about to die anyway.

I scooted away from Michael, sitting atop Sam, who began to fight back. They tussled and rolled across the clearing, shouting when they rolled over roots or banged into the pitiful tree stump. They were evenly matched. Sam was older, but Michael had fury on his side. He never liked seeing me hurt.

Nothing was going to stop me from being hurt, not at that point, so I sat and watched in morbid fascination until they rolled to a stop, panting, lying in the dirt on their backs, beside each other. Their hands joined, something I hadn't seen them do since we were kids back home—young kids at that—and I bit my lip to stifle a cry. A scream. My boys. How I loved them, especially after everything that had happened. I leaned forward and settled onto my knees, a few feet from where they lay. They talked as only brothers do, and I listened, a voyeur at the end of my ropes.

"She bit you?"

"Yes."

"On that leg."

"Yes. You already said that."

"I know. I'm just recapping."

"It's not Jenna's fault. It just happened. These things happened."

"I never should have left."

"Yes, you should have. It's not your fault."

"It's my fault."

As they talked, a ceaseless river of tears spilled from my eyes, no matter how hard I willed them to stop. A light flickered beyond weeds, catching my attention for a stray second. *Must be Rosie and Will,* I thought. *I'll get them after. After this is done.*

There was no question in my mind that Michael had to die. He was bitten. Infected. We couldn't let him become a zombie, especially not one of the mutated ones. He was too smart as it was; as a zombie he'd be a disaster for us to kill.

Sam's eyes were dry when he sat upright. He pulled Michael up, too, and they hugged. My heart broke. I couldn't go to them, but I couldn't stay away. I inched closer, wanting to see them, be with them, smell them, together, one last time. Closer and closer I scooted until I was there, too. But I didn't touch them. This was their moment.

Finally they let go, each wearing a look of determination. They looked at me. Michael nodded to Sam. "We're ready."

Sam stood, and Michael backed up to the stump again, like an accused man headed to the guillotine. "I want to face you," he said. "I don't want you to shoot me in the back."

"Agreed."

I leaped to my feet. "No!"

They turned to me. "What?"

"Not you, Sam. This is my job. He's my husband. I have to be the one to kill him."

Sam looked at me, eyebrows knit with surprise. "But he's my brother. He's my responsibility. It needs to be me. Our parents would want it this way."

Anger, sadness, frustration, all burst out of me in the form of a laugh. "Your parents? Are you kidding? Did you really just say your parents would want you to kill Michael? What's happening here?"

"Jenna, stop." This time it was Michael. I stopped. "It has to be Sam," he continued. "Sam's been through this before. Sam's my brother. You're the love of my life, but he's my blood. I want it to be him."

His words were a bullet, straight through my heart. I gasped, staggering back.

"I'm sorry," he said. "But it has to be Sam."

"I don't want to do it, Jenn," Sam said. "But I have to. The one time before I should have done this for someone else, I didn't. I was too weak. But I can be strong for Michael. Please. Let me."

With trembling hands I reached out and took Sam's. I nodded. "I'm holding you while you do it."

He nodded, curt and business-like. Then he turned to Michael. "So this is it? This is goodbye?"

Michael nodded. His face fell. They stumbled toward each other, toward their last embrace. When they parted, neither could dam their tears. "Guess I'll see you on the flip side, bro," said Sam.

"I'll be waiting."

I stepped forward. "Can I say good…"

I couldn't get the rest out. Michael wrapped me up in his arms the way he always had, and suddenly I remembered all those nights on the road, together, the way we'd sleep all tangled, the way I could barely breathe if I didn't know exactly where he was. Now I was facing a life without him in a grief-shattered world. A life in which I'd always know exactly where he was—there, buried in this godforsaken field. All those nights we'd spent alone since we'd had our falling out. In that moment, in his arms, I hated each of those nights. I sucked in a breath through my nose, trying to pull his scent into me, ignoring the twinge of rot that already emanated from the bite in his leg. I focused on the smell of his deodorant. The smell of his sweat, the oil in his hair. I touched his face, letting my fingers trace the curve of his jaw. I touched his back, his butt, his arms, his fingers. I held him, wishing the moment would never end, knowing it would, all too soon.

Sam pulled us apart. "It's time."

"I know."

Michael's eyes grew a little wild, and his gaze shifted from Sam to me, Sam to me. "So this is it."

"Yes."

"I love you guys."

I was crying too hard to say the words back. But he knew how I felt, and so did I. Finally.

Michael lay back, resting his head against the stump. "Do it fast."

Sam nodded. "I will."

Sam raised his rifle, pointing it at the crease between Michael's eyebrows. The crease I'd kissed a thousand times. I stepped behind him and slid my hands down his arms, stopping at his wrists. I squeezed with my hands and pressed myself against his back. He smelled like Michael, almost. Almost, but not quite. I closed my eyes.

"Do it," I whispered.

Sam drew in a sharp breath.

* * * *

"No!"

In the darkness of the night, amplified by my squeezed-tight eyelids, Will's voice was perhaps the loudest thing I'd ever heard. Chicken barked, braying his dissatisfaction at the interruption, and Sam snapped his head to the side. "What?" His voice was filled with fury. "Can't you see we're doing something important here?"

"Yes," said Will. "But you have to stop!"

He stepped into the clearing, holding Schwartz's notebook and a small penlight. *The light in the weeds,* I remembered. *He's been reading at a time like this.*

Rosie followed him, keeping a careful distance between herself and the scene before her. I didn't blame her. I'd have kept a careful distance, too.

"Why should we stop?" I said, squeezing back the faint glimmer of hope that bloomed in my belly. "We know what's coming next."

"But what if we don't? What if Michael's *immune?*"

Had he taken out his gun and shot each and every one of us, we wouldn't have been more surprised. Michael jerked to attention, leaning forward against his knees. Sam lowered the rifle. We turned to Will.

"What do you mean, immune?" I said. "Nobody's immune. Everybody turns into a zombie."

Will took a deep breath. When he spoke, the words poured out fast, faster than anything I'd ever heard him say. "Yes, but what if we could develop immunity over time? Maybe not a forever-immunity, but maybe long enough that we can figure out a way to save him. Maybe he's been exposed so much, so often, his body knows how to fight it!"

"What do you mean, exposed? I've never been bit before."

"Yes, but you've killed how many zombies? Hundreds? Thousands, I'm betting. I've seen your guys' handiwork. And in all that killing, what are the chances you haven't gotten zombie blood on your skin? In your hair? In your eyes or your mouth? *In an open cut*?"

"But what if it's just the zombie saliva that carries the virus?"

Will sighed. "Maybe. So then, same question. I'm sure you've been spit on by a zombie. Licked, sneezed on, whatever. I'm sure that in the course of blowing zombie brains out, you've been exposed to the virus a hundred times. And yet *you're not a zombie.* Do you see where I'm going with this?"

Like dutiful students, we nodded. We saw. The tiny glimmer of hope blossomed to a full-fledged feeling.

Will kept talking, excited. "Michael, how long ago did the bite occur?"

"About 45 minutes ago, I think? Jenna, is that right?"

"Closer to an hour. You were out for a while when I was carrying you."

Will nodded. "Right. Great. That's great news."

"Why?" Sam pulled Michael to his feet, and together they stared at Will as though he was a god, a savior. Maybe he was.

"Because think about it. How long does the virus normally take to set in? Ten, twenty minutes at best. If nothing else, a person's good and sick after twenty minutes, right? Michael, how you do feel?"

He looked down, ran his hands down his body. "Well, my leg hurts."

"But other than that?"

"My head hurts where the rock hit it."

Will groaned. "But other than *that?"*

"Honestly? I feel sort of fine. Sort of normal. Not…zombie…ish…"

"See?" Will looked smug. Content. Prouder of himself than a boy who's just won a science fair.

I whispered. It was all I could get out. "Are you serious? Don't you mess with me, Will."

Will grinned. "Based on Schwartz's notes, and some theories I've been tossing around for a while, yes, I think I am. He's got some kind of immunity on his side. He won't become a zombie, at least not for a little while. Long enough for us to try to do something."

"So we don't have to kill him?"

"Not today we don't."

"Oh my God, Will, that's amazing!" I darted to him and pulled him into a bear hug. He was smaller than me, and I picked him up and spun him When I put him down he staggered away so I grabbed onto his sister, who'd stood silently by, watching the whole thing play out, tears glistening on her cheeks. I kissed her forehead, and then turned.

There they stood, Michael and Sam, wrapped up in an embrace. Chicken leaped and pranced as though he understood, tugging occasionally in their shirttails. I ran to them, tugging on their hands until they let each other go.

Michael pulled me into his arms. He picked me up. I wrapped myself around him, arms and legs, and he pulled his head back slightly. Our eyes met. So did our lips. We kissed, our mouths eager and open and victorious and happy. It was like no time passed since our last kiss, so many months before. Soon, too soon, Sam cleared his throat and we pried ourselves apart.

"I think it's time we set up camp for the night," Sam said, a silly grin on his face. "Maybe if we're quiet the spirits of all the dead people won't find us."

"The spirits…" began Michael, but Sam cut him off.

"Forget it. It was a joke. Let's quiet down and go to bed. I'll keep first watch. In the morning we'll go salvage what we can from the truck. In the meantime, you kids get some sleep."

His grin turned two a lascivious leer, and I threw my head back and laughed. It felt so good to laugh instead of cry.

* * * *

It took us a while to settle down after all the excitement. Even Michael, normally a champion sleeper, tossed and turned on the ground beside me until he pulled me tight to his chest, twining his legs through my own. He stilled, melting into sleep. I listened to his slow, even breaths, counting each one, long into the night.

I tried to ignore, every time I licked my lips, the lingering taste of death, of decay, left behind by Michael's kiss.

* * * *

The truck was totaled. The next morning when we went back, Sam slipped under the chassis and saw where the oil leak was, where the remaining drips had settled and congealed on the cold concrete overnight. The engine was seized, broken, and nothing we could do would change that fact.

We couldn't go back, couldn't exactly ask Dave for another truck. Instead, we crammed what gear we could into our packs and set out the way we'd begun our journey: on foot, with nothing but a few sketchy maps to lead the way. We had to leave behind the cooler full of "fresh" food, but we carried with us all the MREs, our weapons, and our tents.

And thus began the next leg of our journey east. Three boys, two girls, and a dog. One of the boys had a zombie bite in his leg that oozed and festered no matter how many times we applied antibiotic ointment, but it didn't progress much further than the actual wound. With a crutch fashioned with a pipe from the truck, Michael was able to hobble along with us, barely slowing us down as we trudged onward.

Early on in the journey Will came up with the bright idea to "treat" Michael with an antiviral medication, hoping to help stop the zombie virus from spreading. One night we found a small town, not far from the road we traveled, and Will and I went in under cover of darkness—me for protection, him for drug location. As we headed toward the town, leaving the comparative safety of our tents behind, Will talked.

"We need the *right* antiviral," he said as he ducked beneath a low-hanging tree branch. "Antivirals are pretty target-specific. If we try the wrong one it won't hurt him, but it won't help him either. Let's get a big supply of whatever we find, and that way when we find the right one we'll have enough to keep him going a while."

"You're making a lot of assumptions, don't you think?"

He stopped walking and turned to me, the whites of his eyes bright and wide even in the murky darkness of a foggy evening. "What am I assuming?"

I shrugged and kept walking toward the town. "One. There's going to be a drug store in this rinky dink town."

"Every town has a drug store, Jenna. They have to. Or else where do they get their medicines?"

I ignored him. "Two. That drug store, if it even exists, will have any sort of supply that hasn't already been picked over by a hundred other looters."

"We're not looters, Jenna. We're scavengers."

"Three. Any sort of antiviral drug will have any sort of effect on Michael's bite. I mean, he seems to be doing okay by himself most of the time, don't you think?" I stopped walking and took Will's hand, willing him to agree, hoping he hadn't noticed the smell, the way I had, and the way Michael sometimes spaced out mid-conversation like he forgot who, or what, he was.

But Will looked away. "He's doing okay, yes. My immunity theory is on target, to a point. But I'm afraid the virus will ultimately win, unless we give him a little help. A little nudge, so to speak."

I shuddered, and he squeezed my hand. "But don't worry, Jenna. Not yet. We're going to take care of him. We're not going to let him… you know…zombie."

Forcing a smile, I squeezed his hand back and started walking again, leading him down the road. "I know we won't, kid."

* * * *

The town loomed in the distance: an old, boarded up Main Street and a few scattered houses and trailers. It looked like the whole thing had seen its heyday long before the advent of the zombie plague. A faded sign let us know where we were: Harleyville, Kentucky, population 932.

Below it hung a piece of plywood, spray-painted with the words, "Keep out, or else." Of course the words were written in a jagged print, with the red paint dripping like blood. I sighed. "Sometimes I feel like we live in a bad horror movie."

Will nodded, his eyes focused on the blood-red words.

"We should turn off our lights," I added. "Anyone here could see us coming for miles."

Only the click and the ensuing darkness told me he heard. A breeze kicked up, blowing a cloud in front of the moon, immersing us in a deep, inky black. We stepped onto Main Street, letting our eyes adjust to what we could see.

"There," Will breathed beside me, pointing. "See the R-X sign? That's the pharmacy."

I saw it. Barely. Long-dead neon failed to light the way for us.

"Yup." I gulped. "Let's go."

The windows of the storefronts were boarded up, though glass glinted on the sidewalk beside a few of the buildings, as though the boards were nailed after the windows were shattered. "I feel like I'm in an Old West ghost town," I whispered. Will and I joined hands.

On many of the boards were scrawled similarly ominous messages: *Keep out. This means you. Death to all who enter. Harleyville, Kentucky. Population: 0.*

"Should we turn back?" Will whispered.

Instead of answering, I sped up, toward the pharmacy. Will stayed with me. I hoped I wasn't leading us into some crazy-person trap. Nearby, the breeze blew wind chimes that hung on an unseen porch. The music was soft and eerie, but gentle. I found, after a minute, that I even enjoyed hearing something different than the sound of our voices or the wind rustling tree leaves.

We reached the pharmacy—SMITH'S DRUGS, the sign said proudly, at a drunken angle—and I tried the door. To my surprise, though the windows were boarded up and messaged, the door swung easily outward.

"After you," I whispered.

Will smiled, vague and nervous. "No, after you. You have the big gun. And the bat."

I grinned. "Okay, hold the door for me. Be a gentleman. But I go in first, and quiet. Get ready to run if I say so."

He nodded, and pressed a hand to the door. I raised the Slugger to swinging position and stepped inside, holding my breath.

Glass crunched beneath my boots. I nudged a blue ball aside with my toe. It was the type of ball pharmacies always had on hand to tempt children and annoy their mothers, that wasn't quite balloon, but wasn't quite kickball either. I remembered buying new ones almost every time I went to the store with my mother when I was small, but the presence of this one, in a place so dark and grave, was unsettling. It reminded me of someplace else.

* * * *

I stood at the end of a long hallway, facing what I knew was the medical lab where Chase Franklin, the self-designated leader of post-apocalypse New Orleans, had his goons conducting all kinds of medical experiments, seeking a cure for the zombie virus and an end to the hell. People from his camps who went into the lab never came out, at least not as humans. We heard he used the zombies created in the lab to keep some of the nearby cities populated with undead, serving as gateways protecting his city from people he didn't want.

The hallway was dark, lit only by a flickering EXIT sign at one end, and it stank of death and decay and zombie. Chicken stood, shaking, by my side, ever a worthy companion. I scratched his head as my eyes adjusted and I looked around.

There on the walls were cheerful murals. Clowns, balloons, circus animals. Coat hooks and cubbies stood waist-high, in between each of the wooden doors with windows near the top.

This, the medical lab, was once a preschool.

There, at the end of the hall, I'd find genetically modified zombies. Before I did I'd meet Dr. Schwartz, and his laugh, his broken, devastated laugh, would haunt my dreams for the rest of my life. The sound of his whistle would ring in my ears and soon the zombies—the faster, stronger (but not smarter) zombies—would be hot on my tail as I ran for my life and prayed the lab would explode behind me.

Chicken began to growl, and the sound morphed into a zombie's petulant moan. The moan changed, too. The zombie called my name. Jenna. Jenna.

* * * *

"Jenna? Jenna? Wake up! Come back to me. Jenna!"

Will stood before me, shaking my shoulders. My Slugger hung low at my side.

"*Jenna!*"

"What?" I said. My head wobbled back and forth on my neck, like the head of the zombie that attacked Michael. That bit Michael. Wobble, wobble. "Stop it!"

"Then wake *up!* You're scaring me!"

I snapped back to reality. "Will? What happened?" I stood in the pharmacy, not the preschool medical lab I blew up in New Orleans. "What's going on?"

Will looked terrified. His breaths came like the pants of a thirsty dog, and his eyes bugged open wide. "I don't know. You saw that ball, and it was like you…I don't know. Like you went away somewhere else. Somewhere far away. You scared me."

I shook like Chicken after a sudden rainsquall. "Whoa. Yeah, I think I was just remembering…you know…"

"It was like how Sam does sometimes. When he blacks out. Did you black out?"

"I don't know? I don't think so, but maybe? I mean, it was like I was *there*. Really there."

"Jenna, are you okay?"

"I don't know. Are any of us okay anymore?" He shook his head. "Exactly. Moving on. What time is it? How long was I out?"

Will checked his watch. "Maybe three minutes? Long enough. Too long. I'm worried."

"Shut up. We're here now. Let's find what you need and get the hell out of here. This place gives me the willies."

Will's mouth turned up in an almost-smile. "Don't call me Willie."

"Huh?"

"Never mind. Forget it. Anyway, the prescription drugs are probably in the back. This place doesn't look too badly picked over."

I looked around and laughed. The shelves were mostly bare. "Oh really?"

"Well, I mean, I see a can of soup over there. We should grab that."

We did.

In the back of the store we found a meager supply of prescription drugs. Will let out a deep breath. "Okay, not as much as I'd hoped, but let's see what we can grab."

He rustled through while I kept watch, filling a sack with rattling bottles. Soon we left the way we came in. I kicked the blue ball on my way out the door.

Chapter 15: Will

Attempt 1:

I decided to try Tamiflu in the initial attempt at using antiviral drugs to stop the progress of the virus through Michael's system. The reason was simple enough: the undead virus is spread by bodily fluids, and the flu is airborne. Thus, the Tamiflu shouldn't work.

Right now, my immunity theory needs further testing; the antiviral drugs are secondary to the body's own ability to fight. After all, one does not typically die from the flu, especially not if one has become immune to it via inoculation or otherwise. In the same way, exposure to the flu does not assume infection.

Physical exam notes prior to Attempt 1 (Tamiflu):

On the surface, Michael seems fine. He reports no obvious symptoms beyond pain in his leg, which measures a 5 out of 10. He denies sweats, chills, and does not present with fever.

If we look below the surface, however, we do see some symptomology beginning to develop.

1.The bite wound itself remains red and inflamed at all times. Application of antibiotic ointment has done little to dull the inflammation, though the absence of any sort of pus discharge indicates a lack of secondary infection

2. The entry point is jagged; flesh does not appear to be healing in the least. But nor do I see the blackening of the flesh that is consistent with zombie samples I've seen. Their entry wounds are often decayed until they can barely be recognized as anything resembling human flesh. This does not appear to be happening here. Yet.

3. The smell, however, is growing stronger. While at first examinations revealed a minor whiff of the rot associated with zombies, the smell is worsening. It's exacerbated by pressing on the area immediately surrounding the bite wound itself, which leads me to wonder if the infection is, in fact, progressing somewhere beyond the obvious location. I'd love to have seen the progression of the creature responsible for Michael's bite, as she changed from living to undead. Was her progress this sedate? But as that can't happen, I'll just have to take careful notes.

4. Michael's breath is growing foul, which supports the above theory. Jenna has taken to supplying him with minty gum (how she finds things like that I'll never know, but she's the supply queen for a reason), but I made him spit it out for the examination. As expected, within moments his breath was so foul it was difficult being with him inside a tent, and we moved our exam outdoors.

5. Michael's pulse rate remains strong and consistent, though at times he appears to pant in an almost canine way. When his attention is drawn to the fact, he ceases, and breathes normally once again.

6. His eyes remain clear, pupils normal.

7. This bit is less quantifiable even than the above (most of which is based on observation, with very little measurable due to my lack of medical equipment), but I feel compelled to report it as part of the exam. Most of the time Michael is completely capable of normal, ordinary conversation, responding to questions in expected ways, joking with Jenna and the medical examiner (me) and laughing. But sometimes his eyes glass over and it appears that he "checks out" for upwards of a minute at a time. When he comes back, he has no recollection of any time having passed. This behavior is not all that dissimilar to the behavior exhibited by Sam, who appears to have flashbacks from time to time. I imagine Sam would be diagnosed with some form of PTSD by someone with a medical degree (not being a doctor, I feel odd making a diagnosis, though I'm fairly certain I'd be correct). I wonder if Michael is experiencing these flashbacks, or if this is some symptom of the viral progression. It's worth noting that, when he awakens from a flashback, Sam can typically report what he was seeing/re-experiencing, while Michael seems to not have that capability, which leads me to fear the latter.

Attempt 1 consists of two Tamiflu tablets. As Michael said, down the hatch.

* * * *

"Hey, Will. Whatcha doing?"

Rosie poked her head into the tent where I sat, scribbling in a new notebook Jenna found on one of her magical supply runs. I told her I needed to keep notes on Michael's progress; she came back with three notebooks and six boxes of pens. Her eyes were wild when she handed everything over to me. "Here," she'd said. "I hope this helps."

I snapped the notebook closed. Rosie always liked to read over my shoulder and I wasn't ready to start sharing my research. Not even with her. I forced a smile. "Just writing some notes. What's up?"

She came the rest of the way into the tent we shared each night and sat beside me, pulling her knees up to her chin. We'd taken the day off from hiking to give Michael some time to rest. His leg was a constant source of pain, and he needed to be off it. Rosie had been running around in the woods with Chicken for the past hour or so, searching for mushrooms or anything else we could add to our dwindling food supplies, but now she was back, interrupting me, and smiling as she did it.

"I just wanted to see what you were doing, cooped up in here like this. It's a beautiful day. You should really be out enjoying it."

I shook my head. "Too much to do."

"But it's so nice out! Get some air, Will. It's good for you." She grinned, and I could tell she was trying to be enticing. It didn't work.

"You're starting to sound like mom," I said, and I immediately regretted it. Rosie's face clouded over and her eyes went dark, as if I turned off a light.

She frowned. "Mom would agree with me."

I flinched. "Sorry. I know. You're right. But this…it's important. Research." I gestured toward the tent flap. "Michael and all."

Rosie brightened and reached out. "Can I see?"

"No!"

My voice was sharper than I'd meant and her face fell again. I thought about back-tracking, maybe showing her a page or two, as she stared at me with those big, hurt-puppy eyes, but before I could Jenna's shouts cut through the tension.

"Will! Will, get out here! We need you!"

Sam's voice came next. "Hurry!"

Rosie and I exchanged a look. She tore out of the tent as I paused to tuck the notebook at the bottom of my rucksack.

* * * *

Attempt 1 results: failure...or was it??

Though I didn't expect the Tamiflu to do much to inhibit the spread of any viral infection, I didn't expect Michael's body to react quite so strongly to it.

For 24 hours following the first (and only) dose, Michael's temperature rose steadily. Though I didn't have a thermometer, the presence of fever was obvious. His skin grew flaming hot to the touch. His face reddened. His eyes grew glassy. He had chills that shook his entire body.

Every twenty minutes or so, Michael vomited. At first the vomit was strictly the undigested remains of the food he ate in the hours preceding treatment; as his reaction (for that's what I believe it was) progressed, the vomit was more bile and less food, until there was nothing but stomach acid coming out. Dry heaves continued after that fact, as did diarrhea.

His symptoms mirrored cholera, or ebola, or at least a really bad stomach virus. Sometimes I wish I was already a doctor and understood the nuances better, but there you have it.

I do think his body actively fought the entry of the Tamiflu into his system. I wonder if that's the work of the virus? Perhaps the more violent the reaction (and this was certainly violent), the higher the likelihood the medication was attacking the right thing? Perhaps this was the virus's way of fighting back, or maintaining its presence in its host?

Further testing is required. Especially when, upon examination, the redness of his leg wound was drastically reduced.

After 24 hours Michael's temperature began to regulate, and the vomiting began to ease. He was able to keep in basic fluids after 32 hours. We've now been camped in this location (I believe we're close to Charleston, West Virginia. There are mountains around us and we've left main highways for the cloak of back roads, which are, according to Jenna, safer and more secure) for approximately 50 hours now. I'm hoping to try a second treatment later today.

* * * *

"No."

Jenna and Sam spoke in unison while Michael slept in the tent beside us. Rosie and Chicken were off scavenging again.

"But if we don't try again, we won't know if it was a reaction to the medication, or something else he ate. And did you see his leg? For once it was less red. Maybe the Tamiflu did something. Maybe it's the right drug."

Jenna stood in front of the tent's door, arms crossed over her chest, squeezing her Slugger tight. She wasn't going to let me in, at least not while I was holding Tamiflu in my hand. "Will. Are you crazy? Even if it helped a little, we can't do that to Michael again. We were barely able to keep him hydrated. If he gets sick like that, he could *die.* The cure could kill him faster than the disease. Do you not see that? Besides. I can't go through that again." Her voice shook. She'd spent every moment by Michael's side while he was sick, cleaning his blankets and carrying off buckets of vomit and his other bodily emissions. She was a good nurse, but the experience had been draining. Dark circles ringed her bloodshot eyes.

"But this could be a really important advancement in the treatment of the zombie virus," I said, hoping I sounded firm and not whiny.

Sam shook his head and stepped forward to stand beside Jenna. "No. Dude. It would be one thing if we were in a hospital and could somehow regulate his symptoms, right? I know they'll do that for, like, cancer patients with chemo and whatnot, but this isn't a hospital. Look around. We're in the middle of the fucking woods, in the middle of God knows fucking where, and if Michael gets sick like that again, we'll lose him. So no. No way. Dream on, *kid.*"

"Besides," added Jenna, casting her eyes down. "I'd like to get moving again. I don't like this place. I feel like someone's watching us. All the time."

I nodded. I knew what she meant, actually. The hair on the back of my neck had been on end since we'd stopped in this spot, and I swear I kept hearing things in the distance. Not to mention the fact that we hadn't seen a zombie in days and days, which was, on its own, really weird.

But still. "If we find a hospital with equipment, you'll let me try again?"

She shrugged. "That'll be up to Michael. For now, our priority is keeping him alive, and getting where we're going. But keeping him alive is first and foremost on my list. So don't fuck with me."

I jumped. Jenna never talked to me like that.

From inside the tent came Michael's voice. It was raspy and weak. "Jenn? Are you out there?"

"One sec, babe," she called over her shoulder. "I'll be right there." Then she turned back to me. "I'm serious, Will. No more. We can't risk it. I'm not losing him."

I nodded, and she turned and disappeared into the tent. I heard the low rumble of their voices and the rustling of sheets, so I turned to walk away.

Sam caught my arm, stopping me. "I'm serious too, Will. Don't touch him. Not like this. You'll regret it if you do."

I blinked and swallowed hard. "I thought you were on my side," I said. "I thought you were all about helping me to find the cure. I thought we were in this together."

"Fuck that," he said. "Right here and now, that ends. I'm in this to get home. To find my parents. They're alive, I know it. I've always known it. And if it helps you test your theories on other people, fine. Just keep your hands off my brother."

* * * *

Attempt 2: I'm going to have to try something else. I need to see if a second dose of Tamiflu causes similar reactions. I'll just have to dissolve some in his canteen.

Chapter 16: Jenna

"On the road again…just can't wait to get on the road again…" I hummed as we walked away from the Campsite of Doom, where I thought, for the millionth time, that I was going to lose Michael. But for the millionth time, I didn't. And no matter how much I wondered how long our luck would hold out, I couldn't help but feel a little lighter as we left that incident behind. *Good riddance.*

Michael was skinny, but he'd been skinny before (*like that time in the camp in New Orleans when he literally came back from the dead)* and I'd fatten him up again. Chicken was keeping his distance from him, but that was okay, too. Chicken was always leery of new things, and Michael certainly did have a new funk about him since he got sick. It was making it hard to sleep beside him at night, but that was fine. We'd work through it. Michael and I could work through anything.

He walked between Sam and me, like we were the three amigos once again. It was a good feeling. A safe feeling. And if I still felt like we were being watched (*Oh my God, I remember when we traveled to New Orleans and every time we stopped at a gas station they knew us and by the time we got to Chase Franklin he knew everything we'd done and then I remember the way Chase looked at me, like he wanted to be my Michael, but he was pasty and thick and sick and when he touched me my skin crawled and I wanted to throw up)*, well, maybe that was okay, too. It would keep me on my toes.

I tightened my grip on my Slugger with one hand, and checked my hip with the other. *Pistol. Knife. Extra ammo. We're good to go.*

If my backpack was weighted down with extra supplies that made me stagger beneath them, well, that was also fine. It would make me stronger the further we marched.

I sang louder. "On the road again…just can't wait to get on the road again…"

Michael groaned, and Sam snorted. "Don't you know any other songs?"

I grinned at both of them. "Sure I do. But none that make me quite as happy as this one right now. Now shut up or sing along."

* * * *

But going was slow, especially as we reached the grips of the Appalachian Mountains. We made a quick and conscious decision to follow the Appalachian Trail, its pathways already marked out for us with fading white circles. Though the lack of upkeep in the prior dozen plus months was evident, at least we always knew where we were headed: northeast. Toward home.

Home. Sometimes a scary thought, always an exciting one, at least on a few subconscious levels.

But going was painfully slow. The Appalachian Trail was legendary for a reason, after all. Paths were slim, and sometimes we had to climb near-vertical. And though it was summer, a cool breeze almost always blew, that high up in the mountains. We wore layers, and prayed for no rain, and mostly the weather gods smiled upon us. It was a dry, reasonable summer.

We ran into all kinds of animals, relying heavily on Sam and Chicken's noses and Spidey-senses to let us know if we were finding living or undead things. We tried to use as little ammo as possible, and succeeded, for the most part.

But Michael was struggling. After a couple of days on the trail he sort of receded into this constant daze. Food didn't interest him all that much, and after we busted Will trying to slip a Tamiflu into Michael's canteen, he didn't seem that interested in water either. I tried not to worry—what good would worrying do—and after the hell we raised with Will for that act of betrayal-in-the-name-of-science, I knew we could trust him not to do that again. No matter what, though, I slept with one eye open and a hand on Michael's arm at all times.

We kept plugging away anyway, and the miles melted slowly by. We had to get home, to see if we could find a place for Will to test his theories. And in the back of my mind, even though I knew it was a long-shot at best, I hoped against hope: maybe Michael and Sam's parents really *had* survived. Maybe we'd find them, and maybe we could be a family. Maybe Sam's dreams had infiltrated mine, sure. But maybe, just maybe, there was hope.

The only way to find out was to keep going.

It was just too bad I never lost the creepy feeling someone (or something) was watching us.

* * * *

I awoke to the blackness of night. Michael and I slept alone in the tent as we had for the prior handful of nights. Sam preferred to be outside, beneath the stars. He claimed his reasons were twofold. One: he kept watch over us while we slept. And two: he wanted to give Michael and me some space.

Me? I thought he couldn't handle the stench. Michael was certainly growing more offensive to my nose with each day that passed.

My first thought, in fact, when I awoke that night was that I should open the tent flap to let in some fresh air. The sticky sweet-sour smell of his wounded leg turned my stomach even under the best of circumstances; there, trapped in the tent with the warm moisture of our sleep, it was suffocating. The June heat, even in the mountains, was growing relentless, and it seemed to be expediting the rotting of Michael's leg.

My second thought quickly surpassed the first in urgency. *What woke me up? What was that sound?*

The sound came again. Chicken growled louder.

"Buddy?" I whispered. "Chicken. Come here, to me."

Apart from the sound of his growl, all was still in the night.

I rubbed my eyes. "What are you growling at, bud?"

As I let my hand drop from my eyes, panic setting in my stomach, I gazed around. Light from the moon filtered through the nylon of our tent, allowing me to see two shadows, silhouettes against the light. One was obviously my dog.

The other was a man.

I jerked away, pulling my legs up to my chest, reaching blindly for my knife with one hand and for Michael with the other. For there was a strange man, hunched over in the corner of our tent. Michael needed to wake up and help me fight.

But Michael wasn't there.

Chicken's growl grew louder, more threatening, as I scrambled to the far corner of the tent. I found my hunting knife, its bright neon green handle glowing in the dark. I stared at the man. My heart almost stopped.

"Oh dear God," I whispered. "Michael. What are you doing?"

He crouched in the corner in an unnatural squat. Immobile. Watching.

"Babe?"

My skin prickled with chills, even in the warm stench of the tent. My throat tightened, threatening to close. Like my knife's hilt, the exposed whites of Chicken's panicked eyes glowed, as did his bared teeth. He meant business as he snarled at Michael.

"Michael? Honey, wake up. You must be dreaming."

It was all I could think to say as Michael's eyes shifted from Chicken to me, from Chicken to me. Something was wrong with his eyes, and it was obvious even in the dim light. Maybe it was the speed with which they shifted; maybe it was how dark they were. Maybe it was the way he narrowed them, then widened them, as he glared at us.

Glaring. It was definitely a glare. He stared at me with an inhuman contempt. With fear. With *hunger.* His stance was that of an animal cornered, not a boy sitting in a tent with the girl he loved and their beloved mangy mutt. He sniffed the air, even tasted it, darting his tongue in and out of his mouth. He growled.

"Michael?"

My voice shook. My hands shook. My heart was a kick drum in my chest, beating hard and fast.

It's the end oh my god he's turned I'm not ready to say goodbye again we've said goodbye so many times I can't stand for this to be the final one that fucking zombie who bit him that bitch not my Michael oh my god please don't let this be the end I want to die if this is his end please let it be mine too I don't want to live without him ever again.

"Michael."

Chicken lunged. He darted forward from his corner and lowered his head, ramming into Michael's side. A woosh of air escaped Michael's lungs as he fell backward, crashing into a tent pole, almost collapsing the tent.

So he's still breathing, I thought, wonder mixing with relief. Relief, that is, until Michael swung his arm out in deadly silence, flinging Chicken over to my side of the tent. Chicken yelped, landing in a heap beside me and scrambling to his feet. He hunched back, watching, ready to pounce again at a moment's notice.

"Stay," I hissed. He froze.

We watched Michael as he stared at his arm. Black blood flowed from a wound opened by the tent pole. Michael eyed the blood, waving his arm back and forth before his eyes until he stopped moving and sniffed it.

Oh my god he tasted it he just licked his own wound he's drinking his own blood, what do I do how do I handle this oh my god what do I do here someone please tell me!

But I already knew. This wasn't my first trip to the dance.

I tightened my grip on my knife. With my free hand I grabbed Chicken's collar, hauling him behind me to keep him from attacking again. This wasn't his fight. This was mine.

"Michael," I said, my voice firmer as the calm of battle settled in. "I'm sorry. I have to do this."

I was awkward in the confines of the tent. I couldn't stand, but I needed my hands to be free. I couldn't crawl on all fours. So on my knees, raised up as tall as I could, I shuffled across the small space between us while Michael remained distracted by the tear in his arm. My eyes were clear—free from tears—as I closed the gap. My grip on the knife was firm but not panicked. I was just another soldier in the war.

The back of his neck was the easiest target, his spine exposed as his head stayed bent over his arm while he suckled on his own blood.

Sever the spinal column. Paralyze his body. Then you can take care of the rest, maybe even say a proper goodbye before you do.

I pulled back my arm, the knife honed in on its target. I would strike true. I always did.

In silence, I took one last breath. One last look at the love of my life. I bit my lip.

"Michael."

The word escaped my lips. I hadn't meant to. But it happened.

As soon as it did, Michael's head jerked up, away from his arm.

No.

It was much easier to kill a distracted thing than one itching for a fight.

I braced myself and prepared to shout for Sam.

"Jenn? Jenna, what's going on? Why are you looking at me like that?"

The beast, the creature that had taken Michael's place in the moments leading up to that almost final moment, was gone, almost as if it had never been there, replaced once again by Michael. My Michael.

The knife fell from my hand. Chicken darted forward as though he saw my weakness. His teeth were bared, and he was ready to strike but without thinking I stuck out my arm, knocking him to the ground beside the knife. He stayed there, beside me, unsure of what to do next.

I understood the feeling.

"Jenna, seriously. What happened? Why do I taste blood? What's going on?"

Michael began to cry, huge, heavy sobs shaking his body. "What's happening to me? I just had the worst dream and now here you are, ready to kill me. What's going on? Help me, Jenna, please! Help me!"

"Michael!"

I reached forward and caught him before he fell. His head found a place against my chest and I held him as he cried, but as I did I found my knife again. I kept it back, pressed against my side, but I clutched it, the cold hilt warming slightly in my hot palm.

Less than a minute passed before the tent flap unzipped and Sam appeared in the doorway.

With a direct escape route, Chicken took off, running from the tent with his tail between his legs, wounded by the night's events. I, too, wanted to run and hide, but I wasn't a dog. I was a woman, I was a leader, and I had to stay there and fix things.

"Jenna?" said Sam, his voice barely audible over the thunder of Michael's sobs. "What happened?"

I could only shrug. I tried to talk but nothing came out. Words failed. I dropped the knife again, safe with Sam's presence in the doorway, and I collapsed over Michael.

"He didn't mean it," I said as I cried into his foul-smelling shirt. "He didn't mean it."

I don't know if I meant Michael. Or Chicken. Or both. Maybe neither.

"I didn't mean it either."

* * * *

"So he's changing. He's definitely changing. This confirms it." Sam sounded cold. Almost clinical.

Michael slept in the tent. After such a traumatic night, the decision to spend a few extra daytime hours in our campsite was an obvious one.

"We should have tried the other antivirals," said Will. "You never should have stopped me. This proves it. Michael's immunity isn't going to be enough."

"Shut up! You guys. This doesn't mean anything. Michael just had a bad dream, that's all. And I overreacted."

Sam shot me a look.

"Don't be so stupid," he said. "Even if I thought for a second—and I don't—that you had overreacted, how about Chicken's reaction? What about that? You said he attacked Michael. I've never seen that dog attack anyone other than zombies or me, when I deserved it. He was protecting you."

"Right. Protecting me. Because Michael was having a bad dream and he gave us all a good scare."

Neither of us mentioned the fact that Chicken hadn't been back since. I'd heard him rustling around in the leaves outside of camp a few times, but he had yet to actually step into the clearing. I wasn't sure if it was because of me, or Michael. After all, I'd basically slugged Chicken to keep him from killing Michael, and I'd *never* hit my dog. Ever.

"Jenna." Rosie's voice was surprisingly calm and deep. "Jenna, I can smell him from here. It's getting worse. I think the end is coming."

"Well, what do you know? What do any of you actually *know?* You'll all sit there and team up on me, but what about *Michael*? Huh? What about him? Who wants to go in there and kill him? Huh? Because it's not going to be me. Not while he's still here. He's not a zombie."

"Jenna!"

They all said it, but fuck them, I thought. Fuck them all. They want to kill him before it's time. They wanted to take away the few months or days or even minutes I had left with him before the virus took over and I'd have to kill him anyway.

Fuck them all.

I stormed off into the woods, leaving them all behind. "Chicken," I called as I left the clearing. "Buddy, please come back. I'm sorry I hit you!"

I stomped through the underbrush, tripping over roots and rocks and other things that seemed to jump up out of nowhere. The tears that had barely been at bay all day threatened to explode out of me the further I got from camp without finding my dog. I knew he was out there, somewhere close, but avoiding me.

I came to a small stream and stopped, sitting heavily on a rock that jutted up, seat-like, inviting me to rest a second. So I did. I sat, rubbing my shin which was battered from a collision with a small tree a minute earlier. I tossed a small stone into the water. It splashed and sparkled in the warm sun filtering through the thick canopy of leaves above.

"Careful. You might hurt a fish."

I jumped. "Michael! You could get killed sneaking up on a girl like that," I said, but I scooted over to make room for him to sit. In truth, though I denied it to myself, I'd known he was coming. I'd smelled him. It was impossible not to.

He ignored my comment as he sat down. "I wonder if fish can be zombies. Like, are they infected like all the other animals? Or are they immune somehow?"

"Good question."

He took my hand. "I'm not immune, you know. I know that now."

"Michael." I sighed. "About last night. I'm sorry…"

"No. I'm the one who's sorry. I thought I was dreaming, I really did. It was a nightmare. You didn't look like you. You looked like…well, for lack of any better comparison, you looked like you'd taste like a cheeseburger if I just had the guts to get up and take a bite. I fought it." Michael shuddered. "Oh, god, I fought it about as hard as I could, but I was losing. Jenna, do you hear me? I was losing."

I shook my head. "No. You weren't. It was just a dream gone bad. Just a nightmare."

"But the nightmare is starting to take over in the day as well."

"No."

"Yes. It's true. Right now, I can still feel what I felt last night. I'm more able to fight it because we're awake and talking, I don't know how much longer I can fight. Jenna, I'm turning. Look."

He pulled up the leg of the pants he'd taken to wearing to hide the ugly bite on his leg.

"Oh dear God!" I jerked my head back, away from the smell and away from the sight. He hadn't let me see it in days, now that I thought about it, but there it was. The wound. It had festered, grown. Deepened. I could see bone, stone-grey and splintering, beneath the black, mottled flesh that spread and puckered and oozed.

It looked like every other zombie bite I'd ever seen.

"Someone has to kill me. Soon. I don't know if the virus will let me do it myself."

"What?"

Michael dropped his pant leg, his point made. As it slowly fell down his leg, hiding the putridity of the bite, I hated the relief I felt. So long as I wasn't staring straight at it, his injury was an abstract thing, a thing that could be hidden and forgotten.

He stared out over the water, and tossed in a rock too. "I've been thinking about it. At night, before you come to bed mostly. The easiest solution would be to kill myself. But Jenna, it's like there's this new survival instinct in me, even bigger than the one that's been a part of me since this all started."

"What do you mean? Don't dance around this." I stared at him, the way his face worked while he talked. His jaw muscles clenched and unclenched. His eyebrows knit together. He was working hard to focus, to make sense. Finally he looked up, and everything relaxed as the words poured out.

"I'm saying I tried, Jenn. I tried." He stood and walked out into the rushing stream. It wet his pants up past where I knew that ugly wound was, and I fought the urge to tell him to get out, to keep from infecting the fish. From the stream, with the water seeming to part, Red Sea-like, as though it, too, wanted to avoid infection, he continued. "I tried. Three times. I held my gun in my mouth, and I tried. Oh, God, I tried. I want this to end. I don't want you to have to kill me. I want to end it myself, to spare you, spare Sam. But I can't pull that trigger. When I try, I black out. Do you hear me? The virus is fucking strong enough that it triggers something in my brain to black out when I try to kill myself. And when I wake up the gun is away, back in my bag. The virus is smart and it's going to kill me and then it's going to try to kill you. It wants you, Jenna. It wants you even more than the others. I can feel it."

Before I could say another word, Michael stalked off down the stream, staying in the water, not looking back, and I didn't have the strength to go after him.

It wasn't until he was gone from my sight that I noticed Chicken sitting in his usual place atop my foot. I wondered how long he'd been there, and how much he'd seen and heard and understood.

Chapter 17: Sam

Every night after his episode with Jenna, Michael slept in chains we pilfered from an old hardware store. Jenna almost died getting them. A run-in with two relatively fresh child-zombies and their enraged human parents was almost her undoing. But if a cat had nine lives, Jenna must've had over a hundred. She showed up back in camp with her cheeks blood-splattered and new supplies in a canvas bag strewn around her neck. The funny thing was, none of us even knew she was gone until she got back. It was the middle of the night. Instead of keeping watch like she was supposed to, she ran an errand and almost died. Had I done that, Jenna would have killed me, but for her, it was something she had to do. We had to grin and bear it. Jenna was funny that way.

"We need the chains," she said, her voice hoarse and her hair caked with drying blood. "We need them for Michael. It's the only way to be sure."

He didn't argue. None of us did. We knew she was right.

After that night I stayed in the tent with them, too. Two people are better than one when facing a zombie, and I didn't want to let her out of my sight again.

Or Michael, for that matter. I didn't want to miss the final minutes with my brother. I was pretty sure they were coming soon, to a tent near me.

It wasn't just that one night that told us the end was close. It was the way he walked. The way he talked. The way I'd be having a conversation with him, remember the old times, and he'd suddenly be… gone. Vacant. I imagined it was a lot like talking to an old man with advancing Alzheimer's. Michael was there one minute, gone the next, and frankly, I lived for the moments he was lucid.

* * * *

Days passed. Not weeks. Not months. Just fucking days. Not enough fucking days, in retrospect.

One particularly bright morning we walked through a valley, surrounded by wildflowers yet again. God, I hated the goddamn wildflowers! It was their threateningly sweet stench, and the way they'd grown up as humanity had faltered, as if to say, "The earth is ours, you can't have it anymore. The ruins of your dead will feed our soil for years to come. We'll grow big and strong while you rot in your graves."

I fucking hated them.

And so did everyone else.

Everything bad happened in the wildflowers.

Our steps were slow and cautious as we worked our way through the field. Chicken stayed glued to Jenna's side. Will and Rosie joined hands, walking like two little kids on their way to school, minus the jokes and hijinks. Michael walked between Jenna and me, his eyes glassier than normal and his mouth loose and slack.

The end was definitely nigh. We could all sense it. Had a funeral dirge been playing, we wouldn't have seemed more solemn.

I fucking hated it. But I wasn't ready to say goodbye. Not then. Not yet.

The field stretched for a half-mile before running into a path that headed upward into the mountains. I could see the trail. I could see the trees. The day was crystal-clear, and visibility was perfect. Another day, another walk in the woods. Eat your heart out, Bill Bryson, I thought, remembering the book I'd read in college when I had dreams of being a mountain man, dreams that had come true in the most nightmarish of ways.

Because the hair on my neck refused to settle. The feeling that we were being watched refused to die. My stomach gurgled and cramped.

"Something's going to happen soon," I muttered.

At the sound of my voice Michael started. He turned to me, but he wasn't *there*. He had that vacant stare again.

Jenna turned, too. "What?"

But I kept walking, pulling Michael along beside me, and suddenly he came back, grinning and full of life. "Dude, you worry too much."

"Shut up," I said, shoving him. He stumbled, throwing up a cloud of dust around us. Jenna giggled. God, I loved the sound of her laugh. It was getting so long in between the times I'd hear it.

In the distance, a hawk cried. Chicken flattened himself to the ground. About ten meters ahead, Rosie and Will froze.

"What's the matter, you guys?" I called. "It's just a hawk. We can take it." I laughed. It felt good to laugh, all of a sudden. Michael was *there*, we were in a field of fucking wildflowers, and I was tired of feeling tense. I laughed again.

But Will turned, his face white. "Shut up," he hissed.

I did. I listened. I heard it.

A motor.

"Fuck," I said. Jenna and I exchanged a glance, and then we both looked at Michael. He'd turned pale, gray.

"If it's people," he said, his voice low, "they better not see me. We better hide. Fast. *Now*."

"Right." Jenna and I spoke as one.

"Deeper into the flowers," I called to Rosie and Will. "Hide."

Without another word, they faded into the field like ghosts.

We were another story entirely. We were bigger. Bulkier. We carried more equipment. Michael was unreliable at best. And we had a dog.

Jenna turned first to Michael. "You," she said. "Shut up. Don't say a word, whatever happens. Just keep your mouth shut." She kissed him, square on the mouth, and I hoped he didn't notice the repulsed face she made as she pulled away. He must have tasted awful. "I love you."

She looked down at Chicken. "And not a word from you, either, sir."

She grabbed our hands and pulled us into the flowers.

* * * *

It felt very familiar and ominous, the pulling and tugging of the leaves and brambles at our faces and hands. The scraping and scratching of any area of exposed flesh. The floral smell heavy and cloying, like a funeral parlor's visitation room.

We tried not to leave evidence of our passage but it was impossible not to. Had we placed a neon billboard above our heads, flashing and flickering with a light-up arrow pointing right at us, we probably wouldn't have been more obvious.

But we had to try. We were too exposed, with no natural defenses, to make any kind of a stand against a human enemy. All we could do was wait and see what happened, and hope, if these were indeed enemies, maybe we could slip away into the forest.

The sound of motors grew louder. We ducked down. Jenna trembled, but then I wondered if it was *me* shaking her. Michael stayed pale, his eyes vague and glassy.

"It's okay, Mikey," I said. "It's all going to be okay."

I don't know why I said it. I didn't believe it. But I had to say something.

The rumblings of motors were joined by the gravely call of tires on dirt. All too soon they came to a stop, all too close to where we cowered.

God, I fucking hated cowering. I hated hiding. I hated waiting for them to find us when I already knew they would. I fucking hated everything in that moment. Hated it.

As quietly as I could, I pumped my shotgun, priming it for a fight.

In silence, Jenna jerked around to stare at me, her eyes wide, pleading. *No,* they said, silently pleading. *Don't do it.*

I did it anyway.

I stood up, ready to face whatever we had to face. I pulled my shotgun to my shoulder as three armored cars—small enough to travel on trails, but heavy enough to do some damage when needed—came into view.

The sun reflected off the bright green metal of the cars, and I squinted. It was painful, in a way, and I couldn't see half as well as I needed to.

But a voice spoke. "Well, lookey here. This isn't what I was expecting to see today. Hello, Silverman."

And the bottom dropped out from my stomach as I fell to my knees once again.

* * * *

"Sam. Please, Sam. Do it. Finish it. I can't do it alone. I can't pull the trigger." Ty lay in the darkness, bleeding, his life pouring out of him even as the zombie virus spread throughout whatever was left.

"Please, Sam. Please. I can't pull the trigger."

He reached out to me, his hand dripping blood though the wound that killed him was in his neck. I knew that then. I knew it now. But his hand dripped blood. Gushed blood from the fingertips like a fire hose pointed at flames. It splattered me. Coated me. Insinuated itself in my mouth, my eyes, my nose. I inhaled his blood. I breathed it in and out, in and out, as he begged me to end his life.

But I was paralyzed. Unable to do it. Unable to help him.

Until the single swish of a sword put an end to Ty's suffering, but not to mine.

"You're weak," said Assassin, the man whose real name was lost to a world taken over by zombies. "You should have done that. I shouldn't have had to. You're a weakling, Silverman."

I cried like a baby, like the baby I was. Soon Assassin would chop my head off too.

* * * *

"Sam! Get up. Don't check out on me now. I need you!"

Jenna's voice cut through the darkness and I awoke to find my face wet and to hear the crashing of boots through the field of fucking wildflowers and another voice, calling my name.

"Silverman. I know you're there. Come out, come out, wherever you are!"

"Sam, who is that? How does he know you? What's going on?"

Her eyes were wild, her face panicked. Beside her knelt Michael, awake and vivid and alive, sniffing the air, searching with his eyes for a means to escape. Chicken was nowhere to be seen.

"Sam!"

I sat up, wiping a flood of tears from my face, and I exhaled the weight of the world from my lungs. "How long was I out?"

"Thirty seconds. What's going *on?* Who is that?"

"His name's Assassin. Or it was, a while ago. I don't know what he'll be calling himself now."

Michael exhaled. "Assassin. The one you told me about? The one who…"

"Yes, the one who killed Ty for me." I didn't like to hear anyone else say it. That made it too real, too unbearable.

I wanted to throw up. Because now he was coming for me.

"C'mon, old friend. I'm not going to hurt you. I just want to talk to you. Catch up on old times."

Jenna rolled her eyes. Now that I was awake and she knew what she was dealing with, she slipped into battle mode. "Right. Like we don't know he's lying." She sighed. "How many cars are there?"

I rubbed my head, which was beginning to throb. "Three, I think. Probably at least three people per car, if not more. They're traveling heavy, and armed. We don't have a chance in hell to fight them."

"So we run? Find the kids and run?"

The words were barely out of her mouth when a high-pitched, mouse-like scream filled the air. *Rosie.*

"Jenna!" she cried, and our decision was made for us. As one, as the group we'd always been, Jenna, Michael and I stood to face whatever was coming for us.

About fifty feet away, a tall woman with fiery copper hair pulled back in the tightest of top-knots held Rosie, arms pulled tight across her stomach. I saw no sign of Will, and wondered if he'd gotten away. He was small enough to go unnoticed, and quiet enough too, unlike his little sister.

My heart skipped a beat when I saw the woman. She was beautiful, a goddess, an Amazonian princess unlike anyone I'd seen in years. Beside her, even Jenna looked frumpy. The woman was too beautiful to be real. And fierce. And feisty. And curvy. And….I had to look away or I was going to do something stupid. Between the woman, and the impossible amount of adrenaline pumping through my veins thanks to the unexpected reappearance of my "old friend," I was about to explode.

As I looked away, I spoke the most brilliant, well-thought-out words of my life. "Put her down or I'll kill you. I'm a good shot. Don't test me."

The woman only laughed, and where a second earlier I'd been about to explode, I went limp. Soft.

"Why don't you turn around, buddy," she said, and her voice in every way matched her face, her body. It was sexy. Husky. I wanted to die.

Jenna turned first, and stifled a cry when she found herself face-to-face with the barrel of a massive rifle, the likes of which I'd also never seen before. Compared to it, my rifle, too, was weak. Limp. Flaccid.

"Oh fuck," I whispered when I saw there was one in my own face as well.

Only Michael hadn't turned, hadn't moved really, and with a panicked glance I noticed he was gone. Vacant.

"Oh fuck," Jenna echoed. She knew it too.

"Silverman." Assassin's voice rumbled from my right. He held the gun in Jenna's face, his finger tight against the trigger. "My old Army friend. Whatchoo been up to all this time? Why don't you and your lady friend drop your weapons, and let this be a bit of a friendlier chat?"

He spoke as if we were buddies catching up over a couple of beers, not as if we were engaged in a standoff in which he so obviously had the advantage. I cleared my throat and tried to match his tone as I nodded at Jenna. We dropped our weapons. What choice did we have?

"Oh, you know," I said, trying to see past the big, black hole pointing at my nose. I couldn't. "Just finding some old friends. My brother. And just trying to survive."

Assassin laughed, deep and threatening. "Aren't we all?" I didn't know exactly how many people surrounded us but I guessed it was a bunch or he wouldn't be wasting time talking. He'd kill if he felt at all threatened. That's the way Assassin was, at least how I remembered. "Now, who's the babe?"

Jenna closed her eyes and let out a huffy breath, but she answered before I could. "I'm Jenna," she said. "Jenna Price."

It was like a jolt of electricity passed through our assailants. They jerked, and then fell silent. All eyes turned to Jenna. Assassin's eyes widened, and he stared her up and down, taking in every line, every curve, every feature, in those two or three seconds. Then he opened his mouth and let out a huge, Hulk of a laugh.

"You," he said, gasping for air as laughter wracked his body. "Jenna Price? *The* Jenna Price. That's hysterical. You're joking, right?" He turned his head to his fellow soldiers, and as though it was a signal, they, too, cut up laughing. But as he turned to face us again, a look crossed his face that said to roll with it.

Jenna opened her mouth to object, but though I had my hands full of rifle, I stuck out an elbow and jabbed her in the ribs. She shot me a look, laced with fear and anger and frustration, but I shook my head. Jenna nodded.

"You're right," she said. "I'm not her. I just like to tell people I am. Sometimes it scares them away. My name's…Ashley."

The group laughed louder, saying things like "We're not afraid of her," or, "The great Jenna Price, I'd *like* to face her one day." I felt Jenna grow even more tense beside me, standing statue-still and breathing in tight, shallow breaths. With all the attention on her, we hadn't kept an eye on Michael. He'd separated himself from us by just a few steps, but it was enough that I suddenly noticed his absence.

A low, quiet growl sounded, underneath the laughter that still rang through the air.

"Chicken, down," Jenna said, not taking her eyes off Assassin.

It wasn't Chicken growling, though. I knew that. Chicken was hiding out, probably wherever Will was. Ice froze my heart as I realized what was about to go down.

"What's wrong with the fella beside you, Silverman?" Assassin's voice sounded tighter all of a sudden. Less relaxed. More trigger-happy.

"That's my brother Michael," I said. It was so dumb, such a ridiculous thing to say, as if by claiming him as my blood I'd put a stopper in whatever was going to happen. As if Assassin would care that he was related to me when, in that moment, he was so obviously, painfully zombie.

I stepped back from Assassin's rifle, pulling Michael with me, trying not to cringe when my warm fingers met the cool, dying flesh of his arm. Jenna followed, walking backwards, not taking her eyes off the soldiers and their rifles.

From several steps away, I saw Assassin clearly, hulking and massive. He was flanked by a half-dozen men, each wearing the dark military uniforms of the Roughnecks. *I used to be one of them.*

"I don't like the look of that guy," said the beautiful woman holding Rosie. Her voice had tightened, too. In her arms, Rosie thrashed.

"No! Don't hurt him! That's just Michael!"

"His eyes. Assassin, I can see his eyes."

My heart dropped. A look of panic seeped across Jenna's face; the deep scarlet flush and a glistening sweat were always her tells. She'd never have made it as a poker player. Assassin pulled his rifle off her, and pointed it at the back of Michael's head. I let go of my brother's arm and stepped closer to Assassin again.

"No!" I said. "Stop. That's my brother. He's fine."

"He's bit, Silverman, isn't he?"

"No!"

"Don't you lie to me, man. Don't you lie. We go back way too far for you to lie to me now."

"No!"

"How long, Silverman? How long ago was he bitten?"

"He wasn't!"

Assassin's voice had been rising steadily until he was shouting. I was, too. We were like an old Looney Tunes cartoon, accusing, denying, accusing, denying. Any second and he'd switch sides, until by accident I'd admit our guilt. Our deceit, which we hadn't even intended, hadn't planned, but on which my brother's life now seemed to hang.

Michael didn't move.

"You stop this shit, Assassin. You stop it right now. Something's definitely wrong with that guy." The red-headed woman knew. Assassin knew. But I wasn't ready to give in.

"He's fine!" My voice was a teenage boy's, cracking on the words.

"Stop it!"

Jenna's shout cut the air. She stepped between Assassin and Michael, her hands raised like a POW in an old war flick. "Please," she said. "Please. Don't hurt him. He's fighting it. His body is fighting it. He's not one of them. Not yet."

Michael chose the exact wrong moment to turn around, giving Assassin the first good look at his face. Assassin sniffed. He cringed. His eyes darted from Michael's glassy corneas to the way his lips pulled back, exposing his teeth as he began to growl.

"Oh hell no," Assassin said.

It was over in an instant.

Assassin stepped forward and swung his rifle, knocking Jenna to the ground. Michael lunged at Assassin.

Assassin fired, pointe blank.

Michael fell.

Jenna and Rosie screamed.

From somewhere not far away, Chicken howled.

I never moved as my brother died.

I never tried to protect him.

I let him die.

A millisecond later, everything else fell apart too.

From deep in the field came another howl, but this one didn't belong to Chicken. High-pitched, piercing, it forced the hair all over my body to immediate attention even as I stood still, paralyzed by the sight of my brother's lifeless body on the ground. The trees on the mountainside quaked as though being trampled by an invisible giant. A murder of crows rose from their branches, their caws blending with the howling until it was an orchestra of death and despair. As one, the crows flew at us.

Will appeared from his hiding spot in the weeds as if by magic, and the woman holding Rosie dragged her to us as that other howl, that human-but-not cry of pain and despair, picked up momentum. Other creatures, surely undead, echoed the cries. I raised my hands to my ears, pressing hard to try to drown out the aching sounds. It was an impossible task.

"We're surrounded," shouted the redhead to Assassin, tossing Rosie to the ground like a sack of potatoes. Will raced to her side, pulling her to her feet and tugging on her arm, pulling her toward the weeds.

Assassin's reply was lost in the cacophony of a coordinated attack. Dozens of zombies poured into the clearing, howling and crying and barreling forward like linebackers into an offensive line. The wildflowers, some as tall as me, bent double beneath the weight of the creatures. They worked in a loose formation, some kind of arrow-head shape, with a point position headed straight for our center. All carried weapons, logs and sticks and rocks scavenged from the forest floor. At least one held a bone. I stood before them, frozen, unarmed, and remarkably unafraid. Michael was dead. Nothing else mattered.

Jenna sank to her knees.

"I need a gun," shrieked Rosie. "Come on, you guys. Give us our guns!"

Jenna lay on the ground beside Michael. She was giving up. I readied myself to join her.

The rapid thunder of gunfire sounded as the Roughnecks began to fight. They lined up, weapons drawn, and fired. The first line of zombies fell, but was replaced immediately by another.

Assassin's voice thundered. "Give the newbies their guns. We need 'em. Give 'em to 'em now!"

His was not a voice to be ignored. I stayed on my feet as a Roughneck paused firing long enough to kick our weapons in our general direction. Rosie and Will leapt to action, diving for the nearest ones and starting to shoot. Zombies fell, piling up as the attack continued, more and more creatures flanking our sides. The kids pressed their backs into the Roughneck line and fired in the other direction.

I stayed glued in my spot, as did Jenna. I leaned down. We were the eye of the hurricane, the calm of the storm, as nothing around us mattered. "Jenna," I said, leaning in close enough that I knew she could hear me. "Jenna, what do you want me to do?"

I hoped she'd tell me to fuck off. I hoped she'd tell me to die. It was what I wanted. Instead, it was like I awakened her from a dream. She raised her head from where it rested on Michael's stomach, which had already begun to bloat with death gasses. Her face was pinched and white, her eyes red and bloodshot. They darted from place to place, settling first on the zombies and then on the Roughnecks. They landed on our guns, within our reach. Finally they reached Rosie and Will, each fighting for their lives.

The switch turned. She pulled herself up to her knees and reached out for the nearest rifle. To me, she nodded. "We fight."

* * * *

Then it was just another battle. I shot, I killed, I reloaded when needed. Jenna's body pressed beside mine, jerking with each round she fired. As more zombies appeared behind our group, we killed them all. The air hung heavy with noise and the smell of rancid, decaying flesh, the standard battle onslaught to our senses. Shouts from Roughnecks filled the air whenever the undead came too close, but we four stayed silent. Shoot, kill, reload. Shoot, kill, reload. Chicken appeared in small bursts from his spot in the weeds, knocking down the zombies that strayed too far in our direction. He was an efficient assistant, using his mass to stem the tide of undead. Slowly but surely, the zombies fell, until all that was left to do was to kill the ones who lay, still half-alive, on the ground. We pulled out our knives and dug into the dirty work.

When it was over and the last zombie growled its final growl, I noticed we, the four of us, were the only ones wading in and ending things for the more stubborn hangers-on. The Roughnecks watched us work.

"Damn," said the redhead, standing beside Assassin. "They're efficient."

"They also saved us," he said, shaking his head. "No way could we have killed that many. How'd they…" He trailed off.

I stopped what I was doing and took note. The piles on our side of the battle were certainly bigger, though I would have assumed the Roughnecks could've handled it. But that wasn't the case, I learned. The redhead spoke again. "They'd have overrun us." It wasn't a question.

In my minds eye I saw Rosie and her razor-sharp aim. I saw Jenna, who handled a rifle like she'd been born to it. I saw Will and me, and the way we all fought in a way that used as few bullets, and as much precision, as possible. We'd all learned to fight like that in our time on the farm. We had to. There was never any extra ammo to waste.

It looked like all that training was about to pay off.

"So can we kill them? Knowing what they can do?" The redhead's eyes had narrowed as she watched us work. When Rosie slipped her knife into the temple of a zombie that, when she turned, hadn't been much older than Rosie herself, the redhead flinched. Rosie got up and moved to the next one.

Assassin glared at her. "No. We can't. Of course we can't. The Captain's gonna want these four. Five if you count the dog."

"You can't keep the dog."

They spoke as if they thought us deaf, as if we couldn't possibly be listening to their endless prattle. Though in the heat of battle I'd been able to hide from myself the reality of my brother's death, as I listened to them talk about our lives as though they were casual items to be thrown away at any moment, I remembered everything. I remembered that my brother was dead. I remembered the way Assassin shot him, as though nothing living mattered. I remembered that I wanted to die, and that I wanted Assassin to die, too.

I wasn't the only one. For a few moments Jenna worked, head down, sweat dripping from the few locks of hair that never stayed back in her ponytail. She held her Slugger, preferring its blunt tip to smash in skulls, walking from body to body and pressing down with a dull thump, thump, thump. She neared Assassin, giving no sign she was listening.

Until she was close enough.

Jenna lifted her head. In her eyes burned the hatred of a woman who's lost everything, and is facing the one who took it all.

No, I thought. Don't.

I wasn't ready to see her die too.

She raised her Slugger to swinging distance. She aimed for Assassin's head.

Jenna never had a chance. Before she could swing, before she could even breathe, Assassin stopped her with a punch to the side of her head. Jenna crumpled to the ground, and Rosie shrieked.

"Still want to keep them alive?" said the redhead, her lips pressing together to form a tight, straight line. "I don't think we can trust them."

"No, we can't, but we need them." He turned to me. "One wrong move, Silverman, and you're dead. Come to think of it…"

I hadn't realized I'd walked to them as Jenna fell, but I stood close, my legs protectively straddling Jenna's body. I was close enough that Assassin could reach me. His fist plowed into my head, too, and the next thing I knew I was awake in the front seat of a truck, bound for God knew where.

Lesson 3: Never give up, and never surrender, not even in Undead America

Chapter 18: Jenna

No. He's not dead.

No. I found some way to save him and he's not dead.

No. He's just waiting for me, back in Nebraska. He never left, and when this nightmare is over I can pack up and go home to Michael and Sadie and Allie and Simon as if this never happened. Because it didn't. This didn't happen. Michael's not dead.

Not Michael. Not my Michael. My best friend. Not him.

This can't be happening.

* * * *

I remember the night the zombies came. The night we had sex for the first time and it was awkward and messy and terrible, but also still sweet, and somehow wonderful. I remember how he looked at me, as if he wanted to eat me alive, but it didn't scare me. Not then. Because back then, people didn't eat people, so I had nothing to be afraid of as he stared at me with that ravenous look. He wanted me, wanted me in a way I don't think I'd ever been wanted before.

I remember how we used to sleep, back when it was just the two of us and Michael's hatchback, traveling the country in search of something we never found. Rest? Safety? It didn't matter, we didn't find it. I remember how our legs tangled, sweaty beneath the heat of a southern spring night. I remember being so full of love I wanted to explode.

I remember marrying him. The way we fumbled with the rings. The jokes he made about his being the One Ring. The way it looked on his finger.

I remember his lips, so soft, when he kissed me that day, when Chicken was our only witness when we spoke our wedding vows. I wish I could remember what we said, but that memory is gone forever.

I wonder if Michael remembers.

Remembered.

Michael is dead and this is real and oh my God I wish I could wake up from the hell that is my life and now nothing will ever be the same.

* * * *

It's time to wake up. It's time to figure out our next step.

* * * *

It's time to move on.

* * * *

Fuck you, Jenna. You can never move on.

* * * *

The miles droned by, taking us further from Michael. He was dead, for good this time, and though there had been so many times when I thought his death was imminent, the reality still came crashing down around my ears in the end.

I wanted to die.

Wait for me, Michael. I'll find a way to get to you soon.

* * * *

I sat in a truck beside the one called Assassin.

Appropriate name, no doubt. Michael would've laughed at the irony there.

We were alone but for each other, a cold-blooded killer and his victim's broken wife.

* * * *

More miles passed. Sometimes we stopped. Sometimes we camped for the night. Assassin never left my side, following me even into the bushes when I had to pee.

"I can't let you go, *Ashley*," he said, again and again. "I can't lose you."

Like I was something he loved, something he was afraid to lose.

Or like I was a prisoner, and he couldn't afford to show up empty handed.

I wasn't allowed to be near Sam or Will or even Rosie; they kept us all pretty well separated, though I gleaned from conversations around me that Rosie stayed with Will, which at least let me know they cared enough to keep her safe. A little girl in a camp full of unknown men, all by herself? At least they were decent enough people to protect her.

Not that they were decent. I was traveling with an assassin, after all. An assassin who never, *ever* let me out of his sight. I slept in his tent at night. If anyone came close, he threw a lumbering arm across my shoulders, holding me tight to him. He smelled of sweat and cigarettes, though I never saw him smoke one. And though I wanted to pull away, I stood limp, immune to his touch, immune to everything. Michael was gone. Had he tried to touch me at night, I'd have let him. I didn't care.

But he never did, leaving me to wonder, in a grief-fueled haze, why he was keeping me so close.

One morning as we drove east, east, east, Assassin turned his head to look at me, easing the truck onto the road as part of the six-truck caravan. I sat, hunched, head drooping, staring at the dashboard. My hair hung down in my face in greasy clumps; I was too tired to bother putting it in a ponytail. Besides, Michael always liked my hair down.

Assassin reached across the seat and, with a gentleness that belied his strength and size, he tucked a few strands behind my ear. As his fingers brushed my cheek, my temple, I jerked away.

"Don't touch me." My voice was thick and raspy, and it hurt—everywhere—to speak. But I felt something—revulsion—for the first time in days and I couldn't ignore it.

Assassin's eyes widened, and his mouth opened and closed. He blinked, rubbing his eyes with the back of his hand as though that's all he'd ever intended to do anyway. Then he stared straight ahead again.

"So you do talk." His voice, deep and gruff, wasn't unpleasant.

I spat at him. A gob of phlegm landed on the gearshift; I'd have to work on my aim if I wanted to hit his face. He ignored it, staring up at the rear-view mirror at the rest of the caravan.

"Look, *Ashley*," he said.

Who's Ashley, I wondered, but then I remembered. *Me. Right now I'm Ashley. I just wish I knew why.*

Assassin continued. "I'm trying to help you, believe it or not. Stick close, stay with me, and maybe you'll come out of this alive. I can't say the same for your friend Sam. When the Captain sees him…he doesn't forget a face, that guy. But I'll try." He glanced at the rearview again. "They don't know Sam defected from the Roughnecks, and I for sure don't want them to know you're the real Jenna Price. They'll kill you both before we stop the caravan."

A block of ice filled my stomach solid.

"I'm not Jenna Price," I said, my voice low. "I'm Ashley. And you killed my husband."

Assassin nodded. "I saved your life. *Ashley.* Sam's too. Let's just say you owe me, and I'm gonna help you repay that debt."

"I owe you nothing. You killed Michael."

He sighed. "We can talk more tonight. We'll reach the city soon. Your life is in danger."

It was my turn to sigh. I let out a breath as though I'd been holding it for years. It was foul—even I could smell my own breath, and I wondered how many days had passed since I'd last brushed my teeth. Time had a way of skipping around when I forgot to pay attention to the world around me.

"Who cares about my life," I said. "Michael's dead, the zombies are evolving. The world's fucked. You should just let me die."

The touch of Assassin's hand against my cheek was surprising and gentle. Without thinking I leaned into it, the touch of another human irresistible. "Don't say that," he said. "Your life's important. We need you."

"Whatever. Michael's dead. I don't want to be alive."

With his eyes on the road, Assassin shook his head. He touched my arm, a short, stroking motion with which he seemed to want to comfort me. I turned away, curling up around my rucksack, my head resting against the cool glass of the window.

* * * *

When we stopped that night, Assassin took me by the hand, leading me to a hastily-erected tent as though we were newlyweds. As his fellow soldiers cat-called and whooped and hollered ("Assassin's got a girl! The world's coming to an end!") and Assassin pretended to blush, I cut my eyes frantically around, trying to catch a glimpse of Sam or Will or Rosie. They were nowhere to be seen.

Are they dead too? Why save just me? Why not them?

Assassin pulled me into the tent. I scooted to the far side, and he laughed quietly. "Man, you *are* awake now. For the past few days you just lay wherever I put you. It's nice to see you move a bit."

Quit being so fucking nice. You killed Michael.

I glared at him.

He squatted—he was far too huge to be in such a small tent, his mass taking up most of the free space and, it felt like, all the oxygen—and pulled a small knapsack off his shoulder. From it he pulled a small stash of food: some bread, some hard cheese, and even some jerky. He tossed it to me, respecting the distance I put between us.

"Here," he said, his voice gruff. "I don't know the last time you ate. Go ahead. Eat."

The spicy, peppery smell of the jerky reached my nose, and my stomach lurched. *How long has it been?* But I glared at him.

"You killed Michael. I don't want your food."

A dark look crossed over Assassin's eyes—which were blue, sky-blue, just like Michael's had been—and for a moment he looked angry. It passed quickly, and he reached out, collecting the food. "Suit yourself. You're gonna need to eat at some point."

Jerky-scent wafted beneath my nose again, and my stomach flipped. As if it acted on its own, my hand flashed out and grabbed the jerky package from Assassin. I flushed as it fell open in my lap, pieces of jerky scattering across the tent floor. He grinned.

I picked one up and inspected it. It looked okay. Salivating, I drew it closer to my mouth, but then I stopped. "You killed Michael. How do I know you're not going to poison me? How do I know you're not just biding your time so you can kill me."

Assassin's lips curled up into a wicked smile. He took the piece of meat from me and popped it into his mouth. Chewing, he winked. "You don't. But you're going to have to start trusting me at some point. I'm trying to save you. And your pal Sam. And those two kids. But you've got to work with me."

"But you killed Michael."

I was a record on repeat, a single 45 with one song that played over and over and over. This time Assassin didn't flinch. Instead, he spoke, his mouth full. "He was dead anyway. You just didn't realize it yet. Now eat. Let me help you. Because I need your help."

He turned and left the tent, zipping it behind him, leaving the food behind. As soon as he was gone, I leaned over and began shoveling bits of jerky into my mouth, chewing and working over the meat as the juices began to settle my stomach.

I had to think, and I never thought well on an empty stomach.

* * * *

"So where are you taking me?" I said as soon as Assassin unzipped the tent flap that evening, his watch presumably over and his time to sleep arrived. "And why won't you let me see Sam?"

Assassin stopped with his body partway in the tent, and he grinned. While he was out, I'd polished off most of the food he'd left behind. Then I straightened up my mess, and myself. In the knapsack I found a toothbrush—it still amazed me, the depths to which I'd sunk, sharing a toothbrush with a stranger—and a comb, and I'd done my best to clean up. After all, I'd always gotten further with men by being nice than by being a bitch. It even worked with Chase Franklin, for a little while anyway. I figured if Assassin was going to tell me anything, I'd have to work with him. Or at least pretend to. And then, once I found Sam and the kids, we could high tail it back to Nebraska. Fuck heading east. The trip had been nothing but trouble so far anyway.

Trouble. To say the very least. An image of Michael swam before my eyes, even as I smiled at Assassin.

He slipped the rest of the way into the tent, rather graceful for such a big man, and zipped it behind him. "Glad to see you up and moving, Ashley," he said, a little louder than was absolutely necessary. I nodded encouragingly. "Did you eat?"

"I did. Um, most of it, actually. Sorry about that. I hope that wasn't your whole stash for the rest of the trip."

From behind his back he pulled a protein bar, which he opened and ate in three bites. "Nah," he said, wiping his mouth. "There's more where that came from. Food's not a problem for the Roughnecks, especially not now. Not with all we've got going on."

I narrowed my eyes, trying to ignore the growling of my stomach. It seemed like food would always be a problem for me, and I remembered the way my grandmother never let a single scrap hit the trash can; she ate every single leftover, a product of growing up in the Depression. He noticed, and tossed me a second bar, which, not to be outdone by the bigger man, I devoured in two bites. Assassin laughed.

"So," I said, my turn to talk with my mouth full. "*Where* are we going again? You never answered."

He rifled through his knapsack. "Did you use my *toothbrush?* That's disgusting. Some things are sacred."

My hand tightened into a fist. "Desperate times," I said, no longer laughing. "Stop changing the subject. Where are you taking me?"

"Who wants to know? Ashley? Or Jenna Price?"

I glanced around, knowing full well the tent's walls were thin. "Why are we hiding my identity? Why are you hiding Sam's? What's going on?"

He did the same check as me. There were no shadows nearby outside. We were, it seemed, alone. Then he cut his eyes at me. "Are you really *the* Jenna Price?"

"The one and only."

"Are the stories true?"

"Depends on what stories you've heard."

"Did you blow up New Orleans? Kill that Chase Franklin guy?"

"Guilty as charged." I couldn't stop the pride from billowing up inside me. "Well, I mean, I didn't kill him myself. But I blew up the city. My friend's dad actually killed Franklin. It was a mess there. He deserved it."

"See, statements like that make you about as dangerous to the Captain of the Roughnecks as anyone can be. So we can't let anyone know it's you, until the proper time of course."

"The proper time? What's going on here, anyway? It sounds like you're planning a mutiny. Why not just leave?"

Assassin, for the first time, looked unsure of himself. In fact, he looked scared, all wide-eyed and flushed-cheeks. For the first time, I didn't hate him. His voice dropped even farther. I had to strain to hear him. "I can't *just leave.* We need you, Jenna. We need you to do whatever you do, to make things change back east. We need the Captain out, but he's too strong, too entrenched, too powerful. No one believes anything can change, so no one's going to do anything about him. But you? You've done it before, haven't you? You can help us. I know you can. But not everyone out here wants to be helped. His people are everywhere. It was luck that we found you, and now we need to make that luck last. So you? You're with me for the duration. We can't risk your friends giving you away."

"But why? Why me?" I was afraid of the answer, but I knew I had to hear it.

"Because you're Jenna Price. *The* Jenna Price. And you're a legend in Undead America."

* * * *

Later that night, I elbowed Assassin awake.

"Undead America?"

He groaned. "Yeah. You got a better name for it?"

"I don't know. It never occurred to me to change the name of our country, based on its current…inhabitants."

In the dark, I heard the rustle and crinkle of nylon as Assassin shifted in his sleeping bag, leaning up on his elbow. "Government's gone. Life's fucked. Why not rename it? Own it? Let it be something new?"

"But couldn't we have come up with a better name? A more positive one?"

He groaned. "With everything going on, and everything I told you today, the one thing you're stuck on is Undead America? Really?"

"It's the easiest thing to think about. Doesn't involve any decisions really. Like whether or not to trust you, or whether you're just taking me somewhere just to kill me anyway."

"What, do you think I'm taking you somewhere to be a virgin sacrifice or something?" His laugh was low and soothing. I found myself wanting to like this man who'd murdered my Michael, and hating myself —badly—for it.

"Who are you calling a virgin? I was *married*, I'll have you know."

He laughed. "I don't want to kill you, Jenna. I mean, Ashley. I need your help too bad. Now let me sleep. We've got a long drive ahead of us tomorrow. It's the final leg."

I'd been out of it so long, I had no idea where we were, let alone where we were going. "Final leg to where?"

"New York City. Now will you please let me sleep."

The shuffle of a sleeping bag shifting let me know he didn't need an answer. Soon his loud, heavy breathing filled the tent again, and I was left alone to wonder: *New York City? How the hell are we going to go there? Isn't that the zombie capital of the world? Maybe he really is going to sacrifice me.*

Once I decided I didn't care, I fell asleep, dreaming of Michael's face. His hands. His….never mind. Some things are too private to share.

Chapter 19: Sam

I was crammed with Will and Rosie into a single row of seats in a small military vehicle. Though we were all slight, it was still a tight fit, what with the homegrown armor on each door pressing inward, and the hard-as-rock seats beneath our bony asses. Rosie sat in the middle, partially draped over each of us, and poor Will was green with carsick in the unventilated car, filled to the brim with soldier-stench. Unwashed bodies, stale cigarettes, foul breath—it was enough to make even me nauseous. I prayed Will wouldn't boot all over Rosie, because I had a feeling it would set off a chain reaction, which would be ugly.

"Where are we going?" I asked for what was probably the hundredth time. "We have a right to know."

The driver—the Amazon princess with the flaming red hair—snorted with laughter. "Rights?" she said, almost swerving off the curving road. "What the hell kind of rights do you think you have here?"

She had a point. We were prisoners, after all. Our hands were bound, our doors locked from the outside.

"Fine, then," I said. "Where's our friend? Why isn't she in here with us?"

"You mean Jenna?" She stared at me through the rearview mirror, her eyes bright and blistering.

"Jenna? No, I mean Ashley. She just says that sometimes, if she's cornered. Everyone's afraid of Jenna Price, so why not pretend to be her, right? Makes Ashley feel tougher."

Will shot me a look but I silenced him with a quick nod, one I hoped would be imperceptible to the woman in the front seat. The distractingly gorgeous woman in the front seat.

She noticed, and her eyes crinkled. She looked mischievous. Devious. "Right," she said. "Ashley."

"Yes, Ashley. Where is she?"

"She's with Assassin. I'm sure he's making her feel…right at home. He needs a new lady friend. His last one didn't make it past her first battle."

First battle…

And that was all it took. Suddenly I was there, back at my first battle. I smelled the char of burning, rotting zombie-flesh. I heard the guns, the pop of thunderous grenades. I tasted the ozone in the air.

I closed my eyes, willing myself not to black out.

I can't do this now. I have to protect Jenna. Will. Rosie.

Suddenly Rosie appeared, cutting through the darkness of my vision. She wiggled her way to my side of the seat and took my hands in hers, no easy task considering the way in which we were tied. She pressed her forehead against my temple.

"Stay here," she whispered, her voice sweet yet forceful, her breath warm against my ear. "Don't leave us. We need you."

Like magic, the heat of the battlefield receded into the distance, the smells fading with the sounds as though it was a movie, fading to black. Keeping my eyes closed, I forced a smile.

"I'm here," I whispered back. "And I'm not going anywhere. I won't leave you."

Rosie let go of my hands and looped her arms over my head and around my neck, giving me a tight squeeze. "Thank you."

I almost smiled, almost found a way to squeeze her back. But before I could, from the other side of the small back seat came a gagging, retching sound. Her arms still around me, Rosie groaned. "Here we go again."

From the row of seats behind us came the sounds of groans and shouts, and, unmistakably, another gag. Another retch. And then another. The smell in the truck went from foul to unbearable as vomit flowed around our feet.

* * * *

We pulled over for the night soon after that, at least a hundred miles from where we left my brother's body, unburied and rotting in the warm summer sun. The image of him, falling, and Jenna collapsing beside him kept threatening to choke me, to wreck me, but I did my best to press it down. I couldn't think of it. It was a rabbit hole down which I didn't want to fall, remembering my brother, our lives together before the zombies. I didn't let myself wonder, if by some stroke of insane luck I saw my parents again, how I would tell them their other son was dead.

Rabbit holes were dangerous for a guy like me; it was too easy to get lost forever, to never find your way back home. Rosie and Will needed me.

As the truck slid to a stop near a thick copse of trees, and the chatter behind us reached a head as people clamored to be the first one out of the puke-truck, the woman driver look at me again through the rear view mirror. "Someone's coming to take the kids," she said. "Don't worry, they'll be safe. Unharmed. We won't touch a hair on their head. But you? You're coming with me, Silverman, and we're gonna have us a little chat."

I didn't have a chance to respond. The door beside Will was pulled open from the outside, and a smaller girl—obviously a Roughneck based on the black fatigues and combat boots—stood, ready to pull him out. She flinched, though, taking in the vomit-stain down the front of his shirt, in his lap, and on the floor. Rosie and I were the only two aside from the driver, safe in the front seat with filtered air blowing right on her face, who hadn't gotten ill. I couldn't smell it anymore, but I imagined the stench would be overwhelming to a newcomer.

The girl looked at Will and Rosie with pity as she stepped back, wary of being too close to the toxic fumes. "You two are coming with me," she said in a small, sweet voice. Rosie brightened at the sound of it; it was impossible to be afraid of such a voice. "Let's, um, get your stuff, and get you cleaned up. Please," she said, eyeing Will, "please tell me you've got a change of clothes."

He nodded, and struggled to get his feet under him. He was always wobbly after a bout of carsickness. "Yeah, in my bag."

"If you can untie my hands and point me toward some water, I'll help him get cleaned up. I'm Rosie, by the way." Rosie nudged Will forward, out of the car, and hopped out after him. She was playing the nice girl card, and I couldn't blame her; in a place like this, anything you could use to get ahead was a good thing, and Rosie was naturally sweet and likeable.

Unlike me. As they walked off, following the girl in black, the woman in the front seat did a final check of her equipment before turning to face me, not needing the rear-view mirror anymore. Her eyes pierced better than an ice pick. She made me cold, but it wasn't necessarily an unpleasant feeling. More like the chill on a fall night, when you step too far from the campfire and are waiting to be drawn back into its warmth. Like there was a promise of warmth, somewhere, in the not too distant future.

"So," she said, her lips curving up into a smile, her cheeks pale and freckled beneath the tangle of fire engine hair. "It's just you and me tonight. You're mine to watch, and I plan to watch you. But first we need to get a couple things straight."

She looked at me like she was hungry and I was dinner. I liked it, but I needed to assert myself. Like a dog humping a leg, I needed to show my own dominance. I stretched my wrists as far apart as I could without cutting into them with the flex-ties that bound them. "Hold up a sec," I said, meeting her stare with my own, trying to convey strength and power. "I gotta take a leak. Like, now. Can we postpone the rules talk until after that?"

Beneath the freckles she flushed, and her smile faded. She rolled her eyes. "Just like a guy," she said. "I try to lay down the law, and all you can think about is your dick."

"Well, a guy's gotta go."

She blew a lock of hair, escaped from her warrior's topknot, out of her eyes and sneered. The look was sexy. It worked for her, and she knew it. "Fine," she said. She turned her back on me and hopped out of the truck. Once again, I was impressed by her size. When she opened the door to let me out, I realized she was a few inches taller than me, and I had to look up to meet her gaze.

Around us was a flurry of activity as people got to work setting up camp. Trailers popped up from the back of trucks and tents went up in the ground. The people from our truck all stood together, mopping one another off with water poured from huge old coolers, and I was suddenly reminded of how long it had been since I'd had a drink.

"Well," she said. "Aren't you going to go?"

I shrugged. "Don't have to anymore, I guess. But I *am* thirsty. You gonna help a guy out with that? Some water from one of those coolers maybe?"

"You're going to be a pain in the ass, aren't you? I'm going to regret offering to keep you, aren't I?"

I grinned. "Probably. Annoying girls is my specialty."

"Well, then," she said, shoving me—hard—away from the truck. "Don't think of me as a girl. Think of me as your prison guard. And then things will fall pretty well into place."

We took a few steps toward a small-ish green tent. I followed like a lost puppy, since hers was maybe the most perfect butt I'd ever seen.

"And just so you know," she said, as she leaned over to unzip the tent. "I won't hesitate to kill you. Now get inside. We need to talk."

I opened my mouth to respond, but instead, for once, I shut it, falling down to my knees so I could crawl awkwardly through the opening. A moment later, she zipped us in, and we were alone.

* * * *

"Here," she said. "Open up." In her hand she held a mint.

I opened, grateful for the cool wintergreen flavor that spread across my tongue. Cold, brisk, fresh. It was heaven in my mouth.

"Thanks," I said, as the brief spasm of flavor-joy passed. "My mom always told me, if someone offers you a mint, you take it. They're probably trying to tell you something."

She nodded, and suddenly she was so close I could feel the heat radiating from her body. Her face pressed close to mine. My hands were still bound and the woman reached up and slid my looped arms around her neck. Her body pressed against mine.

"Your mother was right," she said, and gone was the earlier edge of anger in her voice, replace by something else. Something sexy. Something disarming and scary and I wanted to consume it.

"What are you doing?"

"Making use of our time together." She was a kitten, now, purring in my arms, her soft, clean hair spilling across my arms, raising goosebumps across my entire body. "Don't you want me?"

Oh God do I, so much, do I, but what the hell? Am I down the rabbit hole again?

I tried to pull away, but with my hands tied around her, I only succeeded in falling backward, pulling the girl—the woman—on top of me as I lay atop a cushion of sleeping bags and supplies. Something crunched beneath me, and all thoughts of hunger and thirst and exhaustion flew out the tent's flap as her body pressed against mine.

"But I don't even…"

I didn't have a chance to finish the thought. Her lips pressed down against mine, and I was grateful again for the mint as our mouths opened and our tongues met and suddenly nothing mattered but the weight of her chest against mine and the longing I'd felt for so long suddenly finding release, finding escape, as her hands slid down and began to unzip my pants.

* * * *

We lay beside each other, after, catching our breaths, waiting for our heartbeats to re-regulate.

"What's your name?" I said. "I can't believe I don't know your name."

"You don't know anything about me." She spoke low, and husky, the voice of a woman satisfied.

"You're right. But can we start with your name?"

"Yeah, sure." She sighed. "It's Lyra."

"Lyra," I said. "I like it. I like you."

She pushed herself up to one elbow, staring at me, and I felt naked beneath her gaze (probably because I was, at least from the waist down). "I don't like you yet," she said. But then she narrowed her eyes, the prison guard once again. "I don't trust you. So don't fuck with me."

"I…I…"

"I'm going to get something to eat. If you move, I'll kill you. If you try to talk to your friends, I'll kill you. Right now, you're mine, and I can do with you whatever I want. So don't fuck with me."

She stood, hunched over in the small tent, and yanked up her pants from around her ankles. Soon she was gone, leaving me behind, alone, exposed, unable to pull up my pants, and hoping Jenna wouldn't find me like that. And also hoping she would. Because suddenly the weight of Michael's loss pressed down and I didn't want to be alone.

"Michael," I whispered. "Why'd you have to go and die?"

Of course, I knew the answer to that. Assassin. And he'd have to answer soon for what he'd done.

* * * *

I dozed until Lyra returned. She laughed when she saw me, but it was a cruel, sharp sound. "You're still naked," she said, her voice cold. "Put that shit away."

I shook my head to clear it, and stared at her as she glared at me, her eyes every bit as cold as her voice. Gone was the warmth of earlier, replaced by something else, something akin to disdain. I didn't understand it, but then again, I never understood women.

"Untie my hands, then," I said, pulling myself up to sitting. "Or else you're just going to have to deal with the beast, hanging out in your tent all night. Because I can't do shit with my hands tied."

She rolled her eyes, but pulled out a knife. It looked dull, tarnished, in the rapidly fading sunlight that barely filtered in through the thick nylon tent. For a moment, she looked from the blade to me, from me to the blade, and I wondered, briefly, if she considered killing me. From the look on her face, it seemed possible, even likely, that she would.

And though I hated myself for it, I grew excited again. She noticed, and groaned. "Oh, for God's sake, put that shit *away!*" As she spoke she reached over and sliced through the plastic tie on my wrists. I moaned with pleasure as blood flowed unabated to my fingertips for the first time in hours. I rolled over on all fours and proceeded to, with the grace of a three-legged dog, pull my pants up, hiding the evidence that I found her, even in her cruelness, to be the sexiest woman alive. Once I felt like I had a bit of my dignity intact, I sat up, turning to face her.

"So," I said, rubbing my wrists, willing the feeling back into my hands. "Why'd you jump me back then, when you so clearly hate me now?"

"I was horny. And you're fresh meat. But…." She glared at me from across the tent. "That? What happened here? It didn't happen. Do you understand? It did *not* happen. I'll lose my job if anyone finds out."

"So then…"

"No. We don't talk about it because it didn't happen. Now shut up and listen."

I shut up. I listened.

"If you want to survive, you listen to everything I say. You obey everything I say. You're my prisoner, mine alone. The Captain trusts me to protect the clan, and I will do that. If you do anything to threaten that, I'll kill you. I won't even hesitate."

I gulped. This wasn't what I expected, at least not after what *did*, in fact, happen earlier that day. I almost thought we'd be friends, after that. But apparently not.

"We're headed back to the clan, and you look like you could be a good fighter. So I want you to live. But the thing is, no matter what, you're either with us or against us. And if you're against us, you're nothing more than…"

"Zombie food." I finished the sentence for her. "And zombie food must be eliminated."

"How did you…"

"Let's just say this isn't my first run-in with the Roughnecks…but somehow I think it'll probably be my last."

She stared at me, surprised by my confession. "Yes, you're probably right. One way or another, it'll probably be your last." She reached up, tucking a stray hair behind her ear. "Now, are you with us?"

I nodded. "I am."

Even though I'll kill Assassin, and I'll kill the Captain, and I'll kill you all for what you did to Michael.

She smiled, and it was the first bona-fide smile I'd ever seen on her face. "Good," she said. "I don't know what we're going to do with the kids, and I don't know what Assassin's got in store for your little friend Jenna."

"Ashley."

"Right. Whatever. I don't expect she'll live to see the sunrise. But if you're with us, you're with us all the way, and that means you can eat."

From behind her back she procured an MRE and a water bottle, dropping them on the tent floor. My mouth salivated at the sight. Being with them would have its perks, just like last time, and I'd take those perks for as long as they'd last.

But I'm coming for you, Assassin, and you, too, Lyra, because I have a feeling you're on the wrong side of right and I can't wait to see how this whole fucking thing goes down. But in the meantime…

As I tore into the MRE and cracked open the bottle of water, Lyra slid closer. She slipped a hand up my thigh.

"And now, since you're with us, maybe that means what happened before…can happen again."

Despite myself, food became secondary and I leaned into her touch.

"Besides," she continued, her hand sliding higher, higher. "I'd like to see what you can do, now that you can use your hands."

Food forgotten, my hands found her sides, her hair, and our mouths met again. All else faded into the abyss of the present moment.

Chapter 20: Will

Rosie's head rested on my shoulder and Chicken slept on my feet as I leaned against the tire of one of the caravan's armored trucks. Rosie dozed, lulled by the quiet crackling flames of a campfire, jerking occasionally as her dreams ebbed and flowed.

Rosie. My sister. I was so glad we, at least, were still together, especially since I hadn't seen hide nor hair of Sam or Jenna since we stopped for our first night with the Roughnecks. At least I assumed they were still calling themselves the Roughnecks, though no one had said as much yet. Sam knew the big guy he called "Assassin," and Assassin pretended to know Sam from somewhere else. The Army, I thought. Maybe. Since I knew for a fact Sam was never in the Army, I figured something fishy was afoot. I kept my mouth shut as often as possible, because, you know, the tangled web woven by lies. Tight-lips seemed a good policy for the end-times.

We'd been on the road a few days before that night. I leaned my head back, soothed by the scent of Rosie's hair, filthy but somehow still sweet-smelling, and the flickering of firelight. I wasn't about to fall asleep, though. No way. Not with so many other questions ready to explode inside me.

Like, where was Jenna? And where was Sam? And what were these soldiers, these Roughnecks, going to do with us?

At least I knew why I had to call Jenna Ashley. Sort of. Her New Orleans story had grown, fish-this-big style, through the rumor mill of the apocalypse. She was legend. We'd heard it twice by then. But legends never have happy endings, so I'd do whatever I could to keep them from knowing they held the real Jenna Price.

No. They held Ashley from New Jersey.

I closed my eyes in the firelight, pretending to sleep, eavesdropping on the Roughnecks' stolen conversation.

For a while they were quiet, roasting on sticks meat I couldn't identify (Squirrel? Possum?) and digging into coolers full of sodas and beer. I'd have killed for a Coke. Or some squirrel. But surveillance was far more important than my most basic needs.

As the soldiers' bellies filled and they pulled out bedrolls, pillow talk began. These soldiers, it seemed, didn't get to sleep in the tents that popped up elsewhere around our gypsy caravan. They slept beneath the stars, and before they dozed, they talked.

"Fun day," said one girl, stretching her arms way above her head and yawning. "New meat, some good fighting, no casualties. No complaints for me."

Beside her, another girl laughed. It was quiet, but I wouldn't have called it kind. She sounded like a clique-y high school girl. When she spoke, her voice was sharp and nasal. "Fresh blood, too. Just what we needed."

A tall guy with a handlebar mustache reminiscent of the Old West laughed. "What, you actually liked that guy? Are you crazy?" He snorted. "Too bad for you. Lyra's got her claws in him."

Mental note: Sam was with someone named Lyra, whoever that was. I wondered if she was the redhead who grabbed Rosie.

"Whatever. I mean, I saw you looking at that girl, like you wanted her. I mean, she's pretty and all, but I don't see what you guys all saw in her."

"Well," said the tall guy. "She *is* Jenna Price, isn't she?"

The mean girl shrugged. I watched through half-opened eyes. "Assassin said no. Said no way was that her."

Tall guy gave her a look. "Then why's he keeping her? Why isn't she out here? With us? I tell you what, if she *is* Jenna Price, Captain's not gonna let her live once we get back to the city. I guarantee that much."

"Why?" The first girl seemed nicer, more curious instead of jealous. "What did she do exactly?"

"Well," said the tall guy. "I hear she…"

* * * *

Jenna Price (according to the tall Roughneck by the fire) was a cold-blooded killer. A temptress. A destroyer of post-apocalyptic communities everywhere.

New Orleans was a safe haven. He was there, or so he claimed. He had shelter—an old hotel, transformed into a refugee camp—and an employer, a boss, who threw excellent, world-ending fiestas. The end of the world in New Orleans was pretty much like everything else in New Orleans: a giant, awesome orgy.

"You're full of shit," said the mean girl.

"Whatever. I was there. I saw it."

Then Jenna Price showed up and destroyed everything.

Either she didn't like the party lifestyle, or she didn't like the boss. Regardless, she wound up blowing up their lab, where a doctor was working to find a cure for the zombie plague, a cure that would have changed everything. But Jenna didn't care. She destroyed it all.

She also somehow managed to sic a huge group of zombies on the city; the tall guy was lucky to escape with his life.

He never saw Jenna in person; he never saw the boss in person. He just benefitted from good food (better than with the Roughnecks), better booze, and the best blow he'd ever found.

"Seriously, you guys. It was unreal. You could fly for days on that shit."

"Yeah. Right."

Jenna Price destroyed it all. There was no way the Captain'd let her do the same in their city. If it really was her, she would die.

She *deserved* to die.

* * * *

"Do you really believe they were working on a cure?" asked the mean girl, her voice softening with the approach of sleep. She yawned, a sound mixing Princess Leia with a wookie. "Why would she blow it up?"

The tall guy didn't hesitate. "Because she likes this world. She's got a thirst for blood, they say, and she likes being a killer. So why would she want it to end?"

"Do *you* want it to end?"

"Yeah, I mean, maybe. Of course I do. I think. But we've got such a good thing going in the city. Life's so different now. You know, before this, I flipped burgers, trying to save up cash so I could go to college and make something of myself. Now? I think I've made something of myself, without college. Don't you think? I'm one of the Captain's top sergeants now. He counts on me. That says something, don't you think?"

"Sure it does." The mean girl yawned again.

"Whatever they say, and whatever she did, one thing I'm sure of is this: there's no cure. There can't be. Zombies aren't people anymore. They're dead. There's nothing *to* cure. Like the Captain says, the only cure is extermination."

The girls sighed. It was a resigned sound, and I fingered the notebook in my pack. *But I have the cure. I can save the world.*

* * * *

Hours later, when my thoughts quieted, matching the silence that surrounded the dying embers of the campfire, and my eyes began to close, Rosie wiggled her head. In the darkness I turned to her. She opened her eyes.

"You know," she whispered. "I wonder what they'd say if they knew you had the cure in your pocket. Would they want it? Or would they throw it away?"

I shrugged, jostling her head against my shoulder. "I've been wondering the same thing."

She spoke around a yawn. "You know, though, I think it's better, maybe, not to tell them. At least not yet. Maybe we shouldn't tell them anything. I don't trust any of these people. Not yet."

I leaned my cheek against her hair, deepening my recline against the rough tree trunk. "You might be right," I said, keeping my voice low and calm. "We should play our cards close."

Rosie snuggled up against my side and I wished I had a blanket to throw over her. My eyes fell shut as visions danced across my darkened inner eyelids. Rosie, dozing on the couch, with mom tossing an afghan over her as she watched a movie on a Friday night. My dad, snoring in his old armchair. Rosie and me, falling asleep in my bed together, my parents looking in from the door at least twice in the night. Zombies, eating everyone…

My eyes popped open again.

How can I not tell them? They're the ones in charge of the whole east coast. If the Roughnecks can't get me to a lab, probably no one can. No matter what that guy says, everyone wants a cure. Don't they?

* * * *

First thing in the morning, I ignored my sister's advice.

The Roughnecks in charge of us were up and at 'em early, almost before the first rays of dawn crossed the horizon. They were sleepy and quiet as they began to break down camp, rolling up sleeping bags and stuffing pillows into backpacks. Chicken was nowhere to be seen, probably off scrounging up some breakfast. My stomach growled as I slid from beneath the weight of Rosie's head. But for the moment, that didn't matter. She was asleep, and I had a job to do.

I pulled from my pack Dr. Schwartz's notebook, worn and tattered from many months of my reading it, taking notes, folding pages, and taking more notes. The leather was smooth and faded. My eyes burned with missed sleep, and my heart thudded fast against my rib cage. *Pound, pound, pound, pound.* I wondered if I'd be sick on the shoes of the guy whose ear I sought; I wondered if there was anything left in my stomach to eject.

Doesn't matter. I have to do this.

My hands shaking, my knees threatening to give way, I stood. I saw him, the guy who'd spoken the night before. The tall one with the handlebar mustache. Though nothing about what he'd said gave me any sort of confidence that he'd even *want* to talk to me, he seemed in charge of our group. As I approached, as quietly and smoothly as my trembling legs allowed, he glanced over, startled to see me there.

"Hi," he said, his voice tentative. "Um, you should really be back there, waiting for us. You're not supposed to get up on your own."

"Why?" I said. "No one's told us that."

"Yeah, but you're our prisoners, so you have to do as I say."

He sounded so weird, so unsure. Maybe he thought himself important and in charge in this zombie world, but the reality was he was a crappy guard. It wasn't the appropriate time to tell him that though. So instead, I shrugged. "Oh. I hadn't realized. Why?"

"We don't know you. We can't kill you because Assassin told us not to and he's technically in charge, at least when we're out on the road. So until the Captain sees you and decides what to do with you, you're our prisoners. So you have to listen to me." He'd stopped packing, and I noticed we had an audience. Several other Roughnecks paused in their goings-on to see what we were up to.

"Oh," I said again, unsure of how to proceed. This wasn't going how I pictured it, but then again, nothing ever did. "Why do you sound confused?"

The guy shrugged, his massive shoulders moving up and down beneath his dark military coat. The sun continued to rise in the east, lighting down on him like a spotlight with its golden-tinted rays. It was going to be a beautiful day. "Don't know. It's just….it's been a while since I've seen a kid, you know? At least, not a zombie kid. We don't have any back at camp, so I'd have probably killed you on sight. Because what good are kids in this world, right?"

"Oh?" said a voice behind me. Rosie was awake. Her hand pressed into my back, and I felt the urgency of her thoughts. *What are you doing, Will?* But her voice was smooth and confident. "You clearly weren't paying attention when we saved your asses the other day. Give me a gun. I'll remind you how well this kid can fight." I couldn't see her, but I could picture the grin on her face—confident, impish. I knew it wouldn't hide the worry and exhaustion in her eyes.

The Roughneck grinned, and the group around him shook with a low laugh. "Whatever," he said. "That's all for the Captain to decide. Like I said, I'd have killed you, but Assassin told me not to. Apparently, he's trying to help out his old Army buddy or something. And he's taken a shine to that other girl."

He was so unapologetic about the fact that he'd have killed us. He talked in such a casual way of death and murder, it made my stomach flip again. Again I wondered if I'd puke on his shoes before all was said and done.

Before I could work myself up further, he asked the question. Looking down at my hands, at the notebook clutched within them, he raised an eyebrow. "Whatcha got there, anyway? You looked like you were about to show it to me when you first came up. What is it? A book?"

"Well, yeah, I…uh…"

Rosie made a swipe at the book. "No, Will."

I pulled away. Stepping forward, I was vaguely aware of guns being pulled from holsters by the people surrounding me, but I ignored them. My hands shaking visibly, I held out the book like a shield, a talisman. "This is…well….I heard you guys talking last night. I heard you say something about New Orleans, about there having maybe been a cure. Well, what if I told you I have the notes here from the doctor in New Orleans? What if I told you the rumors were true, that he was close to finding the cure? What if I told you I knew how to end the zombie plague? What would you say to a kid saying that?"

The Roughneck's face hardened. It looked like stone, cut and chiseled and cold. "I'd say you're either full of shit, or if you're not, you're holding the most interesting piece of paper in the world. And I'd want to know how you got it, because I'm guessing it would be from your little friend Jenna over there with Assassin. And I'd say, no matter what, you better hand it over."

Behind me, Rosie burst out laughing, a shrill, honking sound that was about as fake a laugh as I'd ever heard. It did nothing to cut the tension surrounding me as the Roughneck stepped forward, hand outstretched, ready to pry the notebook from my fingers that suddenly paralyzed, tightened, gripping it as hard as they'd ever held anything. But she persevered, stepping out and around, stopping between the Roughneck and me.

"I'm sorry," she said, wiping tears from her eyes. "My brother, he's funny, isn't he? He's…hey!"

She stumbled and fell to the ground as the Roughneck pushed her aside as if she wasn't even there. A woman stepped forward and picked her up, holding her in place slightly above the air, and she began to kick her legs. "But wait," she cried. "You don't understand. He's not well… my brother…leave him…"

All this I saw but didn't see, barely noticing out of the corner of my eye as the Roughneck before me took hold of the notebook. Suddenly I realized the precariousness of the situation, the flimsiness of the thin leather binding, the flammability of the pages within the covers. Suddenly I didn't want to let it go.

In a flash, I regretted waking up that morning. I regretted not really sleeping enough to have woken up. I regretted being born smart, born able to understand the complex equations dancing across the notebook's pages.

Suddenly I regretted *everything*.

I yanked the notebook away, clutching it to my chest with one hand while the other fumbled for the leather bag which was the notebook's permanent home. At my side. On my person at all times. "Never mind," I said as Rosie continued to talk about my mental issues with no success at distracting anyone. "Like she said, I'm crazy."

But the Roughneck was in my face. His eyes filled mine. His breath washed over me, stinking of un-brushed teeth and stale beer. "I don't think you are," he said.

I took a step backward and ran into a wall. Or a person. Walls don't have arms that reach around you and pin you in place. At least not walls that I've ever encountered.

The notebook pressed against my chest, pinned by the wall-person's strong arms. The Roughneck reached out and took it, then flipped through the pages. His eyes widened, and I wished desperately for the cover of darkness again to hide the equations on those barely-lined pages, but instead I watched as he saw. He read. Maybe he didn't understand it all, but he *understood.* He got it. He knew what was in there, and he snapped it shut. The sound echoed over and above Rosie's now-feeble cries.

"A cure," he breathed. He stepped back from me, still clutching the notebook. He looked around, locking eyes with each of the other Roughnecks in turn. "Would you believe this kid thinks he holds the key to the cure?" He laughter was a bark, and as though it was a cue, a long, loud growl suddenly filled the air. I barely had time to register the sound before a black flash appeared from a nearby copse of trees, knocking into the Roughneck.

It was Chicken. He attacked with jaws wide, back from wherever his wanderings had taken him. The Roughneck stumbled backward, dropping the notebook. I struggled against my captor, diving for the notebook, but I only succeeded in bringing us both down to the ground. From my spot, pinned, my cheek pressed down against a sharp rock in the dust, I watched in slow motion.

Chicken continued his attack, his grip on the Roughneck's wrist tight until the Roughneck pulled back his other fist and smashed it into Chicken's skull. Chicken's jaws released, and his yelp cut through the dawn. Wherever she was, in that second I knew Jenna heard him. Her cry filled the air after, from a location I couldn't pinpoint. Her voice echoed everywhere, all at once.

"Chicken-en-en-en-en-en…."

Chicken fell to the ground, a piece of road kill on the side of the road, waiting for the vultures to find it. Hatred filled the eyes of the Roughneck who, mere hours before, had seemed almost like a voice of reason. Blood flowed from the bite on his wrist. My notebook forgotten, he zeroed in on Chicken. "You fucking dog! Look what you did, you fucking dog!" He shook his wrist, blood sprinkling like ash to the ground.

He loomed over Chicken, three times the dog's size. He wore boots as big as Chicken's head. He raised one. Its shadow fell across Chicken's face, Gulliver's shadow looming over Lilliput. Chicken's left eye opened. The boot reflected in the deep brown of his iris. His lip curled as though to growl, but then it fell again. Too stunned to fight, he awaited death with the patience of a Buddhist monk.

Pinned to the ground with my face in the dirt, I was helpless to do anything other than watch Chicken die, smashed beneath the Roughneck's boot, another senseless victim in this war of attrition. There was nothing I could do. Death was inevitable for us all. I closed my eyes. Maybe I couldn't stop it, but that didn't mean I had to watch.

Another scream cut through the dawn, painful to my ears. I closed my eyes tighter, as though it would help against the noise. Dirt and dust filled my nose and mouth, offering me the same fate as Chicken: death, only this time by asphyxiation. I welcomed it. I'd see Chicken there. I'd see my parents. Let me die. I was ready.

But then a voice boomed out, and it was like the voice of God. "Freeze!"

After that, everything went blissfully, mercifully silent.

Silent, that is, but for the sound of a deep, frenzied panting. The weight of another human body pressing down against my own eased and I opened my eyes.

The Roughneck's boot was still raised, poised to end Chicken's short dog-life, but between the boot and its destination lay my sister, blood flowing from the corners of her mouth. Her eyes were wild. Nearby stood the woman who'd held her, a bite mark spilling blood from her own wrist. Over them all loomed Assassin, a gun pressed against the mustached Roughneck's temple.

"Now everyone just chill…the fuck…out," said Assassin. "And tell me what's going on here. Because I *know* I left you with orders to watch these kids and this dog, not kill them. So you better talk fast, Preston, or I'll kill you where you stand."

The Roughneck—Preston—gulped. He eased his foot back to the ground, neither atop Chicken nor my sister. Preston pointed at the notebook, lying so close in the dirt I could reach it if only I had use of my arms. They remained pinned at my sides. "That kid said he's got the cure, right there in that notebook." Preston glared at me. "I looked at it. It looks…legit. I tried to take it, and then things…escalated."

"The cure?" said Assassin, his eyes narrowing to cut through Preston. "And I suppose you know enough goddamn science to make a call about it being legit by looking through a tattered-ass notebook? Enough to kill some kids over? Some kids I told you to protect?"

"I…I…"

"You *nothing*, Preston. You nothing. That notebook's a piece of trash, a good luck charm, that kid's been carrying with him for months because he wants to believe in a cure. Ashley *told* me. And you were going to kill him for it. And this dog, the first goddamn uninfected dog we've seen in years, and you were going to kill it. Did you not think about how a dog could help us back home? Haven't you ever seen goddamn service dogs? We need him, and you were about to stomp his face off."

"I…."

"You *nothing.* Like I said. Now get the fuck out of my sight. You two clean yourselves up. And someone get these kids some breakfast. I don't want to hear another word about this kid's fucking notebook. Not another word."

He nudged it with his foot, and I reached out and snatched it. The heavy, still-unseen body lifted itself off me. I was free, and somehow still alive. I pushed the notebook into its pouch, its home, and then I crawled over to Rosie, who leaned over Chicken, tears falling against his fur.

"I think he'll be okay," she said, over and over as she stroked his ears and his nose. A trickle of blood flowed from his ear, but he was breathing. "I think he'll be okay."

"Yes, he will," I whispered, wrapping my arms around both of them. "I'm so sorry."

Assassin stared at us. I met his gaze. His eyes narrowed again, and he nodded. Then he turned to go. "A cure!" he said, his voice loud enough to carry through the woods. "A goddamn cure, they think they have. A cure!" He laughed, but it was devoid of humor. "The only cure for the fucking zombie plague is extermination, and we all know it. The Captain's orders, right, y'awl? Extermination."

He walked away into the woods, and somehow I was left with the impression: he didn't believe a word he said.

Chapter 21: Jenna

"Please," I whispered. "Where's Chicken? Is he…dead?"

Assassin drove while I sat in the passenger's seat beside him, staring out the window as we passed long-dead, rusting cars that flavored the air with the sour sweet scent of death and decay. We were alone in the truck, always alone, as though he dared anyone to mess up the rapport he was trying to establish with me. The main question there, of course, was why.

"Please. Just tell me if he's dead. I need to know. I can take it."

Assassin's cheeks puffed out as though he held something inside, but then he exhaled a swirl of Listerine-tinged air. "How many times do I have to tell you? He's alive. The kids have him. He got knocked around a little, but he's *fine.*"

"I don't believe you."

More cars. More trees. The sky above was a startling blue that once promised a day of beach and sun with Michael, but now promised heat exhaustion.

"At some point you need to start believing me, *Ashley*." He never used my fake name without emphasis. I wondered how anyone could even pretend to believe that was really me. I imagined everyone knew who I really was. They were biding their time before killing me, letting me suffer through my final days, extending my time without Michael, cut off even from Sam and Rosie and Will.

"You killed Michael."

* * * *

The rusted-out cars and overturned semi-trucks gave way to burned out buildings and a sign that cut through me like a spoon through melting ice cream.

Welcome to New Jersey.

I was home, but so far from home. "Where in the city are we going, anyway?"

Assassin let out a sound that was somewhere between a snort and a laugh and the honking of a demented Canada goose. "Like you'd believe me if I told you."

It was weird. In his voice I heard regret, almost, and sadness, but also anger. I couldn't get a feel for Michael's murderer any more than I could have protected Michael from the dangers of evolved zombies. The world was moving away from the one to which I'd adapted over the course of two zombie-filled years, and I didn't like it.

"Try me."

"Penn Station."

"You're lying."

"See what I mean? *Ashley?*"

In awkward silence, we rode onward. We headed steadily north on a makeshift road dug out beside the New Jersey Turnpike. The sights of my childhood —oil refineries and green and white exit signs—still stood as a silent memorial to the past, but even they were old, dried out. Burned up. Just like me.

"Penn Station?" I said. "Manhattan? Not Newark?"

Assassin nodded.

"Well, fuck. How are we gonna do that?"

"You'll see."

"Will I get to see Sam again? Or the kids?" I didn't dare ask about my dog again. *Chicken is dead. They killed him and I have to face that fact, regardless of what Assassin says. Soon I'll be dead anyway, the way things are going, and with Michael and Chicken.*

As if he could read my mind, he turned his liquid blue eyes on me. *His eyes are just like Chicken's eyes, just a different color. He's like a giant of a puppy. If only he was kind like a puppy, instead of a cruel, hateful killer.*

"Yes. Your dog, too. I only kept you apart so no one would slip up and call you Jenna. I want to keep you safe as long as possible, and people are already suspicious. I'm trying to save your life."

"My life's not worth saving. I wish you'd let me see them now so I could say goodbye."

Our truck chugged along behind the rest of the caravan, slow and steady and bumpy, but suddenly Assassin slammed on the breaks. It had been years since I bothered with a seatbelt, and I tumbled forward, crashing hard into the dashboard, forehead first. Tears jolted into my eyes, but I blinked them back even as I sat, dazed, on the truck's floorboard.

It took me a few seconds to collect myself. Rubbing at my head, I turned up to see Assassin leaning over me, his eyes sharp and wild. "What'd you do that for?" I said, hating the whining tone that slipped out in an unguarded, ugly moment.

He stared at me a moment longer, and it occurred to me just how *big* he was. Massive, like an old oak tree that's grown in the same spot for a century. Only he was neither gnarled nor crooked. His neck was thick, his arms and shoulders broad and strong. As he glared at me, the devil in his eyes, I realized: he could've snapped me in two. Easily. I shuddered.

When he finally spoke, his voice was low but choked. He was hanging onto something by a thread, a caged animal desperate in some way that had not yet revealed itself to me. "Jesus Christ, Jenna," he said. "Snap the fuck out of it! Nowhere in the legend of Jenna Price did anyone say what a self-centered little bitch you could be."

"What?" Maybe I hadn't heard him right. Maybe my ears were ringing from smacking my head. Had he just called me self-centered? Me? I did everything for everyone else. I lived to help Rosie and Will and Sam, and I'd lived for Michael.

Or had I?

Assassin didn't offer me a hand as I began to pull myself back up to the seat, scooting as far to the far edge of the truck as was possible. Instead, he shook his head. "I'm sorry, *Ashley*. But you've got to get it together. We need you in New York. Shit's about to get tricky, and I need you awake and alert and with your head out your ass for at least a few minutes before we get there."

Break lights ahead indicated the rest of the caravan realized we were stopped, and seconds later the radio overhead crackled to life. "Everything okay back there, man?"

Assassin kept his eyes on me as he reached up for the handset. He spoke to me. "Yes, everything's fine. *Ashley* back here's just having some trouble today. She's not feeling too good, but I think she's on the mend."

The voice on the other end chuckled. "Hope she ain't knocked up. You been protecting yourself, buddy?"

I opened my mouth to object—loudly—to that insinuation, but then I remembered. I wasn't Jenna Price. I was Ashley, and Assassin and Ashley were a thing, because that's why Assassin kept us alone. I shut my mouth as Assassin threw the truck back into gear.

Assassin's laugh into the handset was forced. "Yeah, man. I'm taking care. She's fine. We're catching up now." The truck lurched forward.

"Good. Cuz we're almost there, and if you look off to your left, there's some trouble I'd like to avoid."

Sure enough, there among the sparse trees was the movement of a herd of undead creatures. They were too far away to know much more about them, but the wide swath of ground they covered let us know it was time to get away, and fast. The truck sped up as we neared the caravan.

"Yep. Ten-four, good buddy."

And suddenly I was lost in a world long ago when Michael spoke those same words and together we laughed and laughed and laughed.

That world was dead.

* * * *

New York City. Manhattan. It really was true.

The skyline loomed ahead of us, dull and foreboding, its skyscrapers covered with years of dust and debris, no longer shining in the brilliant sunshine. Most of the buildings, in fact, were dark, blackened with soot and ash and grime. The unwashed city: yet another victim to the zombie invasion. We waited at the foot of the top level of the George Washington Bridge, a demilitarized zone lined with ten-foot fences, the top of which sliced the sky with razor-wire. Massive, military-issue weapons—cannons, it seemed, and huge machine guns that I couldn't identify but knew Michael would have recognized in a heartbeat—pointed straight at us. A dozen or so soldiers manned the gates, filling me with a dark, sullen dread.

"I don't want to go there," I whispered. "The last time I went through gates like that was New Orleans."

"You have no choice," said Assassin, also whispering. It struck me as funny, then, that he'd whisper, too, but I didn't laugh.

"I'm going to die there."

Assassin didn't answer, but the click of the automatic locks in the truck doors echoed in my ears as we drove forward into the fray.

Soon we were in the city, headed for Penn Station. Memories of childhood train rides into the famed station crowded out the sight of the cordoned off street on which we traveled, a makeshift tunnel created by miles of reinforced fencing and patrolled by countless foot soldiers who walked in well-armed silence, bayonetting any zombies who approached the fences. I had to admit, though: there were fewer zombies on the streets than I'd expected.

Still. Right then I remembered Madison Square Garden and the signs outside on the marquis advertising concerts and Knicks games. I remembered the gentle press of people boarding trains. I remembered waiting for a slice of pizza, or riding in ear-bud silence down a rickety escalator. I remembered the feel of my mother's hand in mine when I was small, and then, when I was older, Michael's, as we struggled to keep together, to keep safe, against the hounding surge of a thriving city.

"How?"

My question was simple, but I knew the answer wasn't. There were so many questions wrapped up in it. How were there so few zombies? Or better, how were there still any? When the zombie plague first broke out, didn't they all die out after a few months, the virus giving up on its hosts and allowing them to fail? But hadn't they somehow, someway, continued to flourish here and everywhere, long after they should have died.

Evolution. That answer was clear enough.

But then, how was a train station in the heart of the city, one surrounded above by city streets and buildings, and below connected to dozens if not hundreds of subway tunnels stretching from Manhattan to Brooklyn to the Bronx to Queens, how was it safe? How?

Assassin only smiled a grim, sad smile. "You'll see. You'll see everything. Very soon. It's coming."

But he wouldn't say what was coming.

* * * *

The radio crackled overhead as we passed an old, blown out brick building. The outside was painted red and black with a message of decay. *The End Times are here.* I wondered if the paint was blood.

A deep, crusty, disembodied voice filled the truck. "Assassin. It's about time you're back. We expected you days ago."

Assassin's shoulders jerked. "Yes, Captain. Sorry, sir. There were… some unforeseen events." His eyes lay heavy on me as he held the handset.

"Yes, so I hear." Disdain dripped from the radio. "You're still late. Report in as soon as you unload. I have a little job for you tonight. A pocket of supplies, out on 57th and Lex. There may be…casualties. You're the man I need for the job."

Cold. The voice made me feel cold. And afraid. Casualties. I wondered why or how, but it wasn't the time to ask.

Assassin's face set into a mask of calm. "Yes, sir. I'll be available in ten. Maybe less, if they let us in without checking us."

A laugh barked from the radio. "You don't get special treatment. No one gets special treatment. This is a war zone. One little slip is all we need and this place is toast. I'll see you in twenty. Not a moment earlier or later. And…bring your new friends. I hear I'll want to meet them."

"My friends? Sir, they're not my…"

But the radio was dead.

Overhead, clouds began to gather in the sky. A chill wind blew through the cracked windows, carrying with it the smell of ozone and rotting flesh. A storm was brewing. Anyone could see that.

* * * *

The truck pulled down a ramp into an old public parking deck, the kind that, in prior years, would have been full of cars. The kind you'd have to dart past when passing on foot, for fear a driver would pull out without looking, which happened all the time. We looped in past the other trucks in the caravan, driving deeper, deeper, until we hit a crudely dug tunnel. Assassin threw the truck into park beside it. As he turned the key in the ignition, he glanced at me, his eyes cutting sharp. "Are you ready?"

"No."

"Too bad."

He took hold of my arm, and with none of the gentleness I'd come to expect from him, he pulled me over to his side of the truck. "Come on, *Ashley*. It's time to meet the Captain."

I gulped down the bile that rose in the back of my throat, Sam's voice ringing through my memory. *The Captain. He was a monster. I hope I never see him again.*

Chapter 22: Sam

The days in the caravan merged together into a crazy blur of miles passing the truck in which I sat while Roughnecks I didn't recognize ignored me, including Lyra, who didn't ignore me at night when she pulled me into her tent, away from prying eyes. They knew what we did in there every night—sometimes twice, if Lyra wanted—but she played coy with them. And with me. I was her plaything, her toy, and though she denied our involvement by daylight, by the light of the moon she'd cry out in my arms and scratch her fingernails down my chest, leaving marks I could still see and feel in the morning. Marks I could have used as proof, had I been so inclined, but I wasn't.

I would kill her as soon as we got wherever we were going, and I was going to kill the Captain and Assassin and anyone else who was in my way as I searched for Jenna and the kids and got us the hell out of Dodge. Because New York? No fucking way. I'd dreamed of going there, dreamed of finding my parents there, but as we approached I realized: that dream was stupid. My parents were dead. So was the city. Nebraska suddenly seemed like heaven, and I'd get us there come hell or high water. Or earth and zombies.

But if I wanted to enjoy the nights with Lyra in the meantime, well, what was I but a man, and a weak and tired one at that.

Lyra kept me separate from the kids after the first day. I sometimes saw them climbing into or out of their truck with their guards, so I knew they were okay. I also knew Jenna was still around because Lyra never ceased teasing me about Assassin and Ashley, and the way Assassin stole the girl who was so obviously mine. I grew tired of explaining to Lyra that *Ashley* (I couldn't say Jenna's fake name without emphasizing it in my head) wasn't mine, had never been mine, and was hopelessly devoted to my brother. *His* corpse lay rotting, in the sun, victim to a zombie attack and the Assassin's murderous bullets.

But I never saw Jenna. No. She was with Assassin, morning, noon, and night.

Finally, one day, as a storm brewed overhead, we reached our final destination.

New York. Manhattan. A burned out city infested with the undead. I lost my voice at the first sight of the city skyline, my heart speeding up and my hands clamping down into arthritic claws.

We drove straight to the heart of midtown through a network of fenced off streets and paths, the tires of our truck crunching over bones and human detritus that littered the cracked and puckered pavement. Lyra kept giving me funny looks as the truck lurched and swayed on the uneven roads.

As we neared our final destination and the talk around me in the truck grew more ebullient—*Showers! Hot food! Beds!* —I felt my stomach cramping and my palms growing moist with perspiration.

This is the city where my parents died.

I was as sure of that fact as I'd ever been of anything. I didn't know why, but I *felt* it. I wanted to die, too, to join them and Michael in the afterlife. Or in the great nothing. I didn't care.

The noise behind us grew louder, the talk among the soldiers boisterous and enthusiastic. They weren't looking at us. Lyra glanced over, taking her eyes off the truck in front of us for the briefest of seconds. "What's up, Silverman?" She sounded almost tender, almost caring.

"Nothing." I stared out the window.

As if the sky changed in response to my rising blood pressure, clouds began to gather overhead. They were dark, black, promising the coming of a storm. Lightning sparked from one to another, and I watched out the window as the wind picked up and the buildings lining the street danced and swayed. Thunder rumbled in the distance. A worm of bile seeped upward through my throat; I swallowed it back.

The caravan pulled into an old parking deck near Penn Station. Around me, the press of bodies shifted as the Roughnecks—whose names were all still a mystery to me because nobody ever bothered to talk *to* me instead of *near* me, and I never bothered to ask—jostled about, gathering their few belongings as they readied to leave the truck. I realized with a start that I never knew why they'd been away since, after they'd picked us up, we'd been traveling. Not scavenging. Not hunting. Just…traveling.

From the front seat, I heard Lyra's voice again. "You ready?"

My hands shook so badly it was difficult to gather my pack, light though it was without the weapons I once carried. A hand slapped my head. "I said, are you ready?" As always, when she spoke it was tinged with anger, sharp and edgy. "Or are you gonna fall to pieces and get killed before you even set foot on solid ground?"

Ice settled in my stomach and my hands stopped shaking. The Captain. I was going to meet the Captain. Nothing else mattered. This was it. This was the day. He'd haunted my dreams for months; now I'd finally face him again. "Yes. Yes, I'm ready."

"Good. Let's go."

* * * *

Lyra kept a hand on my arm as we climbed down a series of stairs and paralyzed escalators. Though the power grid here seemed to be working, running on *something,* with bulbs crackling overhead, buzzing with the semi-foreign sound of electricity, no one had bothered to turn the escalators back on.

"We travel by tunnels in the city," said Lyra, suddenly chatty, as we walked. "Safer and easier to maintain. The zombies don't understand stairs—or at least, not the *normal* ones—and we've killed most of the subway zombies already. So we're safe here. You don't have to worry. It's nice."

"What do you mean, *normal* ones? Are there *abnormal* zombies? Abbie-normal ones?" I laughed at my own joke, but Lyra didn't get it. *Michael would have laughed, but he's dead. I'm going to kill all these people for killing him.*

Lyra shrugged as she hopped over an overturned bench at the head of yet another set of stairs. "You know, the normal zombies are the ones that just sort of lurch around, trying to eat things. The new ones, we see them sometimes on supply runs, and you saw them the first day we found you. They're different. They're a little worse than the normal ones."

A memory of the zombies hunting us in our truck came crashing down. That was before Michael got bit and everything went to hell. Yes. I understood the "new" kind of zombies. "But they're still pretty dumb, though, right? They're still just monsters?"

She shrugged again. "Maybe. Maybe not. I think some of them can *think*. But no one else seems to believe me. I mean, really, I don't want to believe it myself."

She glanced over her shoulder. "But I'm not supposed to talk about any of that. Never mind. Forget I said anything."

"Right. Sure. Whatever you say. You're the boss, right? And we're going to meet the Captain and see what happens after that. Do I have the gist of things?"

Whether it was due to the reminder of the Captain, or the tightness I couldn't hide from my voice, her chattiness left as quickly as it had appeared, replaced once again by her guard-like demeanor. That was fine. I liked her better in official-mode. Made it easier to imagine killing her.

In silence, we climbed down, down, down, until we reached the weirdly comforting sight of an old, white-tile subway station. It smelled like a subway station *should* smell—like piss and body odor. I breathed it in, and for a second it was like going back in time.

At least until I looked around, taking in some other familiar sights: an old newspaper stand, little more than a sagging pile of damp paper and splintered lumber. Posters that once advertised Broadway plays and beautiful women were torn and tattered. White tiles, splattered with blood and other animal remnants. I was back in the present, and from somewhere down the tunnel through which we walked came the panting sounds of a nervous dog.

Moments later, flanked by Roughnecks armed with rifles and grenade belts, Rosie, Will, and Chicken appeared in the station, blinking at the sudden brightness as they emerged from the darkened tunnel. Rosie's face brightened when she saw me. I opened my arms and she ran to them. I'm not going to lie—it was nice to be loved. It was even nice when Chicken leaped up and nipped my hand. I let go of Rosie with one arm and scratched the top of his head.

Will appeared beside us, and I punched him on the shoulder. "Good to see you guys," I said. I dropped my voice. "They hurt you?"

Eyeing her captors from the safety of my arms, Rosie spoke first. "No. They've treated us okay. It's just…"

She didn't have a chance to finish because another set of arms grabbed us from behind. They squeezed, pulling us, Will included, into a crushing hug. "What the…"

"You guys are okay!" It was Jenna. She squeezed harder, almost to the point of pain. At the sound of her voice, it seemed like maybe everything was going to turn out well in the end. I couldn't move, couldn't wrap my arms around her or pull her to me the way I held Rosie—although, really, holding her wouldn't have been anything like holding little Rosie—but she was there. Alive and well.

"Jenn…" began Will, but Rosie stomped on his foot.

Jenna's grip loosened. "Ashley," she hissed.

My eyes darted to Lyra and the other Roughnecks. Lyra's eyes had widened, but the other two didn't seem to have noticed. Their faces were placid, dumb and fleshy. I hated them. Lyra, on the other hand, stood at sudden attention.

Oh well. She knew who Jenna was from the get-go anyway. I think.

The air in the subway station was cool and still. We spread out a little, and Jenna leaned over to pick up Chicken. "You big doof." She spoke into his neck, and he lapped at her cheeks and nose. "I missed you, too. Michael would be…" She trailed off, glancing at Assassin. "Never mind. Rosie. Will. Have they hurt you?"

Jenna's voice was hard. Rough. She touched Rosie's cheek, and then Will's, pausing over each of them to look them up and down while still cradling the dog. It was like she couldn't do enough, say enough, or see enough, in those first moments to ensure that the kids were really intact.

Once again, Rosie spoke for her and her brother. "No, we're fine. We missed you, though."

A sweet, sad smile crossed Jenna's lips. "I missed you, too. I still don't….never mind. We're here now." She set Chicken down on the ground at her feet, and he danced in his happy Chicken way, tongue out and nails clattering against the rough concrete. "And for now, that has to be enough, doesn't it?"

I finally found my own voice. "It's good to see you. *Ashley.*" I reached for her, and she stepped into my embrace, burying her face in my neck. She breathed a deep, shuddering breath, and I blinked back tears. I kissed her forehead, but she pulled away.

"Don't. Your beard. It tickles."

I looked away, almost laughing until my eyes found Lyra, standing nearby, clutching her bayonetted rifle with a white-knuckle grip. Her face was flushed, her lower lip sucked into her mouth. I suddenly remembered the way Lyra melted into me when she was dozing off each night, and for a moment I regretted those sleepy moments. I should have kept more distance between us. I shouldn't have let her care.

Shit's getting complicated real fast, I thought, especially when I saw Assassin's eyes train down on Jenna. *Real fast*.

I let go of Jenna and stepped aside, wondering if she and Assassin were like Lyra and me. But no, that couldn't be, I thought. *He killed Michael. She was there. She saw it.*

Assassin cleared his throat. "Y'all finished?" He didn't sound particularly friendly.

Jenna nodded, reaching out and taking Rosie's and Will's hands. "Yes. Where are we going?"

"I already told you. To meet the Captain. Lyra, Wilson, Ruiz, you come with. He wants to see us all."

"Yes, sir."

* * * *

Before we got ourselves organized enough to walk, single-file, back into the tunnel, a voice filled the vast, cavernous space. "Why are you leaving? The fun here's just getting started. Assassin, what do you have for me? Let me meet your new friends."

The Captain's presence was every bit as odious as I remembered. He appeared as though by magic from an opening in the wall. Though he stood ten feet below where we waited on the platform, he seemed bigger than life. I stepped behind Jenna so I could look at him without, hopefully, his noticing me. I had no idea if he'd even remember me, but God! Did I remember him. Did I remember that *voice*. It cut through me like a knife slipping, unyielding, into a dying zombie's eye. Though I'm ashamed to admit it, my palms moistened with sweat, and my mouth went dry. A flood of memories enveloped me. Ty, my best friend. A little boy with blonde curls who I knew for five minutes before his short life ended in my arms. A man named Amos and a woman named Aida, wise, caring people who died at the Captain's behest for no reason I ever understood.

He was flanked by six soldiers, more heavily armed than those guarding us. I counted quickly. They carried no less than a dozen guns, and wore belts looped with knives and extra ammo. They were ready to battle for the long haul, whenever necessary.

A set of crude wooden stairs connected the base of the tunnel with the platform, and the Captain marched up them with ease. I don't know what else I expected—maybe some part of me hoped against hope that he'd been injured in a battle, that I'd find him crippled and undefended, an easy kill. The demon of my nightmare, though, was every bit as healthy as he'd been when I left him. He still wore the crisp uniform, not a mark on it, and the wide-brimmed drill sergeant hat. When he stood on even ground with us, even his grin was unchanged, full of crooked teeth and foul breath that washed over me from twenty feet away.

Of course, he was armed. Packing. He was ready for action.

"Assassin, front and center," said the Captain. His voice was fingernails on a chalkboard. It was biting down on a piece of tinfoil. My stomach clenched.

"Yes, sir." Assassin appeared before me, the mountain of a man standing at attention, ever the obedient soldier. "I wasn't expecting to see you here, sir."

"Of course you weren't. I wanted to surprise you. You know how much I love surprises." Something about the way the Captain spoke let us all know: he liked anything *but.* "How was your trip? Did you have a nice time?"

"A nice time, sir?"

"Oh, come on, man, take a joke! You do remember jokes, don't you?"

"No, sir." Assassin shook his head for emphasis.

"Right. Well, then, did you bring me what I asked?"

"Yes, sir. If you'll look in the storage truck, you'll find a whole new arsenal."

"Where'd you find it?"

"Arlington, Virginia, sir."

"Good. And….I hear you brought me some new recruits? Are they in, or are they out? Have you asked them yet? Step aside, soldier. Let me see them."

Assassin did as he was ordered, but he stayed silent, ignoring the Captain's question. He stood aside to let the Captain see.

Jenna stood up straighter. I felt her prepare to do her flirty-thing. It always had results for her, I knew, but I pinched her side. It wouldn't work with him. She jumped, though, and turned to me, exposing me for the Captain to see.

"Oh, Jesus Christ." The Captain stepped forward. "You *did* bring me a surprise, didn't you? Welcome back, Silverman."

I didn't see it coming. I should have seen it coming. But the surge of pain and explosion of blood that came as the Captain pummeled me with a quick and violently strong backhand somehow surprised me, caught me off guard. I fell to my knees, my hand pressed to my nose, trying and failing to stem the flood. His aim was good, I had to hand it to him.

Rosie screamed, and the sounds of a scuffle reached my ears. From the corner of my eye, I saw Jenna wrestle Chicken to the ground, protecting him, I assumed, from getting shot when he attacked the Captain. The Captain who, I should add, was pulling back a foot to land a kick probably somewhere in my crotch.

But I was ready for him this time. Time had changed me, for the stronger, the better. I wasn't about to let him get the drop on me again. I fell all the way to the ground and rolled to the left, avoiding his kick with ease. He wasn't expecting me to fight back. I rolled again, getting my feet beneath me, and I pressed myself up to standing. When I pulled my hand from my nose the warmth of blood was nauseating, but that didn't matter. I raised my hands, ready for the Captain.

Ready, anyway, until two more men, Wilson and Ruiz, I supposed, grabbed me from behind. They were both bigger than me, and one pressed a gun to my back. I felt it nudging between my vertebrae. I froze. Even I couldn't fight, unarmed, with a bullet through my stomach.

The Captain's face was aflame as he stepped closer to me. It was all very déjà vu. Very slow-motion. He pressed the brim of his hat against my forehead. His breath blanketed me, stale and rotten, and his eyes bore into mine like a drill bit into soft wood. "You shouldn't have fought back," he said. "I'll kill you for it. But first I want to meet your friends. Let you see what else I find."

I wanted to look away, to close my eyes and not see the Captain befoul my friends with his breath, his stench, but I couldn't. I had to see, like a rubbernecker passing a ten-car pileup. I had to watch, even as the blood oozed forth from my nose and my jaw ached and screamed.

Jenna remained on the ground with Chicken, and the Captain ignored her. For the moment she was safe as he stepped forward to meet and greet the two young ones. Will, who looked skinnier than ever —*my God, has he eaten anything since we were separated?* —stepped out in front of his sister, but of course, she had none of that. She pulled him back. Rosie and Jenna—two peas in a very stubborn pod.

The Captain eyed them. "Kids, eh?" he said. "We don't keep kids here. You should have been killed and burned as soon as my Roughnecks found you." He turned his glare on Assassin. "Care to tell me why they weren't?"

Assassin opened his mouth to answer, but Rosie leaped forward and kicked out with her foot, striking the Captain in the shins. He howled, and then, as casually as if swatting a fly, he swept out his hand and knocked her to the ground. Will was about to attack, fury painted across his face, when the Captain gave him a shove in the chest. Will needed only a stiff breeze to knock him over by then; a shove from the Captain sent him sailing across the room.

Oh God, now he'll kill them, no don't kill them, let me go you fucking bastards you assholes who kill kids like cockroaches. Let me go you fucks!

I pulled and tugged against my captors, spraying the ground beneath with blood as I panted and wheezed, but they held firm. I couldn't move. Down below, Assassin reached an arm around Jenna's waist, and grabbed Chicken with the other. We were pinned down, the both of us, unable for the first time to even pretend to protect our charges.

Allie's going to kill us for letting him hurt the kids.

Never mind the fact that the Captain had already promised to kill me.

I braced myself for the worst. *Goodbye, Rosie. Goodbye, Will.*

But instead of lashing out with one of his many knives, or shooting a gun and ending things, the Captain only opened his mouth and began to laugh. His head thrown back, his jaw hanging down, a trail of spittle latched itself from the top lip to the bottom. His teeth were yellow and full of old, rotting fillings. But he was laughing.

Soon, he settled, just as Rosie began to pick herself up from the floor, looking every bit as pissed off as she'd been when she fell. "Why are you laughing?"

"I can see why they kept you," the Captain said. "You're a feisty one."

"They're good in battle," said Assassin, his arms crossed over his chest. "The littlest one especially. She's the best shot of them, a killer. These kids aren't zombie food."

"It's true." Lyra spoke with a sigh. "They were good on the road, survived out there by themselves for a reason. They're all pretty useful. Even her." She glared at Jenna.

Rosie, in the meantime, was still free. She was hot pink in the face, neck, and ears as she marched to the Captain. I wondered if any of them knew she always hid a knife in her boot. I wondered if any of the Roughnecks had found it yet. I had no doubt Rosie was about to kill the Captain with her bare hands if necessary.

The Captain dropped to his knees, like a parent about to explain something very serious to a child. On her level, he held out a hand to stop her. She froze. In his hand was a pistol, small but deadly. He smiled. "Don't make me use this on you, just when I was beginning to like you."

Rosie nodded.

"Good," said the Captain. "I'm glad you can be reasonable. Now, what to do with you? You're a kid. Kids are zombie food, that's it. No kid can survive out there, and no kid has anything to offer me here but heartache. You're like that dog; I can't get attached, because you're going to die sooner than me. You can't survive."

"I've made it this far, haven't I?" Rosie sounded proud.

"Yes, that's true. Is that your brother back there? You two look alike."

"Yes."

"You'll say yes, sir, or yes, Captain, if you know what's good for you."

"Yes, *sir.*" Rosie clenched her hands, her shoulders shaking. She gritted her teeth.

"Um, Sir," said a voice from behind me. The Roughneck holding my right arm—Wilson or Ruiz, I don't know, he had a mustache—spoke. "There's something you should know. Those kids? Well, one of them thinks they have the cure."

The Captain looked up, raising a single eyebrow. "A cure?"

"Yes, that's what they said. He—the one back there—has a notebook all scrawled with formulas and shit. We were going to destroy it, just in case, you know…we don't want to spread false hope or anything. But Assassin let him hang onto it."

"This true?" The Captain again turned his eye on Assassin. He nodded again.

"A cure." The Captain seemed on the verge of laughter again, and I cringed. His laugh was perhaps the cruelest thing I've ever heard. "You, bring him here."

Lyra, who'd stood silent for most of our audience with the Captain thus far, stepped around and lifted Will to his feet. She half-carried, half-walked him forward to stand beside his sister. The Captain took the time to look at Will, taking in his skin-and-bones exterior, the fire in his eyes.

"It's true," the Captain said. "You do believe you've got the cure. Let me have it." It wasn't a request; it was a demand. When Will didn't move, Lyra reached into his pouch, pulled out the notebook, and handed it to the Captain. Will pulled against her grip to try to take it back, but I could've told him: Lyra's grip was iron. He was stuck.

The Captain opened the book, flipping through the first few pages before bringing it up and pressing it to his nostrils. He inhaled. "Ah, I love the smell of paper. We don't have enough of it around here." He held the book out, reaching into his pocket with his other hand, leaving behind the small pistol and taking out a lighter. "Paper burns," he said. "Did you know? It's great kindling. We could start a bonfire with this book."

"No," said Will, but it was weak. The rest of us just watched. There was nothing we could do.

The Captain flicked his finger and the lighter burst into flame. He held it beneath the book, tantalizingly close to those flammable pages, those pages covered with what could have been key to the survival of the human race. "The thing is," he said, trailing off as he played, and as the paper, damp from humidity or sweat, began to smoke and steam. The Captain's voice was cold. Empty. Dead. "The thing is, there's no cure for the zombie plague. The only way to stop it is to exterminate all the zombies. We can't have word of a false cure, a false prophet, sneaking into the Roughnecks and stirring up trouble. We don't like trouble here."

He sniffed again. "Such a shame. I do love the smell of paper, but I can't have you spreading lies. Zombies aren't human; there's no cure for what ails them. They're beasts, brought upon us by God or the Devil perhaps. Once a human is bit, their humanity ceases. They must all die. That's the only prophecy you need to know."

I remembered the sound of the bullet as it cut off my brother's life. I didn't care what the Captain said. Michael died a man, a man with hope. Assassin killed a man, not a zombie. The Captain wouldn't agree.

"No!" Will's cry grew stronger, more shrill. Lyra worked him into a basket hold, keeping his feet inches off the ground. He was so small and she so tall it was easy for her. "No!"

"There's no such thing as coming back from the zombies. The only cure is extermination, and the sooner you know that, the better."

The flame licked the notebook, kissed it, and then began to consume it. The Captain held it as the fire began to devour its pages. Behind the black smoke that rose from the flames, he smiled.

Will screamed. Jenna shouted. Rosie rushed to her brother's side. She tried to take hold of his cheeks, his face. "It's okay." She spoke above the noise he made. "It's going to be okay. Will. It's going to be okay."

But it wasn't. It never would be. As we watched Will's hope for the future go up in flames and the Captain grinned his manic grin, Lyra gave me a look. Had I closed my eyes, I'd have missed it. It was apologetic, regretful.

She's going to kill him.

But she didn't. Instead, she let go with one arm, and let Will almost get away. Almost. She yanked his arm back at the last second, pulling him toward her as she let loose with a single, well-aimed punch. Will's face exploded in a storm of blood and gristle as his nose shattered beneath her fist. He dropped like a stone. Rosie collapsed on top of him. Jenna screamed. The Captain laughed. Chicken howled.

I lowered my head and prayed for an end.

Chapter 23: Jenna

I prayed every day for an end. For *the* end, whatever shape it would take. And I'm not a praying sort of a girl.

The Captain didn't kill us that day. He threatened, but he didn't. Not even Will, who lay on the ground, a ragged pile of skin and bones and blood, unable to speak after the loss of his notebook, his cure. For some reason, the Captain let us all live, even Chicken. Maybe he liked our feistiness. Maybe Assassin's brief mention of our prowess on the battle field convinced him he needed us. Who knows.

No deed went unpunished, though. For going AWOL the first time he was with the Roughnecks, Sam was publically beaten. Flogged. The Captain himself delivered the fifty lashes with an Indiana Jones-style whip that, had he been aware of anything other than pain, Sam would have appreciated. Rosie and I cared for his wounds for days after, when he burned with fever and we half-expected him to die. He cried out in delirium for his parents, for Michael, for me. I was the only one still alive, so I lay beside him, cradling his head in my arms, kissing the tears when they fell from his eyes. Lyra hovered in the distance, watching, always watching.

As soon as Sam grew well enough to walk, she took him away from us, back to her own little hiding spot, like a child with a treasured possession. I'd have been angry, had I been able to care anymore. But I didn't. Something deep inside me shut down. Nothing mattered anymore. Nothing would ever get better in Assassin's Undead America.

Eventually, when he decided we weren't an imminent threat, the Captain put us all to work. Rosie helped in the kitchen, Will did manual labor as best he could, and Sam and I became Roughnecks, re-armed and dangerous, always surrounded by the soldiers most vocally loyal to the Captain and his men. I spent my days pretending to be Ashley, wondering why no one ever blew my cover. Lyra knew who I was, but she never said a word.

We went on patrols at night, deep in the city streets, searching for supplies and more soldiers, expanding the protected area of our camp. With what we found, hidden in plain sight, we could make a stand there for years. The city fell long before its survivors could make use of its miles of stores and resources. In the city we were well-fed, well-clothed, and well-weaponed. The Captain ruled with an iron fist—Sam's beating was not the only one I witnessed in the tunnels beneath New York. Anyone who spoke against him was killed in the end. I chose to comply with his rules, his regulations. I chose to fit into his world. It was easier that way. I tried to forget the life I left behind. Simon. Allie. *Sadie.* They were all just zombie food anyway.

And so I prayed for the end.

The end that never seemed to come.

* * * *

Assassin came to me at night. Every night. But not like that. Not in that way. He came to whisper.

"It doesn't have to be like this, Jenna," he'd say. "We could stop him. Stop them. We could let Will work on his cure. I can't do it alone. It's why I saved you. Why I need you."

Every night I rolled over, facing the wall, as far from Assassin as I could manage. "There's nothing worth fighting for." He'd leave in silence. Always in silence.

I heard rumors sometimes, rumors about Jenna Price being on the move again. Jenna Price was ruthless, a killer, devastating outposts of survivors up and down the East Coast. Whoever that Jenna Price was, she wasn't me, and no one knew I was there, in their camp. Around the Roughnecks, I was Ashley. Just Ashley. Another zombie slayer. Another rule-follower, surviving day-by-day. No one knew how much I wanted to die, but how scared I was of the hell that could face me in the end. No one knew how many zombies I'd killed, cold and ruthless, and no one dreamed my dreams. No one faced the darkness I faced. Alone. I was alone. With no reason to live, and no courage to die, I treaded water every day.

Until the patrol when I got separated, and everything changed again.

* * * *

The patrol was my idea, which was weird to begin with considering I hadn't voiced a single opinion since the start of our time with the Roughnecks. I should have known right away that things were about to change again. I didn't, though. I sat at dinner that night, mulling over the previous day's run. Combat had been tight, face-to-face with a small herd of smart-zombies. More than once I lacked range even for my small pistol, and my Slugger proved less effective against the more-intact skulls of the less-rotten undead. Fighting with my hunting knife was too close for comfort, even for me.

Assassin sat beside me at the table, along with a few other Roughnecks whose names I never bothered to learn. Rosie placed a bowl of soup in my lap, then went back to refill her tray. My Slugger, my old and trusty Slugger, lay beside me. I trailed my hand down its handle.

"You know what would be nice," I said to no one in particular. "A sword. A big-ass, razor-sharp sword."

Assassin smiled—for some reason, it made him happy when I spoke—and picked up his Samurai sword. "You mean like this one? We can head down to Chinatown for a new one for you. That route's pretty well covered. We'd be pretty safe."

"No," I said, as Rosie appeared with more soup, and Sam and Lyra joined us. "Not a Samurai one. More like…think medieval. Like broadsword. Armor." I paused, thinking, and it came to me. "I have an idea."

Sam grinned, a smile that came close to matching his pre-flogging smile. He was resilient, that Sam. "You're mighty perky tonight," he said. "What's wrong? Are you sick?"

I smiled back, surprised at how natural it felt. "No, I was just thinking. I mean, we do a lot of close combat down in the tunnels, right? A lot of killing face-to-face. So many zombies still. And if all we can do is exterminate—Captain's orders, right? —I'd like something more effective than my Slugger. And bigger than my knife. Skulls are getting harder to bash in lately."

One of the nameless Roughnecks nodded. "Yeah, I've been wondering about swords, too. They'd be really good. I just don't know where you go to buy a sword now." He snort-laughed at his own joke, a noise that reminded me, briefly, of the way Michael used to laugh. I remembered a time we were in the Met….

"That's it!" I exclaimed, almost spilling my soup in the first surge of excitement I'd felt since Michael died. "The Met! They've got an entire Arms & Armor section! We could get some fabulous weapons there!"

"And didn't you used to love their jewelry?" Sam laughed. "I see where this is going."

"Shut up," I said. "I'm serious."

"You don't think someone's got that place claimed already? We've seen some pretty big groups lately," said Assassin. "I don't care to face a group of survivors who've been holed up there with swords for the past two years. They're likely to be territorial."

But the other Roughnecks, Sam included, ignored him, too excited. "Maybe, but maybe not. Ashley's right, though," said a girl with pink hair. I didn't understand dying your hair pink when living at the end of the world, but to each her own, I guessed. At least she was on my side for the moment. "It could be awesome. I'm in. I'll run it by the Captain tonight, see what he thinks. Are you guys in?"

They were. And thus began our longest journey, the one that may never end.

* * * *

All raids and supply runs took place after dark, and our trip to the Metropolitan Museum of Art would be no different. There would be about twenty of us going—Captain's orders for strength in numbers—including the Captain himself. He didn't often go on runs anymore, preferring to stay in the safety of base camp where he could direct both the local goings on, and be there to field communications from the many Roughneck outposts up and down the East Coast. But something about the Met had called him, and he in turn called us to order late that night.

"Roughnecks line up!" His voice was deep and booming.

We complied, shoulders pressed together, each of us clad in black and armed to the teeth. I carried a rifle, grenades, and, of course, my Slugger. It was amazing, the cache of weapons the Roughnecks had. I never ran out of ammo, a minor perk of life under Captain's thumb.

"Tonight we travel to hallowed ground. Our scouts say the Met still stands, which means some of the human race's most prized masterpieces could still be intact. But that's not why we're going there. We're going to find weapons, the most basic of weapons, and if along the way we find zombies or zombie food, what do we do?"

"Exterminate, sir!" The Roughnecks spoke as one. We knew what we were supposed to do, though the taste of the words was bitter to me.

"We're close to full domination on the east coast. This will help us in our cause. We can exterminate, we can organize, and we can control. The Roughnecks will be *the* group in charge of the country, and if anyone else comes calling from the West, like that girl Jenna Price and her comrades, what will we do?"

"Exterminate, sir!"

A chill settled in my spine. "Why can't we all just live in peace" was a question best left un-asked.

He rattled on. "Stay tight, stay focused. The path will be fraught, but we travel together, in the tunnels, and we stay alive. No losses tonight. Not a single one."

"Sir, yes, sir!"

"Roughnecks, move *out*!"

As one, we filed from the subway station, down into the train tunnel. From the side came a voice. Rosie stood, waving. "Ashley! Ashley!" Beside her Will stood silent.

I stepped out of line—the Captain was far enough ahead that he wouldn't see—and stood before her. "What's up? You don't usually see us off anymore."

She nodded, her face solemn. "I have a bad feeling about tonight, and I wanted to wish you luck."

"I'll be fine," I said, but I gave her a hug. Then I hugged Will. He stood board-straight and absorbed it, but didn't hug back. I brushed my lips against his cheek. "Poor Will. One day we'll find a way to help you," I said, though I didn't believe it. "I miss hearing your voice."

Rosie made a face. "He just needs to work. He'll come back to us as soon as he can start working on the cure again. I know it."

"Rosie! You can't talk like that. Someone might hear! Besides, you know we can't. It's useless. There'll never be a cure."

For the first time in ages, I saw something spark in Will's eyes. He reached out and took hold of my hand, pressing it.

I shook my head. "No, there won't. Trust me. Maybe some day a vaccination, but never a cure. Those things? They're not human. I know what we thought, while we were traveling, but we were wrong. They're just monsters. We can't fix them."

From my mouth came the words of the Captain, ringing false in the station. Will knew better. So did I. He squeezed my hand again, harder this time, and my heart skipped. He looked like he was about to speak.

I never heard what he would have said. Assassin appeared behind me, and grabbed my wrist. "Drawing attention to yourself again, *Ashley.* You better follow orders, girl." He pulled me back in line.

As we walked into the dark tunnel, toward the museum of beautiful and deadly things, I watched over my shoulder. Rosie and Will faded into the distance.

* * * *

The walk through the pitch-black subway tunnels was long. The path twisted and turned left then right then left again until I was disoriented and lost. We marched in a single column, though I shifted my way through the line until I found Sam. No matter how much time passed, and how many times he was forced to call me Ashley, together we fought better than alone. He nodded to acknowledge my presence, but that was it. We couldn't speak. Silence was a virtue in the Roughnecks.

I shuffled my feet along the rough, littered ground. Bones crunched beneath my feet. The squeals of rats—zombiefied and otherwise—echoed in the cavernous spaces around us, but even zombie-rats couldn't hurt us. We all wore steel-toed boots, the better for rat-head-stomping. I quickly lost count of how many rats I killed as we marched in the velvet-smooth darkness.

A cool rush of air blew back wisps of hair from my face. I froze. The column before me had stopped marching. I heard the clicks of dozens of weapons being readied, of dozens of safeties switching from on to off. My own fingers performed the battle-rite as if on autopilot. There was trouble ahead. I readied myself for a fight.

Sam stepped out of line—the better to see you with my dear, I thought, choking back the manic laughter that accompanied danger—and craned his neck to see what sparked the delay. In the darkness, his attempt was moot. Though I could make out the shadow of his body moving, his shoulders shifting, I could no more see the color of his hair than I could make out a conflict hundreds of yards away. For information on who or what we fought, we'd have to wait.

The first shot came, a bright flash up ahead, along with the thunder of a hundred more weapons being dispatched at once. Hell was a dark subway tunnel full of trigger-happy pseudo-soldiers. Screams built to a crescendo, louder even than the echoing gunfire. We were surrounded, though by zombies or people I couldn't tell. I dropped to the ground, aiming my rifle to the right as I fell. I fired. As the weapon sparked, I saw bodies lining the walls, but still there was no way to tell: human or zombie? Or...both? One fell beside me, the smell of rotting flesh overwhelmingly zombie, but as another body appeared beside it, the *way* it moved was more human. A hand gripped my right foot. I kicked out with my left. Another creature screamed.

I scrambled to my feet, safer when mobile. Over and above the chaotic screaming and quaking thunder of battle shouted the Captain's voice. "Retreat! Retreat!"

I turned to go, but was pummeled in the side by either a sledgehammer or a linebacker. Who knew the difference, down there in the dark? The thing was moving, though. In the distance, a grenade exploded, filling the tunnel with its aftershock. The sledgehammer-linebacker fell silent. I pushed its body off me and rolled to the side of the tunnel.

I thought I heard my name—my real name—called from the right. I ran to the left. I ran into the darkness, toward the silence. I dropped my rifle. When a hand clamped down on my shoulder, I swung around with my Slugger, knocking a body to the ground. This was an ambush, plain and simple, with bodies living or undead lining the walls, ready to attack us. To kill us. In a flash I knew: I wanted to live. No matter what, I wanted to live. I would live. But to live, I had to escape. I knew when a battle was over before it even started.

So I ran from the mêlée, pausing only once to consider Sam. He'd be alright. I'd find him back at base camp. He always found a way to survive, just like me.

I ran faster, clutching my Slugger before me like a shield or a talisman against the things which went bump in the night. I ran with tears stinging my eyes, blinding me further to the all-encompassing darkness. I ran until I couldn't breathe, until I couldn't move. I saw a flash of semi-darkness above, almost blinding in its comparative brightness. Straining against my body's need to rest, I turned toward it. Maybe it was a path to the streets; the streets were dangerous, sure, full of unmitigated zombie activity, but I'd take my odds of survival in the moonlight over the sureness of death in pitch black.

I stumbled over something large and soft—a body, I was sure—and I tumbled head-over-heels before landing on my feet again. It was quiet.

I could no longer hear the sounds of battle; at some point during my flight, I left it all behind.

I found myself at the base of a stairwell that led to the street, and there I paused. I took a deep breath to ease the searing pain in my lungs, and to quell the panic that threatened to consume me. Moonlight poured down, casting long, grim shadows against the wall behind me. I had no idea where I was, and the chance of street signs above pointing me toward the way home were a slim fifty/fifty. My eyes adjusted to the faint light as I contemplated my escape route. I turned to look back the way I came, and saw the body over which I'd tripped.

It was a man, recently dead. He looked vaguely familiar. *A Roughneck? Yes. I've had dinner with him.*

I leaned over. He was dead from a blow to the head, his forehead concave above his left brow. I reached out to move his head to the side and my hand came away covered with bits of brain and bone.

"Yuck. What happened to you, friend?" I spoke to no one, wanting only to hear something break the insistent silence. "A human would have a gun, and would've killed you with a bullet. A zombie would have torn you apart. So what happened here?"

The hairs on the back of my neck rose as a cool breeze from above wafted down the stairs, carrying with it the scent of the undead. Zombies were close, but I couldn't hear them. I couldn't hear anything, actually, but the faint whisper of the wind.

"This is bad," I said, again to no one. "This is very bad." I didn't know why I said it, why I was so suddenly certain of that fact. But I was. I knew it like a child knows its mother's touch. Something was very bad indeed.

I looked up. The street seemed quiet, and reasonably well-lit by the moon. I stepped back over the body toward the stairwell. I could go up, look around, and hopefully find my way back to our base at Penn Station. From there, depending on who made it home, I'd figure out a next step. Now that I was certain I wanted to live, it was time to start caring about things. *Fixing* things. It was time to stop all the senseless slaughter.

First I had to get out of the underground world. I craved the feel of the moon on my face. I craved the wind. I took another step to the stairs.

The faint hiss of wind changed, morphing into a new sound. A different kind of hiss. A *threatening* hiss. A dare to proceed. I paused.

The wind called, the night called. I wanted it. I wanted out. I stepped forward again, hoping to answer its call.

But the hiss below couldn't be ignored.

"I don't want trouble," I said, this time speaking to someone. Something. "I just want to get out."

Silence fell, and it was deafening. No less threatening.

"See?" I said, taking another step. "I'm just trying to get out of here."

I choked up on my Slugger. So sure was I that a creature lay ready to attack, I changed course, heading behind the stairwell. I preferred facing challenges head-on.

"It's okay," I crooned. "I don't want to hurt you."

Curiosity compelled me as I walked farther and still no attack came. This was decidedly non-zombie behavior. Nor was it human. A human would have challenged me in some other way. Cornered humans were worse than cornered zombies.

Behind the stairs I found a hollowed-out space. Where there may have once been a plywood wall, there was now an opening, a crude doorway to a nook. A hobbit-hole, perhaps. As I neared its entrance, the hissing sound reasserted itself, threatening and angry.

"It's okay," I said. "I just want to see what you are."

I had a flashlight in my rucksack; we were forbidden to use them when on the move as a group, because they could be seen for miles in the darkened tunnels, but it seemed prudent to use it then. I pulled it out with my left hand, still hanging onto my Slugger for dear life with my right. I could do lots of damage one-handed, though I considered dropping it and pulling out my knife instead. I was in a rush, though, dying to see what that little room held. I pointed the flashlight and flicked it on.

Almost immediately, I dropped it. The light flickered crazily through the air, alighting on spider webs and filth in the corners of the little space before landing on the ground with a dull, crackling thud. The beam of light settled exactly where I needed it to.

There, backed as far as possible into the deepest, darkest corner of the room beneath the stairs stood a creature. I say creature because she wasn't quite a zombie—no, her eyes had too much intelligence, and her gestures were far too human for me to call her a zombie—but neither was she human. She was something else. Something different. She held out her arms as she growled and spit in my direction. I took in the sight of her in her tattered clothes—tattered, but covering all the right places a human girl would want covered—until a smaller creature poked its head out from behind her. This one was a child. She, too, began to growl. Were they mother and child? It appeared so, as the elder creature kept the smaller one from advancing on me, protecting her from the deadly force of my Slugger. The mother pressed her skeletal hand against the child's sunken chest, curling her lip, threatening me to take another step inside.

I had no intention of doing that. I held out a hand as well. "I'm staying right here," I said, speaking softly as though calming Chicken down after a fright. "It's going to be okay. I just want to get my light, okay?"

The mother-creature cocked her head to one side, an inquisitive puppy trying to understand my words. The child growled, the sound low and menacing. I swallowed hard, almost choking on my saliva, as I set my Slugger on the ground and picked up the flashlight, shining it around the room.

The mother- and daughter-creatures winced as the light hit their eyes, another reaction I'd never seen in a zombie. The mother tucked the child further behind her as I exhaled. "Whoa."

The room beneath the stairs was their home. In one corner lay a nest of old blankets, filthy and stained. At its summit sat an old doll, one of its eyes missing. The child followed my gaze. She scampered to the nest, snatching up her dolly, cradling the decrepit thing as tenderly as Sadie once cradled Chicken. She watched me watching her, and she sneered.

In another corner of the room lay the remains of rats and other unidentified animals. These creatures weren't eating humans.

"It's okay," I said again, and I began backing up. The mother and daughter weren't zombies. They weren't humans. I didn't know what they were, but I had to find Will. He'd know. He understood genetics and mutations and things like natural immunity, and I had a feeling: if this is what the zombies of the future looked like, maybe there *could* be a cure. The way the mother cared for her daughter, the home they had. They weren't mindless, killing zombies. They were something else, something so much closer to human I couldn't believe it was happening.

"Jenna! What are you doing?"

Sam's voice came from right over my shoulder. Though the creatures had relaxed somewhat as I crooned and soothed, they tensed back up at the sound of Sam's call. As did I, hearing him use my real name, and at the sound of his gun priming behind me.

"Wait," I said. "Look."

He never had a chance to look, though. He never truly saw. Not then. Not until later. For in that moment, the Captain's voice boomed. "Who's in here? Silverman? What's going on? Where's everyone else? What are you hiding?"

My eyes were firmly set on the mother and daughter in their pitiful home. They never knew it was coming.

The Captain always fired first, asking questions later. And that's what he did, there in the dark. He killed them, the mother and daughter who'd made a home for themselves and who feasted on rats instead of humans. The gunfire deafened me, echoing through my pounding head, setting my brain on fire. The last thing I saw before the world went black was the child's dolly falling to the rough cement, its head cracking to pieces upon impact. The last thing I heard was my own voice screaming.

"No!"

Chapter 24: Will

"You've gotta wake up, Will. Snap out of it."

Rosie knelt before me in the tiny nook we called our own. It had once been a newspaper stand, deep in the bowels of Penn Station.

Work for the day was done. Dinners had been served and cleaned up by Rosie and her teammates. My cleaning was over, at least until some Roughneck or other drank too much and puked and they called me to clean it up. I'd become a janitor in the Roughnecks' underground lair.

The janitor. It seemed so fitting for the boy whose dreams had died, to spend the rest of his life cleaning up the swill from everyone else. The drivel. The waste. *That* was my new lot in life. I accepted it, but that didn't mean I liked it.

Rosie clucked her tongue and Chicken emerged, a piece at a time, from beneath the pile of old rags he called his bed. He stayed there most of the time, unless he came on a cleaning run with me. But he was a smart thing, and he knew too many of the Roughnecks eyed him with a greedy-eyed hunger—*fresh meat*—and so he stayed hidden most of the time. I sometimes wondered how those hungry Roughnecks would feel about what Sam had been trying to do back at the house, making human jerky, and I sometimes eyed with suspicion the meat that appeared in the stews and soups Rosie served. Though she assured me otherwise, and I believe *she* believed what she told me, I didn't doubt that at some point meat that didn't come from a can had crossed our lips, and whether that meat was human, stray dog, or even undead flesh never seemed to matter. It all tasted rancid to me.

I rarely ate.

"Seriously, Will. Come on. Come back to us. I need you." Her eyes were pleading, with very little hope inside.

Chicken crawled on my lap. I sat on the hard concrete floor, the chill of the cooling days above seeping up through the thinning jeans I'd worn for months. I stroked the silky fur behind his ears, and he leaned into my touch. I was a sorry replacement for Jenna, who was out on patrol that evening, but I knew he didn't care too much.

I wouldn't look at Rosie, no matter how hard she tried to make me. Her hands found my cheeks. I closed my eyes. Her forehead pressed against mine. I turned away. I couldn't meet her eyes. They were too sad, too accusing. She hated me for giving up.

I hated me for giving up, too. But I couldn't say that. I couldn't say anything, not since the Captain destroyed my notes, destroyed everything on which I'd pinned my hopes for the future. I could never replicate that. Could never even try. Not while we were trapped there with the Roughnecks, eking out a bleak subterranean existence. I wanted to leave—maybe if we left I'd find my voice again—but Jenna (*no, Ashley, call her Ashley)* kept saying no. There was nothing better out there, she said. No reason to go anywhere. So we stayed, day in, day out.

It was quiet in our little patch of subway station that night. With so many Roughnecks out, it was mostly us "support staff" staying behind. Since the Captain had gone out with the soldiers, we all took it upon ourselves to turn in early. I appreciated the quiet.

Except for the fact that Rosie kept bugging me.

"Come on," she said. "All's not lost. I know you. You remember everything in that notebook." Her eyes suddenly took on a bit of a spark, a bit of mischief. Despite myself, I felt my heart speed up a bit.

Maybe my face changed. Maybe she was just so attuned to her big brother that she felt the change too. Whatever the case, her impish grin made its first appearance in weeks. She reached behind her, where her ever-present rucksack sat, waiting for the next time we'd hit the road. From it she pulled an old, spiral bound notebook, and a couple pencils.

"I know it's not the same," she said. "And the notebook's half full. But I thought, maybe if you could start writing again, copying down what you remember, maybe you'd start to feel better."

"He'll kill me if he finds it."

Rosie jumped. I jumped. *So I do still have a voice.* Then Rosie's grin deepened. It broadened. It crept up until it overtook her entire face, crinkling her eyes in a way that looked so much like our mother I almost broke into a million tiny pieces. When she laughed, she *sounded* like our mother, too. "So what. Chances are, he'll kill us someday soon anyway. We're living on borrowed time. Might as well make the most of it, don't you think?"

I opened my mouth to answer, but instead felt my hands move as though they had a mind of their own. My left picked up the notebook; my right, the pencil. I flipped through until I found an open page. Without another thought, I began to write.

* * * *

I'd read his notes and formulas so many times I had most of his notebook memorized. I worked for hours that evening with an intensity I hadn't felt in ages. Rosie faded into the background as she and Chicken snuggled in the corner of our newspaper stand and eventually fell asleep. I kept a lantern burning low as I wrote and wrote and wrote. My handwriting was chicken-scratch, and I'd need to study it carefully later on to translate it into something legible to anyone else, but nothing else mattered as I wrote and rewrote all the formulas I needed to stop the zombie plague.

Vaccination. Inoculation. Maybe I couldn't save those already bitten, but I could stop the uninfected from becoming infected. I knew I could. I needed only to weather the storm of the Roughnecks—just another storm in a tumultuous world—and then I'd find my way to a lab, to supplies, to the cure. I could still save the world. All hope was not lost.

My hand ached and my eyes squinted in the dim light when Chicken leaped to his feet and ran to the door of the newspaper stand. For the first time in hours I looked up from the notebook. I heard nothing but a high-pitched whine from the little dog, and the low, steady breathing of my sister, asleep against the wall.

"What is it, boy?"

Chicken whined again, and then I heard it. Off in the tunnel that ran perpendicular to our little station-home. Footsteps thundered our way, fast and heavy.

"Rosie," I said. "Get up. Something's coming."

She jerked awake, her face immediately alert. "What is it? Is it zombies?" Rosie reached again into her pack and pulled out a knife. I quickly stashed the notebook beneath Chicken's bedding, and stood beside my sister.

"I don't think so. I think Chicken would be growling. But look, his hair's not even up."

We had little more time for speculation. Moments later, Jenna and Sam came crashing into our room. Both were winded, but Jenna looked the worse for the wear. She was crying, her face streaked with a thick layer of dirt and tears. Her hair had pulled out of its usual ponytail and blew in tangled dreadlocks about her face. Sam shoved her forward, rougher than I'd seen him act with her, and looked around. His eyes were frantic, darting here, there, and everywhere.

"Hush, boy." He spoke to Chicken first, dropping a hand to let the dog sniff it. Chicken nuzzled it with his nose. "Okay, Jenna, hush. You need to stop now. Rosie, help her. Will…be Will. Be silent. We're in trouble, but they don't know we're here yet."

Jenna's breathing was the loudest thing in the small space. She was gasping for air, wheezing, like a person submerged in the water for a minute too long trying to clear her lungs of something foul. Rosie went to her and pulled her down to the ground, and Chicken joined them.

"What's happening," I said.

Sam started. "You're talking again? Since when?"

"Since now. What's happening?"

"Jenna hit the Captain with her Slugger. He…something…she saw something she didn't like, and she hit him. So I'd say her time here's pretty well up."

"Holy shit."

"Will, don't cuss." Rosie was helping Jenna back to her feet. "Don't you guys mean Ashley? Who's this Jenna?" She glanced toward the door. So far, apart from our group, we were surrounded by silence.

"I'm Jenna." Jenna panted, still, supporting herself on my sister's shoulder. "I'm Jenna. I'm done being Ashley."

Sam lowered his head. "I know. What happened back there, Jenn? Why'd you do it? You've been so careful, so head-down here. Why'd you go off?"

"So you didn't see them?"

"See what?"

Jenna, too, seemed startled at the sound of my voice. Her wheezing breaths quieted as she stared at me. "Welcome back." She almost smiled. "Will. I'm glad. You need to hear this. There were…there were…it was a mother, a daughter, I think. I mean, somehow I *know.* And they were infected, so definitely infected. Their skin was rotting, the smell was terrible. The *zombie* smell, you know?"

We nodded. We knew.

"But they were different. Different even from the ones who…who killed…the ones who got Michael. They were eating *animals*. Not people. The woman? She was protecting her kid. Pushed herself between her kid and me, and was threatening, but didn't want to kill me. I could tell she didn't want to kill me. She only wanted to be left alone. Will. It wasn't like anything I've seen before, ever. They weren't zombies. I swear to God."

My hair stood on end, raising itself to attention all over my arms and neck. "Are you serious?"

Her face flushed and filthy, her eyes red, she nodded. "Different."

That was all I needed. I picked up my notebook, flipped through the pages. I spoke, though it wasn't to them. I spoke to myself. "The virus is mutating. We know that. We've seen that. Michael was a victim of that. But what if we're mutating too? What if every time we get exposed, maybe we get stronger? What if what I thought about Michael really was true? What if we really can fight it?" I set the notebook back down, and grabbed Jenna's shoulders. She winced, but her eyes never left me. "Jenna. Were they like Michael?"

She shook her head. "No. Not like him. Remember how he was there sometimes, but gone the next? This wasn't like that. It was like they were *almost* there. Like they were gone, maybe, but still knew enough to be….people. When Michael was gone, he was all the way gone. They were gone, but still…here. God, I don't know. I'm not even making sense."

"But you are," I said, shaking her back and forth. Her head was unsteady, and soon Sam pulled her from my grasp. I noticed, but I also didn't. My hands stayed stretched out in front of me though Jenna was no longer held in them. "It's like we're all changing. The virus, the zombies, us. All of it. Our bodies are learning how to fight it, how to stay alive even once we're infected."

"So Michael could've been saved?"

"No," I said. "Listen to yourself. When he was gone, he was zombie. But they aren't, you said. That's what you said, right?"

She shook her head, Sam's arm around her shoulders. "Yes."

"I need to see them. Jenna, I think this is good. I think I can work with this. I can look at their blood, talk to them. Maybe they can still communicate! Jenna! They could be the missing link! They could be the cure! Take me to them?"

"I can't. They're dead."

"What?"

She looked at the floor, and Sam gripped her tighter. "He killed them. The Captain. A shot to the face. Both of them. Close range. They're destroyed."

"Oh," said Rosie. "So you clobbered him."

Sure enough, the bat was, for once, covered with red, human blood instead of black zombie gore. Jenna nodded. "Yes, but not well enough. I hit his shoulder, I think. Not his head. Maybe I grazed his ear. I was too crazy, I wasn't focused." She breathed a deep, shaky breath. "I fucked us all over."

"Yes, you surely did," said a deep voice from our doorway.

We turned as one. Chicken yipped a hello. Assassin's massive girth filled the doorway. Sam glared at him. "You can't have her," he said. "I'll kill you first. Just try me." Sam held a gun, his smaller soldier's rifle, aimed straight at Assassin's face.

Assassin drew, too, but neither fired. Instead, they stood there, Sam dwarfed by Assassin's mass, looking like a child arguing with his father. Assassin spoke first.

"I don't want her for what you think I want her for. Put your gun down."

"No." Sam's voice was deadly.

"I don't want to have to kill you, Silverman. I need you. I need all of you." His eyes settled briefly on me. "Even the quiet one."

"You killed my brother."

"This isn't the time, man. This isn't the time."

"You're here for Jenna."

"Oh, for God's sake." He was quick, like lightning, and before my heart could successfully leap into my throat he had Sam pinned and gunless, face down on the floor. "I told you this isn't the time!" His knee was on Sam's back; he leaned over until his face almost touched Sam's cheek.

Jenna sprang to life. "Get off!" Assassin swatted her like a fly. She fell on her bottom, the wind rushing out of her. "Knock it off, you guys. Assassin, I'm not going without a fight. So you'll have to kill me now. In front of the kids. Have fun living with yourself after that."

"JENNA." It was a roar. Assassin actually roared. Rosie backed away until her shoulder pressed into my side and I slid an arm around her. Chicken crouched and growled. But Jenna sat up straighter. "Would you please listen? All y'all. I don't want to kill anybody! At least none of you. I want to help you! I want you to help me!"

He backed off Sam, who struggled up to sitting. He scooted over to Jenna, and they held hands like children at the principal's office. Assassin rubbed his mouth with his big, meaty hand. "Good. Now that's better. Look, I know what you did, and I know what you saw and why you did it. I also know the Captain's been aware of the un-zombies for a long time. When I found you guys, I was actually on the road to find out how far their reach was. I mean, the Captain thought I was finding new weapons, but it was my own mission. One I gave myself. It was the biggest risk I'd taken so far. I went to all our outposts. These un-zombies are everywhere. Part zombie, sure, but still part human. People can survive this thing. They can live. We can stop this, if only they let us."

"Who wouldn't let us?" Jenna said.

I already knew the answer. I'd seen the way he destroyed Schwartz's research with such a vengeance. Such glee. "The Captain," I said. "The Captain. He must've been a nobody before, and now he's a somebody. I heard some of the Roughnecks talking about something similar one night right after you picked us up. He doesn't want to go back to being a nobody."

Assassin nodded. "Finally. You get what's going on here. The un-zombies are all coming from here, originally. Whatever mutation happened, it happened here, in the city. The Captain's going to keep us here until we exterminate them all."

"Jesus," said Jenna, letting out a gutful of air. "We have to stop them."

"Exactly." Assassin looked straight at her. "I want to help you stop him. I want to shut that fucker up for good. But I'm just a soldier. A follower. A grunt. Always have been. But Jenna? Jenna Price? Everyone knows what she can do. What *you* can do. There are good people here, but they need a leader. I'm not a leader. But they'll follow you."

"Me. They'll follow me." Jenna looked pale, the color draining from her face, leaving her white beneath the filth. "That's why you've kept me close."

"Yes. I just didn't expect things to…climax so soon."

"But what do you really want her to do? I mean, she's not exactly Braveheart? And you're still the prick who killed my brother. Why should we believe you?"

"Because you know in your heart that was the right thing to do, Sam. Because you know he was maybe going to be a smart zombie, but you know he was going. Gone. You couldn't have brought him back." Half of Assassin's mouth curled up in a wry smile. "If I get you guys out of this mess, and you still want to kill me after the Captain's dead, then, go ahead. I'm getting too old for this shit anyway."

Sam nodded. He turned to me. "You still remember any of your notes?"

I reached beneath Chicken's bedding and pulled out the notebook. "You mean these notes?"

Sam grinned. "I don't even want to know what you two have been up to in here." He turned his head to look at Rosie, looking rueful and small but also furious. "You ready to fight, little girl?"

She stuck her tongue out at him. "I'm not a little girl."

Jenna stood and walked over to Assassin. "How do I know we can trust you?"

He only shrugged. "Have I hurt you in any way?"

"No."

"Have I kept you safe so far?"

"Yes."

"And what does your gut tell you?"

Jenna's back was to me. I couldn't see her face. Her shoulders rose and then fell with the deepest of sighs. She reached a hand up and touched the side of Assassin's face. "What's your real name, anyway? I don't like working with assassins."

He looked down at her. I don't know if it was relief, or fear, that crossed his face then, but he nodded. "Pat," he said, his voice deep and tight. "Pat Frame. It's nice to meet you, Jenna Price."

Jenna didn't smile, didn't frown, but stood there, staring at him, as though she could read with her eyes all the things she wanted to know. She couldn't. It was impossible. But finally she nodded back, then, quick as a bee darting from flower to flower, she stood up on tiptoe, craned her neck, and brushed her lips against his cheek. He jerked as though he'd never been kissed before and this, his first kiss, burned, but that was okay. In that kiss, Jenna had said all she needed to. We'd be working with Assassin—Pat Frame, I told myself—from that point on.

Beside me, Rosie began packing her things. Our things. I reached for my rucksack, tucking the notebook deep inside. Rosie grinned, but it was wistful. "Man, I always thought when we finally escaped the Roughnecks we'd be headed home to Nebraska. But we won't see home for a long time, will we?"

I shrugged. "Probably not. Seems like we've got a lot of work to do."

Jenna looked over, surprised. "You know, I hadn't thought of home in ages. Not since Michael." She looked down. "I guess I owe them a letter. I wonder if we can spare a person to send them some stuff, to let them know we'll be a while. I want them to know…" She gulped, swallowing like it hurt. "I want them to know I'm coming home someday. I promised Sadie. I can't believe I forgot."

Assassin nodded. "I think we can make that happen. But first, tonight, we need to disappear. And we need to make some plans."

Jenna stood and pulled her backpack tighter on her shoulders. She slung the Slugger across her shoulders and turned to face all of us. Standing in the doorway, the hysterical girl who'd come into the newspaper stand minutes before was gone. That was Ashley. Ashley was dead.

Instead, we stared at Jenna. The real Jenna. Jenna Price. And she was ready for battle. Cold, calculating, there would be no more hysterics from Jenna Price. Not ever again.

"Well, come on, then," she said, spinning on her heel, those biker boots she'd been wearing for years heavy on the ground. "Let's go."

Chapter 25: Jenna

Dear Sadie,

I hope this reaches you. I really do. My new friend Assassin—you haven't met him yet, but hopefully someday you will. He's not as scary as he sounds—says he'll send one of his best rangers to make sure it reaches you.

Rangers. Heh. It sounds like we live in one of the books I used to love, crazy fantasies with princesses and knights and magic and sorcery. But that's life now, if you consider that zombies are sort of magical. In their own way, I guess.

Here's the thing. We said goodbye going on six months ago now. I still remember the way you looked when we walked away, so small and sad. I thought we'd be back by now. I thought we'd never find anything worth looking for, and that we'd be back in Nebraska by now.

Then I forgot that promise. But I swear I'm going to keep it.

Poor Sadie. You were born too late. You never got to experience the world as it was, as it should have stayed. You had a good life once. You had a mom and a dad and a home that you probably don't remember. When it all fell apart, we tried to build something good for you at the farmhouse. Maybe you're still there. Maybe Auntie Allie is reading this to you from the comfort of the living room chair, and she's kissing your hair. I know you don't have a mom or dad anymore. Neither do I. I guess we're both orphans.

I never really believed in a cure for the zombie plague. I never really believed it was possible. But it's been a long six months.

We met some good people I thought were bad; we met some bad people I hoped were good. And we learned there's a lot of world left to fight for.

Sadie, I want to come home. I want to live out the rest of my life with you by my side. When you're there, my little sidekick, things make more sense. I can pretend we're a family and you're mine. I miss the way you'd curl up beside me sometimes, the way it felt to hold your little body close. You're so sweet and so small. Stay that way, please.

I used to think it was enough, just keeping you and Rosie and Will safe. That was my goal: keep you kids safe so you could live to see another year. Sometimes I'd have settled for another day, things looked so ugly and bleak. And they still sort of do.

But Sadie, now I know there's another ending. Another possibility for life. And I have to fight for it.

What I'm trying to say, Sadie, is that no matter how much I want to be home with you, there's more work to be done before I can come back. There are some very, *very* bad people out there, people who think the zombie plague is a good thing. Maybe they were bad people before the zombies; maybe they were just nobodies. I suppose it takes all kinds, right? My mom used to say that.

We have a fight ahead of us, but we're working hard to stop them, and to find the cure. If I can get more of the city (we're in New York City, can you believe that?) secure, Will can set up shop and begin his research. He think's he's close, and for the first time, I do too. But that's not all we have to do. We have to stop all the bad people from thinking they're in charge. We have to stop the killing.

Sadie, I'm going to give you an important job now. I want you to live. I want you to play. I want you to try to be happy and grow up big and strong and I want you to be there, waiting for me at the farmhouse when I get back. Because I'm coming back. Not this year, probably, and maybe not next year. But I'll be back. I promise you.

Keep watch over the south hill, Sadie. Keep watch there, because I'll come from there. When you see me, I want you to smile, because that'll mean we found the cure, and that the end of these terrible times is on its way. I won't come before that happens.

I love you and I miss you every day. I think about you every day. You're my girl, and one day we'll be together again. I promise you that. We'll be together again.

In the meantime, remember your jobs: Live. Love. Laugh.

And before you know it, I'll be coming over that hill with the best news in the world.

I love you.
Love,
Jenna
New York City, 2017

Epilogue: Sadie

Uncle Simon is dying. Auntie Allie says I should stay upstairs today, that the end is near. She hasn't left his side in days to do anything but bring him broth and clean cloths to wipe his face. She's looking thin, too, but he's thinner. We don't know what's wrong with him, just that he's dying. You can tell. His eyes are dim, his cheeks are hollow.

I carried all my books and drawing stuff up here a few days ago, when things got really bad. Callie downstairs wants me to come down, but I said I have to stay with my uncle. She understands, I guess, but she still made an ugly face at me from the top of the stairs.

I sometimes wish, as hard as I can wish, for a home of our own, without all these other people. Auntie Allie tells me stories of what it was like *before*, when she and Uncle Simon had a little girl named Del, and they lived in a faraway place called Maine. Maine sounds like magic. I'd like to go there someday.

In Maine, they had a house of their own, and their little girl went to school and there were stores where you could go to buy food. We grow our own food now, all summer long, and we can it and put it up in the storage cellar and it keeps us alive through the winters. There aren't stores here.

In Maine, they took vacations and went swimming and drove all over the place in cars that actually moved. Our cars? They don't move. And I'm not allowed to go swim, even in the summer. Not since they found creatures in the swimming hole—undead creatures—stuck deep in the muck at the bottom of the hole. They reached out their arms like they could catch me, and even though I swam way above them, I wasn't allowed to go there anymore.

Doesn't Maine sound like magic? One day I'll see Maine.

But right now, Uncle Simon is dying.

And that's okay, because if there's one thing I know it's that we're all going to die. Sooner instead of later, too. That's just a fact of life, and the sooner you realize it, the better off you'll be.

That's another thing about Maine. People didn't die all the time there like they do here. Can you even imagine?

Poor Uncle Simon. I wish I could make him feel better.

Auntie Allie's dozing off in the chair beside his bed. She's exhausted, poor thing. She doesn't want to lose him. Neither do I but people die all the time. We could die tomorrow. I just have to accept it.

Uncle Simon's awake, though. He's watching me as I sit here in the window seat. I have a book open on my knees, but I'm not reading it. I'm actually just looking out the window at the south hill. Once upon a time, Jenna Price told me to watch the south hill. But that was years ago. She's probably dead.

I make a stink face at Uncle Simon. It always makes him smile, and he does, now. It's a quiet smile, though. A weak one. He's so tired. Poor Uncle Simon. I hope he gets some rest soon.

I turn back to the window. It's a pipe dream, I know. Callie from downstairs tells me that all the time. Jenna Price left me a long time ago. She's never coming back.

And, I mean, I barely even remember her. I just remember the way she held me, the way she hugged me when she said goodbye. I've read and reread the letter she sent me after she left. She told me to wait. I've never stopped waiting.

It's hot out today, but Allie keeps it nice and cool in here. She's wasting electricity running a small air conditioner, and Callie says everyone downstairs is grumbling about it, but I don't care. It's nice in here. Plus, since it's so hot out there and cool in here, there's lots of fog on the windows.

I trail a finger through the fog, cutting a small path of clear glass. I curve it around, making a little curlicue design. Beneath it, I write my name in pretty, curling letters. *Sadie Price.* That's me. Sadie Price.

The design isn't what I want it to be. It's not quite good enough to leave, to let the fog slowly fill back in through the paths. It needs to be wiped clean.

With my full hand—still small, but big enough that I've killed ten zombies all on my own, this year alone—I wipe away the design, clearing the whole window of fog. I press my forehead to the cool, damp glass.

Callie from downstairs says I'm crazy to ever watch the south hill. Jenna Price is dead. Soon Uncle Simon will be too. And Auntie Allie's asleep by his bed.

My eyes are closed. Maybe I'll take a nap too. But just when my head starts to sway and wiggle, and I start to float away into my sleepy space, Uncle Simon makes a sound that startles me back awake. It isn't a grunt, isn't a sigh, but it's enough. I'm awake again.

"What?" I say, turning to him, but his eyes are closed.

I look back out the window, but my eyes are open. My heart's beating super-fast and I don't know why. But something tells me: look out at the south hill.

There's something in the distance! Something's there! I squint, trying to make it out, and it's hard, but there are three shapes—one small, two tall. Together they're moving toward us.

"Auntie, wake up, someone's coming."

But she doesn't wake up, she's sleeping so soundly. Uncle Simon does, though. He leans his head up off the pillow, and I swear he's smiling.

I look back out the window at the south hill. I can see better now. It's a dog, a small black one. He's running toward the house as fast as he can. And behind him: a boy. He's got a big, bushy beard, and he's carrying a shotgun. Beside him is a girl. She's tall, and her hair is blowing in the wind.

My heart skips. From the bed, Simon let's out a sigh. It sounds like, "Jenna."

The girl stops. She stares. She lifts a baseball bat up in the air, raising it like a salute. I know she sees me. I wave, and I smile.

Suddenly, the dog stops running. He sits down, and lets out a long, sad howl. Tears fill my eyes, and I hop down from the window seat. I walk to the bed, where Simon is dead. Just like that. But that's how things work in our world.

"Auntie Allie," I say again, shaking her awake. "Auntie, wake up. Uncle Simon is gone, but Jenna's come home. Everything's about to change again."

Auntie's eyes open, sleepy and bleary at first, but quickly she's alert. She peeks out the window and exhales, her sigh heavy like a blanket. I think it sounds like relief. But then she checks on Simon, and she listens. The dog—I know his name, it's Chicken—is howling. She nods, and tears spill down her cheeks.

"Thank you, baby," she says. "Jenna, Sam, and Chicken are home now, and so's Simon. It's okay. Run to her. Run to Jenna, baby. She'll want to see you. Then bring her here. And tell her I'm glad she's home."

I don't wait to be told twice.

Jenna is home.

The end of the life I've known is here.

About the Author

Leah Rhyne is a Jersey girl who's lived in the South so long she's lost her accent...but never her attitude. After spending most of her childhood watching movies like Star Wars, Alien(s), and A Nightmare On Elm Street, and reading books like Stephen King's The Shining or It, Leah now writes tales of horror and science fiction. Her first novel, Undead America Volume 1: Zombie Days, Campfire Nights, released in the fall of 2012, and its sequel, No Angels, released in the fall of 2013. The final book in the trilogy is coming in 2014. She writes for LitReactor.com, The Charleston City Paper, and for herself at www.leahrhyne.com. Leah lives with her husband, daughter, and a small menagerie of pets. In her barely-there spare time, she loves running and yoga.

* * * *

Did you enjoy *Jenna's War*? If so, please help us spread the word about Leah Rhyne and MuseItUp Publishing. It's as easy as:

•*Recommend the book to your family and friends*

•*Post a review*

•*Tweet and Facebook about it*

Thank you

MuseItUp
PUBLISHING

MuseItUp Publishing
Where Muse authors entertain readers!
https://museituppublishing.com
Visit our website for more books for your reading pleasure.

You can also find us on Facebook:
http://www.facebook.com/MuseItUp
and on Twitter:
http://twitter.com/MusePublishing